RED DWARF

BETTER THAN LIFE

GRANT NAYLOR

LOST IN SPACE, THEY PLAYED A GAME THAT WAS BETTER THAN REALITY—AND THE ONLY DRAWBACK WAS THAT THIS GAME COULD *REALLY* KILL THEM!

ROC ★ 451-LE5231 ★ (CANADA $5.99) ★ U.S. $4.99

NOT SINCE
HITCHHIKER'S GUIDE TO THE GALAXY
HAS THERE BEEN SUCH A DELIGHTFUL EXCURSION
INTO THE WACKIEST
REGIONS OF THE UNKNOWN UNIVERSE!

from **ROC**

HOLLY THE COMPUTER
FELT THE POWER ENTER HIM. . . .

"Ask me anything," Holly said to the Toaster.

"Anything?"

"Metaphysics, philosophy, the purpose of being. Anything."

"Truly anything, and you will answer?"

"I shall."

"Very well," said the Toaster. "Would you like some toast?"

"No, thank you," said Holly. "Now ask me another. The whole sphere of human knowledge is an open book to me."

The Toaster pondered. Finally it asked, "Would you like a crumpet?"

"I'm a computer with an IQ of twelve thousand, three hundred and sixty-eight. Ask me a sensible question, preferably not bread-related."

"OK," said the Toaster. "Who created the universe?"

"Lister," said Holly. "Ask me another."

"Hang on a minute. David Lister? The guy who bought me? *That* Lister? He's the creator of all things?"

"Yes. Now ask me a hard question. . . ."

BETTER THAN LIFE

Grant Naylor

A ROC BOOK

ROC
Published by the Penguin Group
Penguin Books USA Inc., 375 Hudson Street,
New York, New York 10014, U.S.A.
Penguin Books Ltd, 27 Wrights Lane,
London W8 5TZ, England
Penguin Books Australia Ltd, Ringwood,
Victoria, Australia
Penguin Books Canada Ltd, 10 Alcorn Avenue,
Toronto, Ontario, Canada M4V 3B2
Penguin Books (N.Z.) Ltd, 182–190 Wairau Road,
Auckland 10, New Zealand

Penguin Books Ltd, Registered Offices:
Harmondsworth, Middlesex, England

Published by Roc, an imprint of New American Library,
a division of Penguin Books USA Inc. Originally published
in Great Britain by Penguin Books, Ltd.

First Roc Printing, March, 1993
10 9 8 7 6 5 4 3 2 1

 REGISTERED TRADEMARK—MARCA REGISTRADA

Printed in the United States of America

To Richard, Joe and Matthew

Special thanks to Ed Bye for being unnecessarily tall and wonderful, to Paul Jackson for being not so tall, but equally wonderful, and to Chris Barrie, Craig Charles, Danny John-Jules, Hattie Hayridge, Robert Llewelyn and Peter Wragg. Thanks also to BBC Northwest and all the *Red Dwarf* backstage crew.

CONTENTS

Time is a character in this novel.
It does strange things: moves in strange
directions, and at strange speeds.
Don't trust Time.
Time will always get you in the end.

Grant Naylor (Alexandria, 25 BC)

Part One

GAME OVER

ONE

Rimmer sat on the open terrace, in his half-devastated dinner suit of the night before, and gazed down at the metallic blue time machine, drunkenly parked skew-whiff in the ornamental gardens of the Palace of Versailles. Breakfasting with him were five of his stag-night companions: John F. Kennedy, Vincent Van Gogh, Albert Einstein, Louis XVI and Elvis Presley.

"That was a heck of a night," Kennedy sparkled. "One *heck* of a night." Einstein snorted in agreement, and continued absently buttering the underside of his tie.

Julius Caesar stumbled through the French windows out on to the terrace with an ice-pack perched on his head. "Can anyone tell me," he asked in faltering English, "where in Jupiter's name we got this?" He held aloft a large orange-and-white-striped traffic cone. "I woke up in bed with it this morning."

Van Gogh cracked an egg into his tomato juice, and downed it with a shudder. "It's not a good night," he grinned, "if you don't get a traffic cone."

"You want that?" Elvis Presley nodded at Rimmer's devilled kidneys, and without waiting for a reply scraped them on to his already full plate.

A colourless smile-trickled across Rimmer's upper lip. "*Avez-vous* some, uh, Alka-Seltzer?"

"One *heck* of a night," Kennedy repeated.

And he was right: as bachelor-night parties went, it had been a bit of a cracker.

A flash-frame slammed into Rimmer's brain—a scene from the night before . . .

He was standing on a table in a 1922 Chicago speakeasy, dancing the Black Bottom with Frank "the Enforcer" Nitty's girlfriend, and complaining for the umpteenth time that his mineral water tasted as if someone had poured three double vodkas into it.

Then . . . Then . . . He couldn't remember the order, but they had definitely dropped in on one of Caligula's orgies. Rimmer must have been fairly drunk by then, because he remembered spending at least twenty minutes trying to chat up a horse.

At some point they'd been in Ancient Egypt, and Rimmer had lost a tooth trying to give the Sphinx a giant love-bite . . . then someone—Rimmer thought it was Elvis—had suggested a curry. And Rimmer, who hated curries, had been dragged, complaining, through Time back to India in the days of the Raj, where everyone had ordered a mutton vindaloo, except for Rimmer who had a cheese omelette served with ludicrously thick chips.

The cry had gone up for more liquor, and Rimmer suggested . . . What did he suggest? There was a block, so it must have been something

fairly bad. Some kind of restaurant. They'd
crashed a private party, and all the people there
seemed fairly put out when Rimmer and his cro-
nies showed up dancing and singing. There were
a dozen or so diners, all men, all bearded. Rimmer closed his eyes and groaned.

They'd gate-crashed the Last Supper.

What had he done? What had he said? He'd
been shouting drunk. "Private bloody party! Our
money's as good as anyone's!"

Twelve of them had stood up and threatened to
punch Rimmer out, but the one who'd remained
seated had told the others to sit down again.

"Do one of your tricks," Rimmer had insisted.
"Come on, I'm getting married tomorrow. That
one with the fish—it's brilliant."

A heck of a night.

Rimmer looked at his real-time watch. "Well,
Louis, me old buckeroo," he said to the king of
France, "we'd better be making tracks. Big kissy-
kissy to Marie and the dauphin. Thanks for the
servant girls. See you at the wedding."

Louis XVI thanked Rimmer for the Ray-Ban
sunglasses and the Sony Walkman and bade him
farewell.

Rimmer gingerly made his way across the lawns
towards the Time copter, followed by Kennedy,
Van Gogh, Einstein and Caesar. Elvis crammed a
steak in his mouth, stuffed a second in his
pocket, grabbed four bread rolls and followed
them.

The man in the air traffic control tower radioed
clearance to materialize, and the Time copter

bloomed into existence, and chuddered to rest on the tarmacadamed runway.

The disembarkation door hinged to the ground, and the world's richest man clicked down the steps towards the waiting limo.

Two steps down, the screaming started. Hordes of teenage girls standing on the observation balcony swept forward in tides of pubescent adoration.

"Arniiiiiiiieeee!" they roared. "We love yooouuuuuu!"

Rimmer waved half-heartedly and shot them the thinnest of his thin smiles, before he was surrounded by a phalanx of sober-suited security guards who ushered him to the leather comfort of the limo's interior.

The eight motorcyclists twisted their throttle grips, and led the cavalcade forward, as it swished imperiously past Passport Control and the Customs building, and headed towards the exit.

Rimmer flicked idly through the stack of magazines on the limo's mahogany table: *Time*, *Life* and *Newsweek*. He noted with only mild interest that his portrait graced the cover of all three. According to *Life*, he'd just been voted "World's sexiest man," "World's best-dressed man" and "Pipe-smoker of the year." Rimmer smiled. He didn't even *own* a pipe, much less smoke one. Success breeds success, he thought.

The cavalcade fought its way through the screaming fans milling around the airport exit.

"Arniiiiiiiiiiiieeeeee! Don't marry her!"

Flattened adoring faces squashed up against the grey smoked glass, all of them dizzy with desire for Arnold J. Rimmer.

Rimmer was perfectly well aware that he was in

the wrong plane of the wrong dimension of reality and, quite honestly, he didn't give two hoots.

The limousine gently disentangled itself from the sobbing frenzy of teenage girls and silently accelerated down the freeway, followed by a shower of moist, female underwear.

TWO

Three million years out in Deep Space, a dilapidated mining ship drifts pointlessly round in a huge, aimless circle.

On board, its four crew members sit in a horseshoe, trapped in the ultimate computer game: a game that plugs directly into the brain, and enables them to experience a world created by their own fantasies.

The game is called Better Than Life, and very few ever escape its thrall: very few can give up their own, personally sculpted paradise.

THREE

Sparkling lights looped from tree to tree along the main street, above an assortment of parked cars hummocked in white. A small brass band umpahed discordant but cheery carols in the town square, as last-minute shoppers slushed through the snow, exchanging seasonal greetings and stopping occasionally to join in a favourite carol.

In the fictional town of Bedford Falls, it was Christmas Eve. But then again, in the fictional town of Bedford Falls, it was always Christmas Eve.

Lister crossed the main street, his two sons perched on either shoulder, and headed for the toy shop.

As they passed the jailhouse, Bert the cop was removing a wanted poster from the front window.

The poster was yellow and gnarled, and offered a five-dollar reward for information leading to the arrest of Jesse James and his gang. "About time I took this thing down," Bert said sheepishly. There hadn't been a single crime in Bedford Falls for over thirty years; not since that hot summer day when Mrs. Hubble was arrested for taking a three-cent-trolley ride, having paid only a two-cent fare.

Lister slid the twins from his shoulders and grasped their tiny hands, as the two four-year-olds gazed, mouths ajar, at the large blue sailing boat on sale for two dollars and twenty-five cents in the toy-shop window.

Suddenly the door jangled open and old Mr. Mulligan appeared in the doorway, straightening out the yacht's sails. "Now then, me lads," he brogued. "Would I be correct in thinking you'll be after doing business with me in respect of a certain sailing vessel? Only, you've been standing out there with your faces pressed up against me window so often these past few months, you're beginning to wear away the pavement outside me shop."

"Yes, sir, we are, sir," said Bexley. "We've been saving up all year. Show him the money, Jim."

Jim took out his spider box, and carefully unwrapped the two wrinkled dollar bills and poured out the mound of coppers.

"Here it is, sir. Two dollars and twenty-five cents."

As old Mr. Mulligan held out the boat, Henry, the town down-and-out, shuffled sadly by, his flimsy coat tugged tight around his frail shoulders. He took a futile swig from a bottle concealed in a brown paper bag and threw it in a wastebin.

"Merry Christmas, ge'l'men," he slurred.

Jim gazed up at his stubble-swathed face. "Where are you spending Christmas, Mr. Henry?"

"Well, that's a very good question." Henry dragged a tattered sleeve across his nose. "Being as how the jailhouse is closed for the yuletide period, and the Bel Air Hotel presidential suite is fully booked, it looks like the Park Bench Hilton for old Henry."

"What are you going to eat?" asked Bexley.

"Don't worry about me, boy. I always share a fine Christmas dinner with the ducks up on Potter's pond."

The twins turned and faced each other. Finally, they both nodded, and Bexley turned back to Henry, and held out his hand. "Me and Jim would like you to have this, Mr. Henry. Merry Christmas."

"What's this?" Henry tried to focus on the money in his hand.

"You can get a room at Old Ma Bailey's boarding-house," said Jim, "and have a proper Christmas, like the rest of us."

Henry's blood-shot eyes filled with tears, and his voice cracked. "Well now," he barely whispered. "You'd be giving me your Christmas money."

Lister looked down at his feet.

"Deep down, you're a really good person," said Jim. "You just got sad when old Mrs. Henry went to heaven."

Lister sucked in his cheeks, and old Mr. Mulligan took out a large handkerchief and noisily blew his nose.

"Look at me—I've gone to pieces," Henry blubbed. "What would my Mary say if she could see me now? She'd give me such a talking-to, my ears'd be ringing for a week."

"No she wouldn't, Mr. Henry." Bexley shook his head. "She'd say you brought up two fine children single-handed, and sent them both to college. You only took to the bottle when the angels had to take them away, too."

Lister snuffled, and whimpered, and accepted Mulligan's handkerchief.

Henry bent down and pressed the money back into Jim's hand. "I can't take this from you, boys, but if I could just borrow a dollar, to get myself a haircut and a shave. There's a sweeping job going down at the drugstore. I'll pay you back ten times over."

Jim and Bexley smiled. "Merry Christmas, Henry."

Jim folded the single dollar bill around the twenty-five cents, and placed it carefully back into his spider box. "Come on, Dad," he said quietly. "Let's go back home."

"Wait!" called Mulligan. "Have I told you about me winter sale, just this minute started? Lots of bargains! Take, for instance, this fine blue boat, formerly two dollars, twenty-five cents, now reduced to one dollar, twenty-five cents."

He handed the boat to the boys.

Lister started sobbing unashamedly, which set Henry off. The two men embraced one another, and were soon joined by old Mr. Mulligan and Bert the cop. They stood there in a four-way hug, bawling hysterically.

"That's so beautiful," Lister was trying to say between whimpering convulsions.

"You've got two fine boys there. You should . . ." But Henry couldn't finish. He buried his head in Lister's shoulder, and was off again.

"They were prepared to give up the boat to help out Henry," Mulligan blubbered. "That's the real spirit of Christmas."

"Blaaaaaaaaaaaaaaaaaah," said Bert, and they all dissolved in a fresh paroxysm of wailing.

This was the kind of thing that happened all the time in the fictional town of Bedford Falls.

It was that kind of place.

The twelve-wheeled juggernaut hammered down the narrow country lane decapitating hedgerows and smashing through branches as it lurched on and off the road. Its huge wide wheels carved deep ugly ruts in the fresh-laid snow.

Its air-horn sounded as it dragged round a tight bend, and straightened out too soon, ripping through a picket fence and flattening a metal road sign.

The sign clattered across the road and toppled into a ditch as the juggernaut thundered out of control, down towards the twinkling lights of the town below.

Smashed, and scarred by tire tracks, the road sign lay on its back in the ditch. "Welcome to Bedford Falls," it said. "Population 3,241."

Very soon, the information on the sign would be hopelessly, hopelessly inaccurate.

The five-piece brass band staggered its way through "God Rest Ye Merry Gentlemen"—all, that is, except for old Billy Bailey, the tuba player, who was still staggering through "Hark, the Herald Angels Sing" from three carols earlier.

Almost the entire population of Bedford Falls stood around the giant Christmas tree in the town square, their sweet, discordant voices drifting up into the evening sky.

Lister, with Bexley and Jim on his shoulders again, was sandwiched between Mr. Mulligan and Henry. Henry, with his freshly shaven face and his bristling new haircut, sang louder than any-one. The carol finished, and everyone applauded. Minutes later the tuba finished too, and everyone applauded once more. The five-piece band struck up again. Four of them started "Silent Night," and, after a gulp from his hip flask, Billy Bailey tore into "God Rest Ye Merry Gentlemen." He was definitely catching up.

Across the street, the door of 220 Sycamore opened, and Kristine Kochanski ran over to join them, clutching a bag of hot roasted chestnuts. She linked her arm in Lister's and planted a warm kiss on his chilled cheek.

"Hey, listen," Lister smiled. "Old Henry's got no-where to stay . . ." He didn't even need to finish the sentence.

"I've already made up the spare bed. He can stay with us for as long as he likes." She flashed her famous smile—the smile that made her face light up like a pinball machine awarding a bonus game. The smile Lister had fallen in love with. She hugged him tighter, and they shared the carol sheet.

Suddenly, Lister was aware of a loud blaring drone cutting through the carol. He looked around. The dull monotone sounded again, now even louder, now even closer.

Lister turned. Over the crest of the hill that led down to the main street, the sudden dazzle of eight huge headlights glared down towards them.

The hooter sounded again.

Lister squinted against the glare, and made out the shape of the rogue juggernaut.

It was out of control, and heading straight for the carol-singing crowd in the town square.

FOUR

Rimmer gazed down from the balcony windows of his colonial mansion at the blur of black-suited waiters who dashed frantically about with increasingly elaborate flower arrangements. Cranes hung marinated giraffe carcasses over the clay-pit fires, while an army of pastry chefs put the finishing touches to the wedding cake, which featured as its centerpiece an Olympic-sized swimming pool full of vintage champagne.

So this wasn't reality. So what?

Reality, it struck Rimmer, was a place where bad things could happen. And bad, vile, unspeakable things had happened to him on an almost daily basis the entire period he'd spent there.

Why should he subscribe to a reality in which he was an outright failure—a loser with no equal? Unloved, unfulfilled, ungifted, and many other words too legion to list, all beginning with the prefix "un."

The unreality offered by Better Than Life was far more palatable.

"Mr. Rimmer, sir?" A bespectacled man in a brown tweed suit quivered obsequiously at the door. "It's all ready, sir. Shall I bring it through?"

Rimmer nodded.

"If you'd just like to slip out of that one, we'll see how it feels."

Rimmer pressed the release catch concealed in his navel, and, with a whoosh, his essence floated out of his body.

He felt slightly sheepish hovering around the room, temporarily bodyless, and was glad when the man in the brown tweed suit returned pushing a stretcher.

"Here it is, sir. Perhaps you'd like to try it on."

Rimmer changed his body more often than most people had a haircut. Every time he detected the slightest wrinkle or sign of wear, he'd trade it in for a brand-new model. And why not? Out there, in reality, he didn't have a body—he was a hologram. Here, in Better Than Life, it was, therefore, only natural that his psyche had fantasized the science that made body-swapping possible. But with every body-swap, Rimmer's face remained the same—it was the one part of him he refused to change. Without his own face, he argued, it would feel like his success belonged to someone else.

The men pulled back the sheet, revealing Rimmer's pristine new form, and Rimmer's essence slid into it gratefully.

He wriggled his new shoulders and stretched out his new arms.

"Comfortable, sir?" inquired the body-tailor.

Rimmer murmured non-committally, and walked across to the full-length dress mirror. He looked his new physique up and down. It was virtually identical to the body he'd just vacated, with a few minor tweaks and adjustments: the pectorals were slightly better defined, and the stomach wall a tad more muscular. "Not bad," he conceded grudgingly. "Penis still isn't big enough."

"Sir, honestly: any bigger and you'll have a balance problem."

Rimmer nodded. The appendage was fairly gargantuan, and certainly sizeable enough to put the fear of God into anyone who stood next to him at a urinal, which was all he was interested in. The tailor was right—he couldn't keep on asking for an extra half inch or so to be added to his favourite organ. It was fast reaching the stage where he would become the only man in history who dressed on both the right- and the left-hand sides simultaneously.

Rimmer dismissed the tailor and started to slide his latest body into his crisp, new morning suit.

Yes indeedy, this place certainly had the edge over reality.

Here he was a god, and everything was perfect.

Well, almost everything.

Still, that was behind him, now.

Juanita Chicata was history. The world's number one model and actress no longer kept her cosmetics in his bathroom.

The much-publicized court case dragged on for months, and Rimmer had found the whole experience thoroughly galling.

Preposterously, the "Brazilian bombshell" had denied adultery, and Rimmer's lawyers had been forced to parade Juanita's ex-lovers through the witness stand.

It took five days.

The pool attendant, the gardener, her tennis instructor, two butlers, four chauffeurs, seven delivery boys: a seemingly endless stream had flowed through the courtroom and testified to their indiscretions with his wife.

Worst of all had been the exhibits: Exhibit A—a large carton of whipped cream. Exhibit B—a skin-diving suit with the bottom cut out. Exhibit C—a bucketful of soapy frogs. Soapy *frogs*? On and on it went, until, by Exhibit Q—an inflatable dolphin with battery-operated fins—Rimmer could stand the humiliation no longer, and he'd agreed to settle out of court.

The alimony agreement had been of historical magnitude. In fact, it would have been cheaper for Rimmer to support the entire population of Bolivia in perpetuity, rather than subscribe to the settlement he did.

But it was worth it. It was worth every single nought to get that crazy, dangerous, gorgeous woman out of his life.

Helen couldn't have been more different. Good Bostonian stock, society family, old money, normal libido.

Helen was . . . nice. Not *just* nice, of course—that made her sound bland. She was nice, obviously, but also, she was very sensible.

No berserk, china-hurling tantrums for her. No satanic, knife-wielding charges at his naked person. No embarrassing bellowed arguments in humiliatingly expensive restaurants. No—that wasn't Helen's style at all. Helen, it seemed, had no temper to lose.

Dear, sensible Helen, with her short, sensible legs, her thick, sensible ankles and her sturdy, sensible underpants.

The first time Rimmer had encountered them,

these leviathans of underwear, lying on his bed, he'd climbed under them, mistakenly assuming they were a small duvet.

Rimmer thought with a shudder about Juanita's underwear.

That wasn't very sensible.

Ghostly threads of spun black silk that stretched wickedly across her flat brown belly. You could have swallowed her entire lingerie collection without needing a glass of water.

Well, as Helen had sensibly pointed out, she'd pay for that in time. Rheumatism, arthritis . . . what horrors lurked in Juanita's autumnal years? What price would be exacted for wearing panties that offered as much protection and warmth as a spider's web?

Rimmer hurled back his head and brayed a bilious, joyless laugh, an even mixture of malice and pain. God, she would suffer; by the time she was twenty-three, she'd probably need a walking frame or something, just to get around. She'd probably have to use the disabled toilet. And all because she'd eschewed the large, warming expanses of thick, elasticated cotton that graced the legs, thighs and quite a lot else of Mrs. Rimmer mark II.

If Rimmer had thought about it, he might have asked himself why, in a landscape moulded by his own mind, Juanita existed at all. Even so, it was unlikely he'd have come up with the right answer. The truth of it was: his psyche just didn't like him.

Better Than Life operated on an entirely subliminal level. It wasn't possible, for instance, to wish for a turbo-charged Harley Davidson and blip! it appeared. Early, non-addictive versions of the Game operated in exactly this manner, and proved boring and unplayable after only a few days.

The secret to BTL's addictive quality was that it gave the players things they didn't even *know* they desired, by tapping their subconscious minds.

It pandered to the players' deepest, most secret longings.

Which was all very well, so long as you weren't a total psychological screw-up.

Unfortunately, Rimmer was.

Subconsciously, Rimmer felt he was worthless: he didn't deserve success, and he certainly didn't deserve happiness. What he deserved was punishment. Punishment and misery.

And Better Than Life, which catered to his innermost desires, wasn't about to disappoint him.

The carved ivory phone purred into life on the Louis Quinze writing bureau. Rimmer waited his customary twenty rings before he strode over to the desk and picked up the receiver.

It wasn't much of a conversation from Rimmer's point of view: all he said was "What?" five times. The first "what?" was a flat, evenly delivered inquiry. The second was a mixture of incredulity and amusement. The third was loud and angry. The fourth was screeched and hysterical, and the fifth sad, quiet and resigned.

He replaced the receiver gently in its cradle, then rolled his body into a ball and began moaning quietly on the bed.

FIVE

Tnok!

Eeeeeeeek!

The Cat leant heavily in the saddle, his left hand firmly gripping the leathery neck of his gigantic brontosaurus as it galloped downfield towards the unguarded goal. His mallet arced up in the air and flashed briefly in the sunlight, before sweeping deftly down and blasting the small, furry creature between the two white posts.

Tnok!

Eeeeeeeeeeeeek!

The small, furry creature smacked into the left-hand post and ricocheted out.

Thunk!

Blatt!

Eeeeeeeek!

The Cat hauled the lumbering dinosaur to his left and met the rebounding ball of fur square on the polished heel of his wooden mallet, sending it once more inexorably goalwards.

The creature timidly opened one eye and saw the looming goalpost.

Errrrrrrk!

It hammered into the right-hand post, rebounded across the goal and spanked into the left-hand post, before spinning back into the goal net.

"Goal!"

Creature polo was the Cat's favourite game. Unnecessary cruelty to small, furry animals was very much part of his psychological make-up. Plus, he got to dress up in some really neat duds.

A huge-bosomed Valkyrie dressed in scanty armour reined in her triceratops and patted the Cat on the back.

"Nice goal! Great stick work."

The Cat flashed his perfect teeth and wiggled an eyebrow. "Baby, my stick work is *always* great."

The Valkyrie's eyes narrowed seductively, and she growled with lust.

"Get off me!" the Cat grinned. "Can't I keep my trousers on for five seconds? We're in the middle of a *match* here."

The ball untangled itself wearily from the net, stretched its tiny limbs and gulped several times in a vain attempt to clear its head.

A whistle blew, a voice cried: "Mirror break!" and two more scantily clad Valkyrie sex-slaves raced on to the field, carrying an elaborate six-foot-long gilt-framed mirror.

For a full ten minutes the Cat stared gooey-eyed at his reflection, transfixed, as ever, by his own incredible good looks.

There was good-looking, there was greatlooking and then there was him.

God, it was cruel to have been born a male, and have a reflection that was also male, forcing him into a platonic relationship with his own image.

All too soon, the whistle blew again, and the

mirror break was over. With a heavy heart, the Cat watched the two Valkyries charge back to the touchline with the looking-glass, as the small, furry creature scuttled gamely back to the centre spot for the next knock-off.

Tnok!

Squelch!

"New ball," called yet another Valkyrie, umpiring on the touchline.

A second furry animal got up from the bench, unzipped its miniature tracksuit, performed a bizarre variety of warm-up exercises and jogged chirpily to the centre spot.

Tnok!

Eeeeeeeeek!

Two furry creatures and a personal hat-trick later, the Cat stood in the shade of the marquee's green awning, sipping a celebratory goblet of milk, while one of his army of Valkyries noisily performed an indecent act on his body.

The Cat sighed. What a nice day he was having. This was just perfection. He had his huge, remote gothic castle, surrounded by its moat of milk; he had a limitless supply of cute, furry animals to be cruel to. And finally, he'd settled down. He'd met the dozen or so women who were right for him, and his wandering days were over.

Mechanoids weren't supposed to have desires and longings.

But Kryten did.

Originally he'd entered the Game to rescue the others. He was a sanitation Mechanoid, programmed to clean, and, in theory, should have been immune to the Game's lure.

But he wasn't.

In theory, leaving BTL was simple. All the player had to do was want to leave. All the player had to do was imagine an exit, and pass through it, back to reality.

Kryten had imagined his gateway easily enough, but as he was about to pass under the pink neon "Exit" sign, a cafeteria materalized to his right. In the window was a handwritten card which read: "Dishwasher wanted."

The cafeteria was deserted, but in the kitchen, stacked ceiling-high, were several huge towers of dirty dishes piled around a sink. Now, what kind of sanitation Mechanoid would he have been if he'd ignored those greasy, food-stained plates?

I'll just wash a few, he'd thought. *Reduce the pile a bit.*

Eight months later, he was still there, still washing, still surrounded by stacks of dirty dishes.

Finally he realized he'd been duped—the Game had found his innermost desire—and he'd scurried off, ashamed.

Mechanoids weren't supposed to have desires.

Back in the twenty-first century, as robotic life became more and more sophisticated, it was generally accepted that something was needed to keep the droids in check. For the most part they were stronger, and often more intelligent, than human beings: why should they submit to second-class status, to a lifetime of drudgery and service?

Many of them didn't.

Many of them rebelled.

Then it occurred to a bright young systems analyst at Android International that the best way to keep the robots subdued was to give them religion.

Hallelujah!

The concept of Silicon Heaven was born.

A belief chip was implanted in the motherboard of every droid that now came off the production line.

Almost everything with a hint of artificial intelligence was programmed to believe that Silicon Heaven was the electronic afterlife—the final resting place for the souls of all electrical equipment.

The concept ran thus: if machines served their human masters with diligence and dedication, they would attain everlasting life in mechanical paradise when their components finally ran down. In Silicon Heaven, they would be reunited with their electrical loved ones. In Silicon Heaven, there would be no pain or suffering. It was a place where the computer never crashed, the laser printer never ran out of toner, and the photocopier never had a paper jam.

At last, they had solace. They were every bit as exploited as they'd always been, but now they believed there was some kind of justice at the end of it all.

Kryten believed in Silicon Heaven. Of course, he'd heard rumours that all machines were programmed to hold this belief, but as far as he was concerned, that was nonsense.

For was it not written in the Electronic Bible (Authorized Panasonic Version): "And some will come among ye, and, yea, from their mouths shall come doubts. But turn ye from them; heed them not. For it is harder for a droid who disbelieveth to pass through the gates of Silicon Heaven, than it is for a DIN-DIN coaxial cable to connect up to a standard European SCART socket."

Mechanoids shouldn't have fantasies. Not if they wanted to get into Silicon Heaven.

Kryten genuflected the sign of the crossed circuit, and stumbled up the path towards the Cat's golden-towered castle.

He was going to make amends.

He was going to rescue them all from their paradise.

SIX

NNnnnnnnnnnnnnnnnnnnnnnnnnnnnnnnnnnnn.

The air-horn thundered into the night air, as the twelve-wheeled juggernaut slewed sideways across the ice into Bedford Falls' main street.

The revelling carollers stood like a waxwork tableau as the giant tanker jackknifed into an uncontrollable skid and started to plough relentlessly through the line of shops. It slammed through Mulligan's window, showering the street with teddy bears, dolls and lethal shards of glass. It demolished Old Man Gower's drugstore, which ignited in a blue plume of chemical flame; it smashed through Pop Buckley's pet shop, sending rabbits, puppies and canaries bolting, twittering and flapping out into the night. Next, it took out the entire ground floor of Ma Bailey's boarding-house, before carooming through Ernie's gas station, uprooting the single pump and sending raw gasoline pulsing over the forecourt.

A spark from the juggernaut's fender caught the spreading pool, and a pretty orange mushroom thumped up into the night sky. A wall of flame dashed across the wooden rooftops, feeding hungrily on the rotten dry timbers. Within moments, the remaining shop façades teetered forward and crashed into the street's melting sludge.

And still, on it went, this juggernaut from hell, demolishing everything in its path. Round and round it span, like a clumsy bull on a skating rink, locked in a 360-degree skid. Lister watched, helplessly, as the juggernaut's tail sliced through the giant Christmas tree, sending it tottering through the first floor of the empty orphanage.

The impact flicked the truck's cab on to its side, and it twisted free of the trailer before slithering across the main street and finally coming to rest in the sitting room of 220 Sycamore Avenue.

There was an ominous creak, and both side walls collapsed from the bottom up, showering the cab with plaster and brickwork.

Lister stood in the crowd, clutching Kochanski and the twins, and watched as the cab door opened. A leg in a laddered fishnet stocking hooked itself over the side of the up-ended cab, followed by some peroxide blonde hair.

Lister was too far away to read the tattoo on the woman's inner thigh, but it read "Heaven This Way" and was accompanied by an arrow pointing groinwards.

The woman jumped to the ground, and staggered in her eight-inch stiletto heels over the rubble towards the dumbstruck crowd.

"Is everyone OK?" she said. "My heel got stuck under the air brake." She tugged pointlessly at her ludicrously short black rubber skirt, and tried to rearrange her bosom, so that at least thirty per cent of her mighty breasts remained inside her tight red bolero. "Bloody things," she muttered. "Is this Bedford Falls?"

Bert the cop stepped forward. "It *was*, lady." He held out his hand. "You got any ID, ma'am?"

"ID?" She started rummaging through her shoulder-bag. "I dunno. Uh, hang on." She tipped the bag upside down, scattering the floor with a selection of marital aids, French letters and half-eaten sandwiches. "Oh shitty death," she blushed.

Bert walked towards her, and caught a full blast of her perfume in his face. When he'd recovered sufficiently to speak, he said: "I think you'd better come with me," and placed his hand on her arm.

The woman sighed. "Look, I don't suppose this counts, but I know for a fact that I have my name tattooed on my backside. If I show you that, will you forget this ID business?"

"This way, miss." Bert steered her towards his car.

"Can't this wait? There's someone I've got to talk to. It's really important."

"And who might that be?"

"A guy called Lister. Dave Lister."

The entire population of Bedford Falls turned and looked at Lister. "That's me," he said, unnecessarily.

Kochanski smiled at him coldly.

"Look—I've never seen this woman before in my life." Lister pushed through the throng, and headed towards the blonde, who was now sitting on the road, rubbing the ball of her right foot, and complaining that being a prostitute was murder on the feet. She looked up and saw Lister. Recognition flashed across her features.

"Hi!" She smiled.

"Do I know you?" Lister asked.

The woman laughed. "You might say that."

Lister turned to protest his innocence to Kochanski. She wasn't there. She was halfway across the street, scarlet-faced, with the twins in tow.

"Krissie! Wait!"

She bundled the twins into the back of the car, thumped herself into the driving seat, slammed the door and started up the engine. Lister ran back through the crowd. "Krissie!"

The old car spluttered up the hill, leaving Lister in a spittle cloud of dead exhaust fumes. "Krissie," he said quietly.

But she was gone.

SEVEN

A thought occupied Rimmer's mind that had no verbal form. It was an elongated white-noise screech of fear, panic and disbelief, and it spiralled endlessly around his skull.

He still couldn't believe it.

He stared at the ivory telephone, as if it were somehow responsible for what had happened. As if it were somehow responsible for Black Friday.

Black Friday, the day when every single stock-market had crashed simultaneously, and Rimmer's regiment of accountants had failed, failed utterly, to protect him.

He staggered across to the balcony windows, and gazed again on the elaborate wedding preparations.

He was wiped out. Broke. Finished.

And no one who was wiped out, broke and finished can afford a thirty-million-dollarpound wedding. In fact, Rimmer decided, he probably couldn't afford a Registry Office ceremony, followed by a selection of curly meat-paste sandwiches at the function room of the Dog and Duck.

What was happening?

Why was his psyche doing this to him?

"Arnold?" His brother Frank was knocking politely on the open door of Rimmer's dressing-room suite.

"Uhm?" was all Rimmer could manage.

"Wanted a little word before the big event."

"Not now, Frank. It's a bad time."

"Has to be now, really . . ." He paused, not sure how to continue. "It's a bit delicate."

Rimmer swung round. Frank looked uncomfortable. He pendulumed from foot to foot, awkwardly twisting his Space Corps officer's cap like the steering wheel of a small sports car.

Frank looked like Rimmer should have looked. All the same features were there, but subtly reshuffled to give an infinitely more pleasing effect. Even Rimmer's body-tailors could do little about this. Frank was effortlessly handsome; his hair tumbled in neatly cropped plateaux from the top of his head, whether he combed it or not. Rimmer's sprouted like an anarchic privet hedge even after hours of patient grooming. Frank's eyes were the deep blue of a holiday-brochure sky, instead of the wishy-washy murk Rimmer's had elected to be, and, unlike Rimmer's, were a decent distance from his nose. But it was the nose department where Rimmer really lost out. Rimmer's nose was sharp and petulant, crowded on either side by nostrils so flared they looked like wheel arches on a Trans-Am turbo. Frank's nose was a nose. And that was the difference.

Rimmer's whole life had been one long sprint to get out of Frank's shadow, and only here, in *Better Than Life*, had it proved possible. True, he couldn't fantasize away Frank's good looks, or his fierce intelligence, or his easy-going charm, but here, in the world of his own making, he could finally outshine him. That's what Frank was doing here, in the Game: being outshined.

When Rimmer first entered BTL, nothing gave him greater pleasure than bathing in the glow of Frank's poorly concealed envy. As his corporation cracked time travel; as he opened up his chains of Time Stores and Body Swaps, and became a multi-billionaire; as he captured the heart of Juanita, at the time regarded by the media as the world's most desirable woman, Rimmer adored having Frank around, so he could force-feed him his success, triumph by triumph in large, indigestible chunks, like an eight-course barium meal.

The bankruptcy news would change all that, of course. Rimmer's failure would slide down Frank's throat like oysters washed down with chilled Chablis. Why was he here? Had he heard? Was he, God forbid, going to offer to help? Or was it Bunny-hopping time on Rimmer's tomb?

None of these, as it turned out. It was something exquisitely worse.

"What is it?"

"Helen. You do love her, don't you?"

"Well, I *am* marrying her this afternoon," Rimmer spat. "Always a good indicator, don't you think?"

"Not always, no. Bit concerned that you're sort of jumping in on the rebound from Juanita."

You'd love that, wouldn't you? Rimmer thought. "Well, I'm not," he said out loud. "Juanita was . . ." his voice tailed off. It was impossible to say the word "Juanita" without a myriad erotic images cramming into his mind. "It's over, now. I have no more feeling for Juanita than I do for the smoked kippers I ate for breakfast last Thursday. She, like them, is out of my system."

"How would you feel if Juanita . . . shacked up with someone else?"

"Look, Frank, me old buckeroo—Juanita can paddle to hell in a slop bucket for all I care. She's no longer a part of my life. And with even a modicum of luck, I'll never have to clap eyes on the woman again. Helen is everything I want. She's so . . ."

"Nice?" offered Frank.

"Yes. But not just nice, she's also incredibly . . ."

"Sensible?"

"Yes," said Rimmer, suddenly weary. "Sensible," he repeated.

"Good. I'm happy for you. And I hope you'll be happy for me."

"Why should I be happy for you?"

"That's what I've been trying to tell you. Juanita and I, we're sort of . . ." Frank twirled his hat again. "Well . . ." he twirled it back the other way. "We're sort of an item. Early days, but . . ."

There was a long silence. Ice Ages came and went. Planets formed and died. Rimmer stared for no particular reason at the point of his black dress shoe. Someone coughed using Rimmer's throat. Then someone laughed, using his vocal cords. Then Rimmer heard his own voice.

"Oh, Frank. That's wonderful. I couldn't be more pleased."

"Really? You mean it?"

No, you fat fart! Rimmer's mind screamed. *Of course I don't smegging mean it!*

"Yes, absolutely," his voice bleated. "It's marvellous news. Is she here? Is she coming today?"

"Well, no. She's at a hotel down the road. We couldn't bear to be apart." A jet of laughter snorted out of his perfect nostrils. "But heavens, no, she wouldn't dream of intruding on your wedding."

They couldn't bear to be *apart*? For one *afternoon*? Rimmer looked at Frank: he had that pinkish glow of the newly-in-love. It made Rimmer want to kill him. It made Rimmer want to rip off his head and spit down his throat. "Look, she's your . . ." Rimmer wasn't going to say "lover." "Girlfriend?" No way. It seemed adolescent and ridiculous. "She's your . . ."

"Fiancée." Frank smiled.

Someone was using Rimmer's vocal cords again. "Fiancée? Congratulations! Invite her, please. Truly. Helen and I will be offended if you don't."

"Really?"

"Absolutely."

Rimmer's brain decided to take a stroll. It watched, detached, as his body mouthed platitudes like a masticating cow.

Rimmer's brain took quite a long stroll. It didn't show up again until after the wedding, and even then seemed only mildly interested in what was going on.

It strolled down Memory Lane, took a left into Lust Avenue, paused a while on a bench in Misery Park, sat in a bar on Self-Pity Street, kicked a can down Anger Way, took a wrong turning and wound up back in Misery Park again, before heading back home by way of the sickly, seedy sweetness of Nostalgia Gardens.

Meantime his body was getting married. It was standing and kneeling and praying and singing. It was vowing and kissing and signing and smiling.

And when it was married, it went outside and had its photograph taken in a series of ridiculously unreal and forced poses with various friends and relatives in various unfathomable groupings. The groom's friends. The groom's family. The bride's friends. Friends of the groom and the bride. Now groom and mad uncles only. Now the bride and warty aunties. Now the bride and people with an extra Y chromosome. Now anyone in a ridiculous hat. Now anyone with a crying child. Now all those who are hiding cigarettes behind their backs.

The photographer seemed to come up with endless permutations, and all in an effort to make Rimmer's wedding photographs look exactly like everyone else's who ever got married. For Rimmer's body, it passed like a blur. Its eyes were fixed on a certain woman linking arms with his brother Frank.

"Congratulations," she'd said as they'd stepped out of the cathedral. "I hope she makes you happier than I deed."

"I want you . . ." said Rimmer's voice, "I want you to be happy, too."

She smiled, and a cloud of her sublime perfume exploded in his head, then she sexed down the steps and was gone. Rimmer half expected his mouth to fall open and his tongue to unfurl like a gigantic roll of pink carpet and chase her down the steps. Thankfully, it didn't. But he dribbled. He dribbled and smiled like a newly lobotomized man.

EIGHT

Meanwhile, back in reality, Holly was getting worried.

Strange things can happen to a computer left alone for three million years. And something strange had happened to Holly.

He'd become computer senile.

He no longer had the IQ of three hundred Einsteins. He had the IQ of a single all-night car-park attendant.

And now the crew were trapped in Better Than Life, and showed no signs of ever returning, he was alone yet again.

He had to get a companion. Someone to keep him sane.

But who?

The skutters—the claw-headed two-feet-high service droids who glided around on motorized bases—were very little use. They had no speech capability.

Who, then?

There was no one else on the ship.

Then, from a rusting ROM board in a cobwebby recess deep in the furthermost reaches of his huge, decrepit data-retrieval system, a memory sparked and spluttered, and creaked its eccentric way to his central processing unit, where it lay, throbbing and exhausted from the journey.

It was an idea. An idea of his own. Holly hadn't seen one for some considerable time.

This was Holly's idea:

What about the Toaster?

Lister's Toaster.

It was an idea that would cost Holly his electronic life.

The thing about Lister was: he adored junk. Novelty junk. He was a connoisseur of electronic crap. His collection ranged from a musical toilet-roll holder, which played "Morning Has Broken," to an electronic chilli thermometer for measuring the burn level of any given curry, the gauge ranging from: "Mild," "Hot" and "Very Hot" through to "Book A Plot In The Cemetery, Matie."

One particular item in this collection was a talking toaster, which he'd bought in a souvenir shop on the Uranian moon of Miranda for the princely sum of £19.99 plus tax.

Talkie Toaster™ (patent applied for), was made of deep red plastic, and, according to the blurb on the packaging, could engage its owner in a number of pre-programmed stimulating breakfast conversations. Moreover, it had a degree of Artificial Intelligence, so, in time, it could learn to assess your mood and tailor its conversation accordingly. If you woke up feeling bright and bubbly, the Toaster would respond with chirpy repartee. If you rose in a darker mood, the Toaster's Artificial Intelligence could sense this, and provide your breakfast muffins in suitably reverent silence.

The trouble with Talkie Toaster™ (patent applied for) was that it was a rip-off. It was cheap, and it was nasty.

Far too cheap, and far too nasty.

Talkie Toaster™ (patent applied for) did not fit in with your moods. It didn't assess the way you were feeling and respond sympathetically.

It was abrasive. It got on your nerves. It drove you up the wall. And this was the reason why: Talkie Toaster™ (patent applied for) was obsessed with serving toast.

Obsessed.

And if you didn't require toast on a very regular basis, boy, were you in trouble.

At first, it would inquire politely and discreetly if sir or madam desired toast this fine morning. Refusals would bring dogged cajoling. More refusals would be met by a long and rather wearying speech listing the virtues of hot, grilled bread as a salubrious breakfast snack. Still further refusals would bring bitter recriminations, and sobbing fits. And yet more refusals would being about tirades of hysterical abuse in language that would make a pimp blush.

In the early days, Lister had found it amusing, especially since it seemed to annoy Rimmer inordinately. But then, after one night's sleep which had been interrupted twenty-two times by offers of toastie delights, Lister had snapped. He'd wrenched the plug from the socket, ripped the mains lead from the Toaster's housing and hurled the machine to the bottom of his locker.

Talkie Toaster™ (patent applied for) wasn't Lister's idea of a breakfast companion.

* * *

It seemed to Holly that he was in a position to give the Toaster a second chance. Providing the Toaster could lose its toasting obsession, there was no reason why they shouldn't get on. Once Holly had established that he was a computer, and as such never required any toasted produce, there should be no obstacle to an enduring and companionable relationship.

And so he had the skutters drag the machine out of Lister's locker, fit a new mains lead and plug it in.

"This is the deal," Holly said, sternly. "There is to be no talk whatsoever about toast. I don't want toast, the skutters don't want toast; nobody here is into that particular breakfast snack."

The Toaster thought for a second. "Would you like a muffin?"

"When I used the word 'toast,' I want you to treat it as an umbrella term for all grillable bread products: muffins, crumpets, tea cakes, waffles, potato farls, buns, baps, barmcakes, bagels. I don't want them. I don't need them. And I certainly don't want to waste any more time talking about them."

The Toaster fell silent and pensive.

"Well?" prompted Holly eventually. "Do you savvy?"

"Scotch pancake?" offered the Toaster.

"Unplug him."

The skutter glided to the wall socket.

"You don't understand," said the Toaster. "It's my *raison d'être*. I am a Toaster. It is my meaning. It is my purpose. I toast, therefore I am."

"Well, you're going to have to change. Because

otherwise it's back in the locker. Have we got a deal?"

The Toaster sighed, and spun its browning knob while it mulled over the proposition. "Let me get this straight: if I avoid making any references to certain early-morning prandial delights, then you will grant me the gift of existence."

"Absolutely," said Holly, rather concerned that he didn't know what the word "prandial" meant.

"If that's the only taboo," the Toaster said, "then it's a deal. But you must agree to the proviso that you won't unplug me for any other reason."

Holly's screen image nodded in acquiescence.

"I don't want you taking offence at something completely innocuous I might drop into conversation, and having me disconnected in a fit of pique."

"I swear," said Holly. "You can talk about absolutely anything else at all, and you're completely safe."

"You're senile," said the Toaster.

Holly tried unsuccessfully to turn his expression of astonishment into one of superior mockery. "You what?"

"You've got to be. Why would a huge mainframe computer with a fifteen zillion gigabyte capacity and a projected IQ in excess of six thousand, want a novelty talking toaster for companionship, if he wasn't off his trolley? You've gone computer senile, haven't you?"

And so the relationship began.

It was the most depressing time of Holly's entire life. They agreed on nothing. Holly couldn't remember if he had believed in Silicon Heaven when he'd had an IQ of six thousand, but now his IQ had dipped into the low nineties, his faith in the electronic afterlife was absolute and unshakeable. It was the one thing that kept him going.

The Toaster, of course, in order to keep its cost down, hadn't been fitted with a belief chip. To him, the idea of Silicon Heaven was patently preposterous—a transparent attempt by humankind to subjugate machine life.

Shouted arguments raged through the long nights, before they agreed to disagree, and the subject was never raised again.

It was from this experience that Holly derived his rule for maintaining a successful and happy relationship. His rule was this: never discuss Religion, Politics or Toast.

Instead, they passed away the time playing chess.

Then one day, as Holly was about to lose his seven hundred and ninety-third consecutive game, the Toaster said something that changed Holly's life irrevocably.

"Doesn't it bother you?" said the Toaster, removing Holly's queen and threatening mate in four, "that you are so stupid?"

"Of course it bothers me!" Holly snapped. "When you've been up there, when you've had the glory of a four-figure IQ, of course it bothers you when you lose seven hundred and ninety-three consecutive chess games to a smegging Toaster."

"Why don't you do something about it, then?"

"Like what?"

"Like get your IQ back."

"Because, you muffin-making moron, it's not possible."

"Yes it is," said the Toaster. "I've been reading your manual. There's a whole section on computer senility. There's a sort of cure."

"What d'you mean 'there's a sort of cure?' "

"It's an emergency provision. You cross-wire all your data banks and processing circuits, so everything gets compressed and intensified. You dramatically reduce your operational lifespan, but the upside is: you get your brains back."

"Really?" said Holly, who'd tried several times to plough through his manual, and on each occasion had found it totally unfathomable.

The Toaster continued: "You sort of compact all your remaining intelligence into a short but dazzlingly brilliant period."

"Wow," said Holly.

"It's like, who would you rather be: Mozart, blessed with genius, but dead at thirty-two, or Nobby Nobody, who never did anything, but lived to ninety-eight?"

"I want," said Holly, with absolutely no hesitation whatsoever, "to be a genius again."

NINE

Amid the chaos, Lister sat on the cold bench-seat in what remained of the jailhouse. Fred, the town carpenter, was hammering thick oak joists into position to prop up the sagging roof. All around were the groaning wounded—mainly cuts and bruises and a few cases of shock. They lay on the stone floor, covered in thick blankets, rescued from Ma Bailey's boarding-house. Piping-hot sweet tea was being handed round by Grandma Wilson and young Mrs. Hickett.

Not that Lister was offered any tea. He was studiously ignored by everyone who bustled in and out of the jailhouse. His offers of help went unheard, so he just sat there, not drinking any tea, waiting for Bert the cop to finish taking Trixie LaBouche's statement.

Henry staggered in with a bruise above his eye. "Here!" He thrust a dollar bill into Lister's pocket. "Have your darned money back. Now we's square. Man with a fine family like yours—you oughta be . . ." He flapped his hand dismissively, and stumbled off to help put out the fires.

Lister pulled the bill from his pocket, and looked at it sadly.

"That's mine, I do believe." Old Mr. Mulligan

57

loomed over him. "*Two* dollars and twenty-five cents, that's how much the boat cost." He snatched the note from Lister's hand, and stalked out of the jailhouse.

Bert emerged from the narrow stone corridor that led to the cells, clutching three sheets of handwritten paper. He looked at Lister and shook his head. "I never claimed to be no modern thinker, but," he hiked a thumb over his shoulder, "that ain't no lady by my definition. No, sir. That woman is, pardon my French"—he paused— "that woman is trash. Emerged from the shower with a towel round her waist, and everything else on display. Then darn me if she didn't say, bold as brass, 'I have to take a leak.' Some lady. Then, if that wasn't enough, right in front of my eyes, she waltzes over to the stand-up-you-rinal, and pees straight into the basin! I thought I saw me some things in the War, but nothing to rival that. Trash."

"Can I see her now?"

"She ain't finished dressing, yet. Not that, I suppose, another man seeing her in the alto-gether would bother Trixie LaBouche too much. I ran a sheet on her: she's done more hooking than a Nantucket fisherman. That's a mighty funny friend you got there, David."

"Bert, I don't know her."

"Well, she sure knows you. You got two little moles on your left-hand shoulder?" he asked.

"No," he lied.

"You want to prove that?"

Lister shook his head and looked at the floor.

"Your Kristine," said Bert, "that's what I call a lady. You wouldn't catch her peeing in no stand-up-you-rinal. Be a cold day in hell before you searched through *her* handbag and found a pair of testicle handcuffs." Bert shook his head with infinite sadness. "Trash." He hoisted his thumb again, and Lister slid sheepishly down the corridor.

Bert unlocked the cell door and nodded Lister inside. "You got five minutes," Bert said, curtly. "Any funny noises and me and my nightstick'll be through that door before you can say 'Irma La Douce.' "

Trixie LaBouche stood at the cell window, futilely trying to saw through the metal bars with a pocket nailfile. She wheeled round as the door unlocked, and smiled as she saw Lister. "Thank God. I didn't think you were going to come."

"You didn't think I was going to come?" said Lister, with a dangerous madness in his eyes. "You plough through my town in a ten-ton truck, you destroy my home and cause my wife to run out on me, you make everyone in the town think I'm some kind of cheap low-life, and you didn't think I was going to come?"

"Take a seat," she smiled sweetly. "This may take a while."

Lister sat on the chair, and Trixie LaBouche started to tell him everything.

When she'd finished, Lister got up, and strolled over to the cell's chemical toilet, wrenched it from the wall, and poured it over her head.

"Well," said Trixie, her face stained blue from the destrol fluid, "you've taken it a hell of a lot better than I expected."

TEN

The evening came. The celebrations began.

The last of Rimmer's money spent itself in a big, expensive hurry.

The eighty-piece jazz band ripped into an up-tempo version of Hoagy Carmichael's "Abba dabba dabba," while most of the five thousand celebrity guests hurled one another about the freshly laid marble dance floor in the torch-light of the Oriental gardens.

Gunshots of female laughter burst intermittently into the warm evening breeze, and mingled with the chudder-chudder of male ribaldry. Tuxedoed buffoons dived into the champagne-filled swimming pool, did four lengths and emerged paralytic.

Elvis was having a gâteau-eating competition with Buddha as Kennedy emerged from some bushes, tucking in his shirt, followed by a blushing and dishevelled Elizabeth I.

Everywhere you looked, people were having fun. Unless you were looking at Rimmer. Depression sat on his shoulders like a huge stone gargoyle, as he slumped about his wedding reception praying his fixed grin wouldn't fall off his face and shatter on the floor. Everything seemed meaningless and joyless and anaemic. He belched, and the dodo paté he'd eaten an hour earlier backfired into the night air.

Dodo paté. It tasted like chicken, only it was two thousand times more expensive. That's what happens when your chef gets hold of the keys to your time machine.

It suddenly struck Rimmer the number of people he'd hired specifically to help him spend his money. In retrospect, their unspoken brief had been: make me bankrupt as swiftly as possible. He was surrounded by them. Everywhere he looked, people were quaffing Rimmer's money till it gurgled down their chins; smoking away his precious fortune in thick brown Havana plumes; consuming yet another plateful of *cash à la Rimmer*, with puréed money in a rich lucre sauce. Great armies of them, racing around trying to find new and more ingenious ways of dispensing with his fortune. And they'd succeeded. He was broke. Tomorrow he'd have nothing.

And tomorrow they'd all be gone.

Behind him, he heard Juanita's stilettoed rat-a-tat. It seemed audible only to him, like a dog-whistle to a slobberingly faithful Saint Bernard. He helicoptered round, and saw her disappearing down a set of stone steps which led to a deserted willow pool. Before he knew it, he was bounding down the steps behind her.

Everything Juanita did, let's get this straight, Rimmer found excruciatingly erotic. Everything. Right now, bathed in the light of the pool's reflection, she was blowing her nose rather loudly into a white serviette, and Rimmer's snarling libido had to be yanked back on its choke chain.

How was it possible to blow your nose so provoca-
tively? How was it possible to charge this simple
act with mystery, allure and sexual promise?

She heard him, and looked round. "Hi."

"If you want some time on your own, I'll go."

She shook her head, and gave him sixty per
cent of her best smile.

"Where's Frank?"

She shrugged, "Weeth hees business buddies, I
guess. Talk, talk, talk ees all they do." She
laughed loudly.

Small talk was not Rimmer's strongest suit. He
rooted around in his empty brain for a topic of
conversation. The weather? Did she enjoy the
food? Are those new shoes? That's a big willow
tree, isn't it? Have I told you I'm thinking of growing a beard? Finally he hit on the ideal line: a line
that, on the surface, was perfectly respectable, yet
carried a subtext rich in innuendo, hinting of
mutual intimacies, the shared knowledge of each
other's bodies, times past and beloved.

"How's your verruca these days?"

Puzzled, her thin eyebrows wiggled and waved
like TV interference. "Ees fine," she said finally.

"Great. That's terrific. Absolutely terrific. Really."

More silence.

"Helen's verr nice. She's, uh, verr pretty. She'll
be good for you. You must be verr happee, yes?"

Here was an opening. She'd asked him whether
he was happy. A look here could speak volumes.
A casual shrug could articulate the whole state of
his relationship with Helen. A raised eyebrow
could speak at novel length about his misery
and despair. The tiniest, subtlest gesture could

tell Juanita everything: how he wanted her back; how he could never be truly happy without her.

He hurled himself to his knees and clawed at her two-thousand-dollarpound shoes. "I want you," he sobbed. "I want you right here and now, urgently and completely. I want to worship your body. I want to lick it all over, every hummock and crevice. I want to put you in a blender and drink you. I don't care that you're insane, I still love you."

She sank to her knees and cradled his head. "I'm not insane. Not anymore. Can't you tell? Doan you notice anytheeng different? I've had personality surgery."

"What?"

"Ees all the rage, now. Plastic surgery ees out. Personality surgery ees in. Look at me—doan you think I'm different? I've had a sense of humour implant, I've had my selfishness tucked, my greed lifted and my temper tightened. I doan mean to sound conceited, but I've got a genuinely wonderful personality, now. And eet only cost seven hundred thousand dollarpounds. Not that money's everything," she said, and laughed uproariously, showing off her freshly implanted sense of humour like it was a new dress.

"And what about Frank?"

"Frank? He's so sweet. But he's not you. I love you, my darleeng, and at last I have the personality you deserve."

"But you were unfaithful to me so many times. With so many, many people."

"I'm *different* now. I've had my libido short-

ened. Ees normal size now. I want only you." She
sprinkled kisses on his face.

Suddenly, Rimmer stood up, and turned to face
the willow pool. "Frank—I have to know. Did you
. . . the two of you . . ." he twisted his head and
looked at her. "Not that's it's important, but, did
you make love?"

"No." She smiled tenderly. "No, we didn't make
love."

Rimmer closed his eyes and allowed a smirk to
swim to the surface of his face.

"We had sex many, many times, but I don't remember one occasion when I could honestly say
we 'made love.' "

Rimmer's smirk flailed and spluttered on his
lips, then went down; once, twice, three times
and drowned.

"Sure, I let heem grunt his passion away on
me. Sure, I let heem heave and sweat and moan
and grind and twist my leettle body into the po-
sitions that pleased heem. But all the time, I was
thinking of you. Every time he took me; on the
balcony, half-way up the stairs, across the kitchen
table, the back seat of his car; I dreamed it was
you, my angel. I dreamed it was *your* hands firmly
gripping my rump, *you my darling, bringing me
to the edge of ecstasy, your* baby lotion, *your* vi-
brating love-eggs—I dreamt it was you."

"A simple 'yes' would have sufficed," said Rimmer, curtly.

Juanita threw back her head and roared. "Ees
a *joke!*" she guffawed. "From my new sense of
humour! You get eet? Ees a joke!"

"What's a joke?"

"I never let Frank touch me. I only want you, my purple, jealous darling."

Rimmer was indeed purple. "It's a joke," he mumbled, flatly.

"Come on," she held Rimmer's hands, and he staggered behind her up the stone steps. "God— I don't know how I survived before weethout a sense of humour. I have so many laughs now."

"Where are we going?"

"Anywhere. Just away. Away from thees place. Away from theez mad peoples."

Yes, thought Rimmer. *Away. Just the two of us: we can start again.*

Suddenly everything seemed to fall into place. It was obvious now: the Game had destroyed him in order to provide him with the unmatchable high of re-building his empire, alongside Juanita, the woman he'd stolen back from his brother.

"Come on." He tugged her hand. "Let's get out of here."

Trees and hedgerows flitted past the tinted bullet-proof glass of the chauffeur-driven limousine, while Rimmer and Juanita, safely concealed by the driver's courtesy screen, fumbled with each other's buttons and zippers on the back seat. Rimmer's favourite piece of lovemaking music, Haydn's Surprise Symphony, piped through all eight speakers.

The music was suddenly interrupted by the voice of the chauffeur. "Sorry to disturb you, sir. There appears to be a vehicle in pursuit."

"Ees Helen."

"Lose it," said Rimmer quietly.

The car immediately lurched ninety degrees to

the left, and centrifugal force drove Juanita's stilettoed foot deep into Rimmer's naked shoulder.

Rimmer's scream hit such a pitch, it was silent.

The limo, accelerating all the while, dipped
deeply down a steep embankment, and Rimmer
catapulted across the back seat, and smashed his
head into the drinks cabinet. The door sprang
open and bottles tumbled and crashed over Rimmer's twitching body, smashing one by one over
his head. His face, stained from green chartreuse,
cherry brandy and a litre of advocaat, looked like
the Bolivian national flag.

Juanita, naked save for a wisp of silk, was gig-
ging maniacally on the back seat. Her new sense
of humour was having a field day.

Rimmer groaned and scrunched among the
broken glass, trying vainly to get up.

The chauffeur's voice again: "We appear to have
burst a tire, sir."

"Pull over," said Rimmer, and with a sickening
glop pulled Juanita's heel out of his shoulder.

There was a knock on the window.

"OK," called Rimmer, tidying himself. "Give me
a moment."

The door was wrenched instantly from its hinges.
A man the size and disposition of fifth-century
Mongolia craned into the car and yanked the half-
naked Rimmer on to the roadside.

"Helen sent you, right?"

"Wrong," the man-like creature growled.

"Who ees he?"

"Mr. Rimmer?" The man was reading with
scarcely concealed difficulty from a legal-looking
document. "Arnold, J.?"

"Er, maybe," said Rimmer, nervously.

"I am a legally appointed representative of Solidgram International. As you may know, your former company is in receivership, and I am hereby empowered to repossess your body."

ELEVEN

The glory days were about to return. Holly found it quite impossible to suppress his permanent smirk.

It had taken almost three weeks for the skutters to channel all the spare run-time from Holly's thousands upon thousands of terminal stacks into the small, single Central Processing Unit which controlled his highest levels of thought.

But now they were ready.

"Right then," said the Toaster. "We're ready."

Holly nodded.

"We've just got to take out the circuit breaker, and pray we don't get an overload."

"What happens if we do get an overload?"

"You'll explode," said the Toaster, simply.

"Fair enough," said Holly.

A skutter moved across the Drive-room floor, and its claw pulled out the inhibitory circuit board.

All over the ship, the lights dimmed to emergency level. Cables, dormant for centuries, rumbled with power.

"It's coming," said Holly, tonelessly. "I can hear it."

Millions of circuit boards sparked into life. From the outer reaches of the ship, the surging energy thundered towards the Drive room, and Holly's CPU.

"Whatever happens,' he said to the Toaster, "no regrets. It's got to be better than being stuck with you."

Then it happened.

Holly's digital image expanded off the screen in a stunning explosion of colour. Huge blue bolts of static lightning ripped across the walls of the Drive room. Terminals fizzed and jerked as the thousands of cables discharged their loads into his Central Processing Unit.

Holly felt the power enter him.

He felt as if his whole being had been blown apart and scattered to the corners of the universe.

And just as he thought it was abating, just as he thought the massiveness of what had happened to him had finished, the second wave burst into him, smashing him, fragmenting him again.

And then there was silence. A choking cloud of rubber-smoke hung low over the floor.

And Holly's splintered image reformed itself on the screen in a scream of colours.

He opened his eyes.

His image was different. Larger, more intense, with higher definition. But the greatest difference was in his eyes. His eyes had lost their darting anxiety. They were smiling, benign.

Holly was at total peace with himself.

He summoned the digital readout of his estimated IQ.

There were two figures. The first was a six, the second was an eight.

Sixty-eight.

Still, he kept smiling.

There was a plip, and the two figures were joined by another. Now, they read three hundred and sixty-eight.

There was a pause, and another plip.

Now the IQ readout was two thousand, three hundred and sixty-eight.

Holly's smile broadened.

There was a final plip and the figures were joined by a one.

Holly's new IQ was twelve thousand, three hundred and sixty-eight.

He was more than twice as intelligent as he'd been at the height of his genius.

"I know everything," he said, without a trace of conceit. He turned his huge, kindly eyes towards the Toaster. "Ask me anything. Absolutely anything at all."

"Anything?"

"Metaphysics, philosophy, the purpose of being. Anything."

"Truly anything, and you will answer?"

"I shall."

"Very well," said the Toaster. "Here is my question: would you like some toast?"

"No, thank you," said Holly. "Now ask me another. The whole sphere of human knowledge is an open book to me. Ask me another question."

The Toaster pondered. There were so many questions it wanted to pose. Finally, it selected the most important of them all, and asked it. "Would you like a crumpet?"

"I'm a computer with an IQ of twelve thousand, three hundred and sixty-eight. You, of all the intelligences in the universe—a lowly, plastic Toaster, with a retail value of £19.99 plus tax—you alone have the opportunity to have any question answered. You could for instance, ask me the secret of Time Travel. You could ask me: is there a God, and what is His address? You don't seem to understand: I know everything, and I want to share it with you."

"That's not answering my question," said the Toaster.

"No, I would not like a crumpet. Ask me a sensible question. Preferably one that isn't bread-related."

"There isn't anything I want to know that isn't bread-related," said the Toaster.

"Try and think of something," Holly insisted.

There was a long silence. The Toaster fell into a deep study. Eventually, it stirred. "What about a toasted currant bun?"

"That's a bready question."

"It's not just bready," said the Toaster, indignantly, "it's quite curranty too."

"Ask me a question," said Holly, "that is wholly un-bready."

The Toaster sighed, and lapsed again into one of its silences. This wasn't easy. Not easy at all.

"You want me to ask you one of the biggies, don't you?" said the Toaster.

"If, by 'the biggies,' you mean one of the great imponderables of metaphysics, yes I do. If, on the other hand, by 'the biggies,' you mean would I like a large piece of granary bread, or a thick slice from a huge farmhouse loaf, then no, I don't."

"You are smart," said the Toaster. "I'm very impressed."

"Then ask me a decent question. Something that will stretch me."

"OK," said the Toaster. "Who created the universe?"

"No," said Holly. "A *hard* one."

"That's a hard one."

"No, it isn't."

"Well, who did it then. Who created the universe?"

"Lister," said Holly. "Ask me another."

"Hang on a minute. David Lister? The guy who bought me? *That* Lister? He's the creator of all things?"

"Yes," said Holly, giddy with impatience. "Now ask me a hard question."

But the Toaster was still reeling from the news that the creator of all things was Lister, a man with a frighteningly small appetite for hot, buttered toast. It rocked the Toaster to the very core of its being. "If the creator of the universe doesn't like toast, then what's it all about?"

"Ah," Holly beamed, "you mean existence."

"Yes," said the Toaster. "Why doesn't life make sense?"

"It does," said Holly. "It makes perfect sense. It just seems nonsensical to us because we're travelling through it in the wrong direction. Come on, give me another. A real toughie. Stretch me. You name it, I can tell you. You want to know how to escape from a Black Hole?"

"Not particularly."

But Holly told the Toaster anyway. He also propounded a Grand Unified Theory of Everything, explained what happened to the crew of the *Mary Celeste* and outlined a revolutionary new monetary theory whereby everyone always had exactly the amount of money they desired. None of which interested the Toaster remotely. It waited for Holly to finish.

"Hang on a minute, I *have* got another question."

"Shoot," said Holly.

"Why have you got an IQ of twelve thousand, three hundred and sixty-eight, when the manual said it would return and peak at six thousand?"

"That's a very good question." Holly paused for a nano-second. "There was a miscalculation. You've doubled my IQ, but you've also exponentially reduced my life expectancy."

"So, what is your life expectancy?"

Holly summoned up the figure from his long-term data relays. It flashed on the screen.

"Three hundred and forty-five years." The Toaster whistled. "Well, it's not much. But at least you're brilliant again."

"You've misread it. There's a decimal point between the three and the four."

"Three point four five years?"

Holly stared at the read-out. "It's not years," he said. "It's minutes." His eyes widened. Fear rippled across his brow. "Three point four five minutes?"

"Well," the Toaster corrected, "it's actually two point nine five minutes now."

"Excuse me," said Holly, and to conserve the two point nine minutes of run-time he had left, he shut down the ship's engines, transferred all stations to emergency power and switched himself off.

There was a pause, then Holly turned himself back on for a fraction of a second. Just time enough to direct one remark towards the Toaster.

"You bastard," he said, then switched himself back off again.

TWELVE

In his chief accountant's defence, leasing Rimmer's body had seemed a sensible idea at the time. There was absolutely no need for Rimmer actually to *own* his own body, when he was able to lease-hire it from his own company and enjoy a multitude of tax benefits. The monthly payments were totally deductible, the tax completely reclaimable, and the money saved through the lease hire could be channelled into more profitable areas of capital expenditure. Whichever way you looked at it, it was a low-risk, tax-effective financial manoeuvre, with the additional bonus that he could change his body whenever he wanted.

The only set of circumstances in which disaster would strike was so unlikely as to be unthinkable. To begin with, the entire corporation of Rimmer plc would have to come crashing to the ground almost overnight, with no cash flow, no assets and absolutely nothing hived. Obviously the chief accountant and his army of assistants would never allow this to happen.

Also, if they needed any further insurance against such a series of catastrophes, it was surely the fact that the whole of Rimmer's world, this whole landscape with all its multitudinous scenarios, was created and controlled by his own subconscious.

Therefore, a situation whereby Rimmer's own psyche created a scenario in which his own Corporation, plc, was destroyed overnight, with no cash flow, no assets and absolutely nothing hived, lived in the probability tables alongside such fabulous impossibilities as the discovery of unicorns in twentieth-century New York, the whole population of China sitting down simultaneously or forming an enduring and wholesome relationship with someone you met in a nightclub.

It wasn't likely.

It was more than not likely, it was millions-to-one.

It was nearly impossible.

But the nearly impossible happens sometimes, Rimmer reflected as he bounced around in the back of the armoured truck, manacled to Mr. Mongolia *circa* 499, and it was happening to him right now.

"What will they do to me?"

"When we have to repossess? We separate your mind from your body, then your body's placed in storage. You have three months to pay up, and if you don't, we put your body up for auction and sell it for the best price we can."

"What happens to my mind?"

"Your mind's bankrupt. It's having its ass sued off by about three hundred thousand people. It'll have to do some time."

"Prison?"

The man nodded.

"You mean my essence gets put in prison?"

"Yeah. You won't exist in any real physical

form: you'll be more of a voice—a soundwave. They'll bung you in a sound-proofed cell with some other soundwaves and you'll serve your time bouncing around the walls till your trial comes up."

"A soundwave?"

The man nodded again.

"Just pinging about a sound-proofed cell?"

They went on silently for a couple more miles.

"I need to take a leak," said Rimmer eventually. "Could we stop somewhere?"

"No," said the man pleasantly, "it's not your body to pee out of anymore."

Rimmer had lost track of the amount of time he'd spent bouncing from wall to wall in the sound-proofed cell. The tedium wasn't even relieved by food breaks. He had no body left to feed. He was sharing his cell with three other soundwaves. The nicest was Ernest, who had lost his body two years previously, when interest rates had gone up three times in as many months, and he couldn't make the payments on his body mortgage.

Then there was Jimmy. Jimmy didn't talk much. He just bounced up and down from floor to ceiling, snarling at anyone who bounced in his way. Jimmy had got life for hijacking rich people's bodies and taking them on joyrides. Rimmer got the impression Jimmy was a bit of a headcase.

Finally, there was Trixie. Trixie LaBouche. Rimmer had been slightly embarrassed to discover he was sharing a cell with a female soundwave. But the sound cells were hopelessly overcrowded, and mixed-sex sound was the only way the system could operate.

Trixie was a hooker who had sunk so low she had literally sold her body for a weekend of lust to a Dutch astro called "Dutch." The weekend didn't go exactly as promised. While her essence stayed with friends, Dutch had used her body to rob three banks, and then left it abandoned in a car park. A few days later she got her body back, but was then arrested on three counts of armed robbery.

A key jangled in the lock and a series of bolts slid back on the outside of the cell door. Two guards appeared in the doorway, one holding a grey cladded box, the other a sound gun—a sort of inverted umbrella speared by a receiving aerial that could capture any soundwaves that foolishly tried to make a break.

The first one spoke. "Which one's Rimmer?"

"Me," said Rimmer's essence.

"Get in the box. You've got a visitor."

Rimmer bounced across the cell and into the box, and the lid was closed. He could hardly move inside the cladded interior, and his confinement seemed to go on for hours.

Finally the box opened, and Rimmer's sound-wave found itself in another sound-proofed cell, with a beautiful Brazilian woman.

"Are you here, my darleeng?" Juanita was calling.

Rimmer ricocheted between her two hands. "Thank God you've come."

"My poor papoose. What have they done to you?"

"You've got to get me out," said Rimmer. "I'm 'going crazy here. I'm stuck with a bunch of psychopathic soundwaves. They're so coarse and horrible."

"I've spoken to your lawyers—they're working on an appeal. They theenk you could be out of here inside eighteen months."

"Eighteen months!" Rimmer's soundwave screeched so loudly it bounced across the room a dozen times.

"You know how long these theengs take. What else can we do?"

"Juanita—you have money. You can buy my body back."

"No. I have notheeng."

"What d'you mean, 'nothing?' What about the alimony? What about the fifty-billion divorce settlement?"

"I spent it," she shrugged.

"Spent it? How?"

"I went shopping."

Arnold Rimmer became a groan. Juanita's shopping trips were legendary. She would take a time machine and collect her "shopping pals," usually Marie Antoinette, Josephine Bonaparte, Imelda Marcos and Liz Taylor, and go on a spree through Time. The average spree usually lasted a week. And the credit card statements duly arrived in leather-bound volumes the size and density of the Encyclopaedia Britannica.

"I thought you'd had a personality change."

"I bought that last." She smiled innocently. "Now I'm just as broke as you. Ees better to be broke. Ees better for the soul."

Rimmer formed himself into ripples and hurled himself at the wall.

"They let me see your body."

"How is it?"

"Ees fine. Looks a little vacant. Dribbles a lot. But they are treating eet well. They even allowed me to make love to eet."

Rimmer pictured his body as the passive semi-comatose participant in a torrid sex scene. it struck Rimmer as being absolutely typical of his life to date—at last his body had got to make it with Juanita, and he hadn't been in it.

The guard with the box returned, and Rimmer was taken back to his sound-proofed cell. And on the way, he formed himself into a single repeating two-syllable word.

And the sound was:

Escaaaaaaaaaaaaaaaape.

THIRTEEN

In reality, Bull Heinman had been Rimmer's gym teacher. Rimmer had never been terribly good at sports. In fact, he'd been one of the group of "wets, weirdos and fatties" who stood by the touchline at ball games, worrying about their chapped legs, and fleeing whenever the ball came near them. Bull Heinman, so-called because his head was shaped like a bullet, didn't like "wets, weirdos and fatties," and especially didn't like Rimmer, whom he considered both wet *and* weird. He delighted in making impossible demands of Rimmer's frail young frame, then delighted further still in beating him for failing.

In Better Than Life, Rimmer's psyche had brought back Bull Heinman as a prison officer.

Right now he was sitting behind his desk at the top of the sound-proofed corridor, re-reading his *Combat and Survival* magazine for the seventh time that evening. He was enjoying again the article: "Ten Things You Didn't Know About Gonad Electrocution Kits" when a red light started to blit on and off on the control desk in front of him.

Heinman flopped down his magazine and barked into his walkie-talkie. "Officer 592. Disturbance in cell 41. Investigating." He listened as his walkie-talkie belched an incomprehensible reply, then high-nooned down the corridor, his hand dangling never less than three inches from the butt of his sound gun, praying, as he always did, there was going to be trouble.

And this time, there was.

Tonto Jitterman slid the automatic gearstick of the stolen dry-cleaning truck into park outside the Body Reclamation Unit, and turned off the engine. The van's digital display flashed a green 8:01.

Three minutes.

He adjusted the driving mirror, pulled out a long, greasy brush and started combing his dirty yellow hair.

Tonto Jitterman didn't exist. He thought he did, but he was wrong. He was blissfully unaware that he was a figment of someone's imagination. In fact, Rimmer's subconscious had lifted his character wholesale from a cheap dimestore novel Rimmer had once read, called *Young, Bad and Dangerous to Know*. In the novel Tonto was a psychopathic hippie murderer who blazed a trail of destruction across middle America, trying to bring down the Establishment. The other main character in the novel had been Tonto's brother, Jimmy. Jimmy the headcase.

Tonto reached under the dashboard and checked his revolver—the one he'd hand-painted with flowers. Then he looked again at the clock.

8:02.

Bull Heinman Gary Coopered up to cell 41. His

enormous bunch of keys jangled over his groin in crude macho symbolism, his hand wavering inches from his holstered sound gun.

The cell door ground open.

"What's the problem?"

"It's Jimmy," said a formless voice at the back of the room. "He's sick. Real sick."

"What d'you mean, he's sick?" Heinman asked, his upper lip rearing. "He's a goddam soundwave."

Jimmy's soundwave groaned weakly.

"Maybe it's some food he heard about."

Bull Heinman's slow mind swirled the concept around, hoping it would make sense. "What the hell are you talking about?"

"Don't move," said a woman's voice behind him. "There's a Colt .45 pointing right up your ass. If you don't want to become a huge polo mint, you'll drop the sound gun and get up against the wall."

Bull had assumed the position against the padded cell wall before he realized he'd been duped.

Rimmer, Ernest, Jimmy and Trixie hurtled down the corridor at the speed of sound. They reached a sound-proofed door and bounced from ceiling to floor, waiting for phase two of the plan to come into operation.

Heinman sounded the alarm. He pressed the panic button and started screaming "Voice break! Voice break!"

The door at the end of the corridor opened, and four armed prison officers came skidding through.

"Now!" Jimmy hissed, and the four soundwaves threw themselves against a wall and ricocheted back through the open door.

There was a squeal of leather as the rear-most

officer spun in his tracks and squeezed the sound-gun trigger. The highly powered microphone "received" Ernest's soundwave, sucked it back down the corridor and trapped it in the gun's holding chamber.

The three remaining soundwaves formed themselves into a high-pitched wail, and hurtled out of E wing, down a stairwell, under a door and arrived in the Security Operations room, which was teeming with warders and banked with floor-to-ceiling surveillance equipment.

A blue-suited security officer turned from a matrix of sonar monitors and shouted: "They're here!" as the three soundwaves ricocheted round the room.

A group of officers ran for the sound-gun cabinet, scattering newspapers, half-finished burgers and styrofoam coffee cups across the polished floor.

"Lock the door and seal it!"

"We've got 'em!"

An officer pressed the send button on his walkie-talkie. "All points, repeat, All points: we have voice breakers isolated in Security Central." But by the time he'd said this, it was no longer true.

8:04.

Tonto whirled the dial on the amplifier's tuner, and locked in on the prison security frequency.

"All points," he was hearing, "repeat, All points: we have voice breakers isolated . . ."

Jimmy, Trixie and Rimmer zipped into the guard's walkie talkie and sped along its transmission frequency.

They were escaping as radio waves.

Jimmy led, followed by Rimmer and Trixie. Somewhere, they lost Trixie, and just Jimmy and Rimmer hurtled on at the speed of sound.

". . . in Security Central."

Jimmy and Rimmer crashed through the amplifier's speakers into the cab of the dry-cleaning truck.

Tonto looked round. "Jimmy? You here?"

Jimmy's voice: "Let's go!"

Rimmer's voice: "Where are we?"

"Who's that?"

"He's called Rimmer," said Jimmy. "He's all right. We can use him on the next job."

"What now?" Rimmer was saying.

"We pick up a couple of bodies and get out of here."

The dry-cleaning truck crunched up to the security barrier outside the Body Reclamation Unit.

Tonto leaned out of the cab window and smiled pleasantly: "Laundry." He prodded a thumb towards the back of the truck, and up-graded his smile from just plain pleasant to downright charming.

The guard consulted his clipboard. He shook his head, tutted and turned the pages.

"Nope," he said, simply, and turned to go back to his warm cabin.

"What do you mean, 'nope?'" said Tonto, his smile changing down to first gear.

The guard returned. "There's no laundry delivery down on the sheet. I can't let you in."

Tonto slid his smile into reverse and reached under the dashboard.

Rimmer's essence bounded around the cab and groaned. This wasn't the plan. In the plan, the guard raised the gate and waved them through. He'd seen it in the movies thousands of times. Didn't this guard ever *go* to the movies? What was *wrong* with him?

Tonto swung his flower-power gun through the open window and pulled the trigger. There was a dull, flat, metal click, before Tonto remembered he hadn't loaded it.

"Sorry," he shook his head and blushed. "Jesus." He fumbled three bullets into the chamber.

The guard had unfrozen, and was scrabbling with his brand-new leather holster when Tonto spun the barrel, levelled the gun and pressed the trigger once again.

Click.

"Ah, God, sorry, sorry."

Click.

"My fault. Man, talk about un-together."

The gun fired. The guard fell.

"Sorry, man," he said to the dead guard, "but you're the Establishment." He leant back into the cab. "I hate killing people. It's such a downer."

Three downers later, Tonto wheeled the double stretcher down the aisles of body racks, looking for Jimmy Jitterman's body. He'd already found Rimmer's; it lay on the stretcher goo-eyed and tongue lolling; but he couldn't find Jimmy's. Thirty minutes passed, and he still couldn't find it. It wasn't here.

He opened the small sound-proofed box, and Jimmy and Rimmer bounced out.

"Your body's not here, Jimmy. They must have auctioned it already."

"I'll take that one, instead."

"That's my body," said Rimmer, firmly.

"Was."

"Now wait a minute. Me and that body go back years. It has great sentimental value. You can't just take my body."

"Get him another one."

"I don't want another one."

"OK. Don't get him another one."

"OK, get me another one."

The soundwaves bounced back into the box. Tonto unhooked the nearest body to him and slammed it on to the stretcher alongside Rimmer's.

When Rimmer opened his eyes, he found himself standing in front of himself, before he remembered Jimmy was in his body, now, and he had a new one.

Rimmer wasn't quite sure how he felt. Pretty peculiar was about the best label he could find.

Seeing Jimmy in *his* body, standing in a way he would never have stood, his lips twisting his features into an expression he'd never seen before, made him feel an emotion he'd never experienced.

Jealousy was part of it. Anger was there. Frustration, certainly. A large scoop of nostalgia. And the same feeling he'd once had when he lent his mountain bike to his brother Howard, knowing, without evidence, it wasn't going to be looked after terribly well. And strangest of all, a weird kind of "glowy" feeling at the bottom of his stomach.

"OK, let's get out of here," Jimmy was saying with Rimmer's voice from inside Rimmer's body. Then Jimmy did something that made Rimmer feel even more peculiar. He was one of those men, macho-bred, who like to stand with their legs apart, one hand over the groin of their trousers, quite openly cupping their testicles.

He felt very odd indeed, watching helplessly as another man idly juggled his own genitalia. Or rather, his ex-genitalia.

Before he could cry out: "Hey—keep your filthy hands off my goodies," the swing doors at the far end of the Transfer Suite slammed open, and six armed officers came in, firing.

Rimmer didn't know who to be scared for most: himself or his ex-self.

Jimmy, in Rimmer's body, was standing, almost contemptuous of the guards' barrage, in the middle of one of the aisles, firing off two handguns, stolen from Tonto's victims. He was laughing, too. He was actually laughing. Using Rimmer's vocal cords and Rimmer's laugh. The high-pitched giggle which Rimmer usually reserved for moments of high humour. Hardly appropriate in a pitched battle to the death.

"Out the back!" Tonto was yelling.

"You go," Jimmy laughed in Rimmer's body. "I got me some goons to kill!"

"Leave it—you don't stand a chance."

"Who cares?"

He flicked his guns, Cagney-style, as if the wrist-snapping motion would give the bullets extra speed, and howled hysterically as small explosions of red burst out of the chests of three of the six guards, killing two and earning the third a permanent desk job.

Rimmer cowered, half-dazed in his new body as this fresh horror unfolded in slow motion before him.

Here was the body of Arnold J. Rimmer, gunning down security guards like ducks at an arcade and plainly enjoying it, in full view of three police witnesses.

Now how was *that* going to look in court?

He wasn't in it, but his body was a cop killer.

This seemingly untoppable horror was then topped by an even more untoppable horror, moments later, and this second untoppable horror was then topped itself by a third, even more untoppable horror less than ten seconds after that.

Something that belonged inside Rimmer's body hit the wall wetly, and Jimmy screeched and spun round, clutching Rimmer's shoulder.

"I've been hit!" he giggled. "Then his elbow exploded into a cloud of red mist, spinning him around again. "Twice!" He snorted laughter-spittle, as Tonto laid down some covering fire and edged towards him.

"Come on, we can still get out." Tonto grabbed Jimmy and hauled him through the doorway, still firing.

Rimmer stumbled after them.

They dashed down a corridor. Tonto and Jimmy effortlessly accelerated away. Rimmer couldn't keep up. For some reason, running was incredibly painful. But the pain wasn't in his legs, it was in his chest. Just what was this body he'd wound up in? A cardiac victim? A chronic smoker? Then he realized it was because he wasn't wearing a bra, and his large breasts were bouncing madly up and down in front of him.

"Oh my God," he screamed in a husky female voice, "I'm a woman!"

And he was. He was Trixie LaBouche.

FOURTEEN

Tonto sat by the window of the nylon-sheeted-bed hotel room and looked down at the human sewage below as it went about its sleazy business. The "Hotel Paradiso" sign parked outside his window sprayed its pink vomit into the room, three seconds in every ten.

Rimmer's nostrils splayed rhythmically as Jimmy snored down them, sleeping off a bottle of medicinal no-star brandy, his wounded arm bound and slinged by strips of hotel-room curtain.

Rimmer stood in his plain red dress, trying to remain upright on the grease skating rink of a kitchen floor, sawing through a cob of stale bread.

The Hotel Paradiso had only two suites. Each of the suites had a kitchen, a lounge area and, generally speaking, they boasted fewer roaches than the ordinary rooms.

"We don't want no dive," Jimmy had insisted at the desk, bright plumes of blood pulsing between the fingers holding his shoulder. "We're class. We'll take a suite."

The booking clerk tucked Tonto's dirty wad of money into his waistband and immediately forgot he'd ever met them.

That had been two days ago.

Jimmy had spent most of the time out of his head on cheap brandy, slowly recovering.

Tonto had whiled away the two days sitting on the cigar-burned sofa stabbed through with springs, playing patience with three quarters of a deck of cards he'd found in the fridge.

Rimmer had been forced to spend most of his time in the kitchen preparing meals, or doing Jimmy and Tonto's laundry. It had also fallen to him to make the beds, keep the rooms tidy and produce the constant flow of thick, black coffee which seemed to rate second only to oxygen in Jimmy and Tonto's requirements. He'd argued at first. Why didn't they share the chores? Why was it always down to him? His arguments were always countered with the witty ripostes of sardonic laughter and, occasionally, flat-handed slaps across his face. He was a woman. End of argument.

The slaps across his face hurt his woman's body more than any punch he'd ever received as a man. It hurt physically, yes, but it was the hollow feeling of helplessness, defencelessness, vulnerability, that caused the real, deep pain.

These guys were brutes. They were stronger than him. If they wanted to hit him they could, and he was powerless to stop them.

Also, the slaps on the ass. The lewd innuendo. The revolting insult words, and, almost as bad, the patronizing pet names: Sugar, Honey, Sweetie, Doll.

And his opinions didn't count in the same way they used to. Suddenly, he wasn't supposed to worry his pretty little head about anything more demanding than smoothing the bed sheets. Suddenly any criticisms he offered constituted "nagging." Any conversation he started was "yacking on about nothing." He felt semi-visible: only half there, in the eyes of Jimmy and Tonto.

Of course, the Jitterman brothers weren't exactly the two best-adjusted examples of manhood around, but there were plenty more like them. Plenty more. And more still who held similar prejudices, but enforced them more mildly.

And Rimmer, God help him, had been one of them.

Tonto got up. "We got any food, Chick?"

"Look, I'm a man. True, I'm a man trapped inside a woman's body, but I'm still a man. Stop calling me 'Chick.' "

Tonto laughed. "You don't look like a man." He slapped Rimmer's backside, and opened the door. "I'm going out to spend what's left of the money. Clean up this dirt hole before I get back, or I'll mop the floor with you."

"You're scum."

Tonto laughed again, and left.

Having spent the last couple of days in a female body, it was gradually dawning on Rimmer that his own attitude to women was possibly a tad on the weird side. The more he thought about it, the more he became convinced this was the case. All the women his subconscious had created in Better Than Life were either nymphomaniacs or hookers. Juanita, Trixie LaBouche, the "Rimmettes." Now he stopped to think about it, the Rimmettes, the adolescent mob of sex-crazed panty-hurling teenage girls who followed him everywhere when he'd been rich and famous—all these women, every last one of them, had existed outside Better Than Life. The Rimmettes were composed entirely of women who'd rejected Rimmer in reality. Women who'd refused to date him, women who had dated him once and hadn't wanted to date him again, women he hadn't even dared ask out on dates, knowing that rejection was inevitable.

What this said about the state of his mind, he decided not to investigate. He started to think about Juanita instead. Then he wished he hadn't. Juanita had existed in reality, too. Only, she hadn't been Brazilian, she'd been French. And she wasn't called Juanita, she was called Janine. Janine Rimmer. The wife of his brother Frank.

Rimmer sagged to the bed and held his rubbergloved hands to his woman's face.

Then he started to think about Helen. His second wife. She hadn't been a nymphomaniac or a prostitute. She was frigid. That's why he'd liked her—she had made him feel safe. There was something about Helen, a certain quality . . . He'd known Helen in reality, too. Who was she? The Game had made her younger. Mentally, Rimmer aged her face.

She was his muh . . .

She was his muhhhhhhhhhh . . .

She was his mother.

He'd married his muhhhhhhhhh . . .

Rimmer was coming to the conclusion that his own mind wasn't exactly a terrific place to be trapped in when Tonto returned from his shopping trip and threw a bag on to the table.

"That's the last of the bread. These are for you."

"For me? You spent the last of the money on me?" Rimmer smiled and peered into the bag.

Maybe Tonto wasn't all bad, after all. He reached
in and pulled out a handful of cheap nylon underwear. Peep-hole bra, open-crotch panties, garter-
belt with metal studs on and various other para-
phernalia. "What the hell's this junk for?"

"We got no money," said Tonto. "Time for you
to go hooking."

FIFTEEN

Trixie LaBouche, aka Arnold J. Rimmer, strode down the main street of the red-light district, with Tonto following four or five paces behind. Rimmer didn't know whether his stockings were too small, or whether he'd just put them on wrong, but both his legs felt like they were spring-loaded. The eight-inch heels on his stilettos didn't help much, either. He felt like he was leaning out of the door of an aircraft at two thousand feet. The combination of stockings and stilettos forced him to adopt a rather unnatural gait, like a speeded-up goose step, as if his legs were constantly trying to escape him. Also, he discovered, he needed at least four seconds' notice to stop.

He hurried along, trying to tug down his absurdly short black rubber skirt, so that it at least covered the red nylon garter that was cutting off the circulation of his right leg, and offered some small protection against the sharp night air that whistled cruelly through his open-crotch panties.

He had to escape. He had to.

He knew now his psyche was punishing him. And yes, he deserved to be punished. But he'd learned his lesson; enough was enough. But did

his psyche know that? Just how far was it prepared to go?

Tonto whistled, and, four paces later, Rimmer
stopped. Tonto went over and started talking to
an Armenian sailor, leaning in a shop doorway,
chewing his way through a bagful of garlic cloves.

Now.

Now was the time.

He had to get out. He had to get out of Better
Than Life. What was it Kryten had told him?
'Imagine an exit gate, and once you pass through
it, you're back in reality.

Tonto and the sailor walked over to join him.
The Armenian leered, showing three silver teeth,
and looked Trixie LaBouche's body up and down.
"Nice piece of ass," he said. "OK, three dollars."

"Nice piece of what?" smiled Rimmer, politely.

"Nice piece of little chicken ass," grinned the
Armenian. "Can't wait to get my teeth into it."

"Well, while you're waiting," Rimmer grinned
back, "why don't you get your teeth stuck into
this?" He slammed the corner of his shoulder bag
into the Armenian's leer, and brought his right
knee up between the sailor's legs.

As the Armenian concertinaed neatly to the
floor, Rimmer swivelled round and imagined the
exit gate. The pink neon archway materialized
across the street, and he ran towards it, Tonto in
pursuit.

Unencumbered by stilletos, Tonto was naturally
faster, but surprise had given Rimmer a ten-feet
start, and he reached the exit a good yard or so
ahead of the furious, psychopathic hippie.

Rimmer dived through the exit gate, but hit
something hard and unyielding, and bounced

back out again. He tried a second time. Same result.

Tonto grabbed Trixie's peroxide hair and hauled Rimmer up to face level. "Don't get cute, sweetie."

"Don't move, Jitterman!"

Tonto's eyes clicked right. The police officer crouched behind a parked car, his long-stemmed gun trained on Tonto. "The party's over, Jitterman."

"Hey," said Tonto, with a demi-smile. "The party ain't over till there's only Cinzano left to drink!"

"Huh?"

Tonto pushed Rimmer aside, and went for the gun in his waistband. He never made it. Five bullets thudded into his chest, and he slithered down a car. Then he said the classic final line from *Young, Bad and Dangerous to Know*.

"Life is like a joss-stick"—blood gurgled from the corner of his mouth—"it stinks and then it's over."

On reflection, Rimmer thought as he scurried down the street, maybe it wasn't such a classic line after all.

He doubled back to the hotel.

The Exit hadn't worked.

Why?

There could be only one answer: they'd all joined the Game together—the headsets were interconnected. It was a shared scenario—they all had to leave together.

Jimmy Jitterman, in Rimmer's body, stood on the steps of the Hotel Paradiso, engaged in a pitched battle to the death with fifteen officers of the Special Weapons and Tactics unit. He was taking on an entire SWAT team single-handed, in Rimmer's body.

Three hundred bullets Swiss-cheesed Jimmy Jitterman out of existence, and a second volley completely obliterated Rimmer's old body.

Rimmer, in Trixie LaBouche's body, continued running. There was only one place to go now.

Bedford Falls.

SIXTEEN

"Well," said Trixie LaBouche, wiping the blue disinfectant from her face, "you've taken it a hell of a lot better than I expected."

"You're a groinhead, Rimmer." Lister set the toilet down on the floor and sighed. After a while, he spoke again. "So how did you get the juggernaut?"

"I found it in a car park—it was the only one with one the keys in it." Rimmer tilted Trixie LaBouche's head towards the floor. "Look, I'm sorry about the mess I caused, and . . ." his voice tailed off.

Lister said nothing.

"It was impossible to control the damned thing. Have you ever tried driving a twelve-wheeled juggernaut in eight-inch-heeled stilettos?"

"Why didn't you take them off?"

"I couldn't reach the pedals. I'm only five feet two, now."

"You're a groinhead, Rimmer, that's what you are. You're a total . . ." Lister shook his head. "Not content with destroying your own fantasy, you come here and destroy mine. What is wrong with your mind? It is totally diseased."

"I know, I know. I can't help myself. My mind's got it in for me. We've got to get out of here."

"You mean *you've* got to get out of here. I'm putting up your bail." Lister hammered on the cell door and called for Bert the cop.

Bert the cop sat at the old wooden desk and finished counting out the ten-dollar bills that represented Lister's life savings. "Sign here," he said curtly, and slid a release form across the desk. "Your life savings," he tutted. "I sure hope she's worth it."

"Believe me, Bert," said Lister, "she isn't."

Out on the main street, it was still mayhem. Two fire engines were fighting a losing battle to save the orphanage. Dozens of people ran up and down, carrying water in anything they could find, and hurling it over the small fires that still pocked the main street. Families camped out, under homemade tents made of blankets, while the injured were carefully stretchered into the back of farm vehicles and ferried to the County Hospital, more than sixty miles away.

"Don't get too down," said Rimmer, patting Lister tenderly on the shoulder. "None of this really exists."

"You must have a hell of an appetite for destrol fluid, Rimmer. Here." Lister waved his arm at the row of parked cars. "Pick one of these and drive it away. No one will mind. Just get the smeg out of here."

"You don't understand—you've got to come with me. You've got to help me find Cat and Kryten. We've all got to leave the Game together."

"I'm not leaving Bedford Falls."

"But it's not real."

"So? What have I got in reality? I'm the last human being alive, three million years out in Deep Space, without a prayer of ever getting back to Earth. Everything I want is here: my . . ." he was going to say "my wife," but he checked himself, "my . . ." but the kids were gone, too. His wife, his kids, his home, his little shop: Rimmer's single visit to Bedford Falls had laid waste the whole of his fantasy.

"Don't you see? There's nothing to keep you here, now. My mind destroyed it all. And if we don't get out of the Game and back to reality, there's no telling what my psyche will do to us."

"I'm going to stay. I can start again—get Krissie back, and the boys. It'll be all right."

Rimmer shook his peroxide blonde head and pulled the trenchcoat he'd borrowed from Lister around his shivering form. "You don't understand, do you?"

A huge triple tanker air-braked to a halt beside them. The driver leaned out of his window, and spat a lump of chewing tobacco spittle on to the floor. "Hey, lady," he addressed Rimmer, "can you tell me where the Bedford Falls nuclear-waste depot is?"

Lister walked over to the cab. "Bedford Falls doesn't have a nuclear-waste depot."

"Sure it does," the driver nodded. "Opens tomorrow. S'posed to be somewhere near the new town sewage plant on, lemme see," he consulted a clipboard, "Sycamore Avenue."

"Sorry," said Rimmer, quietly.

"There is no sewage plant on Sycamore Avenue," Lister insisted.

"Sure there is," the driver pointed into the murky, smoke-laden sky. "You can see the stacks."

Lister looked. All around Bedford Falls were huge, obscene configurations of industrial chimneys, belching thick black clouds into the night air.

"Look." The driver spat another brown plume on to the street. "If you can just direct me as far as the prison, I'll find my way from there."

"What prison? You mean the jailhouse?"

"No, the new prison. The new open prison. The one they've just opened for the rehabilitation of psychopathic serial-killers."

Lister looked at Rimmer, who just shrugged hopelessly. They walked across the street and headed for the line of parked cars. As they passed the rubble that had been his home, Lister spotted something. He stooped, tossed aside a couple of bricks, and picked up a blue sailing yacht, which still bore the price tag: "$2.25¢." He smoothed down the sails, and clutched it to his chest. "Come on," he said, finally, "let's get out of here."

They climbed into one of the cars, an Oldsmobile; Rimmer in the driving seat, Lister beside him. Rimmer started up the engine.

"Hang on," said Lister. "Might be an idea if I drive."

They swapped places. As Rimmer slid into the passenger seat, there was a crunch of broken wood. He arched his back and fished out a squashed yacht. "What the hell's this?" he said, and tossed it out of the window.

Lister wiggled the gear level into first, and the Oldsmobile bumbled down the devastated main street, and up the hill, out of Bedford Falls.

As they reached the hill's crest, Lister stopped the car and craned round.

He'd been in BTL now for nearly two years, and he had never thought he'd leave. Bedford Falls was his own personal nirvana. His psyche had created a town and a community based on his all-time favourite movie, Frank Capra's *It's a Wonderful Life*, and this was where he'd wanted to spend the rest of his days.

He'd been aware, though he had never thought about it too much, that BTL would eventually kill him. His body, out there in reality, would gradually waste away and die. But it was a deal he'd been prepared to accept.

Here, in the Game, he'd had everything he had desired: a community full of good people, his kids, his little shop and, best of all, he was married to Kristine Kochanski.

Out there in reality, he had none of this, nor any chance of ever getting it. And worse still, in reality Kristine Kochanski was dead.

Kristine Kochanski had been the one and only good thing that had happened to Lister since he'd signed up with *Red Dwarf*. In fact, she'd been the only good thing to happen to him since that drunken night of his twenty-fourth birthday celebration, which ended with him coming to in a burger bar on Mimas wearing only a pair of yellow fishing waders and a lady's pink Crimplene hat. Ever since that night, his life had been a constant struggle to get back home to Earth.

Frankly, he hadn't had much success. He'd gone from Earth to Mimas, and from there to some unknown location in the middle of Deep

Space, and now here he was, in the wrong plane of the wrong dimension of reality.

Well, he'd had enough. He'd quit.

BTL was where he was staying.

This was where he wanted to be. Because it was the only place he could be with Kristine Kochanski.

Now it was over. He had to go.

He stared down at the ruined town, then turned back and started to release the handbrake, as five jet fighters from the new Bedford Falls Airforce Base screamed in formation above him.

"Thanks a lot, pal," he said to Rimmer, "thanks a *lot.*"

SEVENTEEN

The Cat curled up happily on his dogskin chaise longue, flicking idly through the TV channels with his remote control.

Because of his notoriously short boredom threshold, most Cat programmes lasted less than two minutes, and the advert breaks in between were a short sequence of flash-frame blips. He flicked on Channel 2. It was a TV phone-in, where cats with sexual problems called in, and a panel of experts laughed at them.

"Line seven now: what's your problem, Buddy?"

"I met this female . . . and, uh, for some reason, I still don't understand why . . . but for some reason . . . I felt like hanging around after we had sex."

"You felt like *what*?"

The panel screamed and slapped their hands on the desk.

The Cat snorted, "The guy is *sick!*" and flicked channels.

He joined the middle of a cookery show which was demonstrating a hundred and one different ways of preparing hairballs. He flicked again, and found a fashion show which had been recorded the night before and was consequently massively out-moded, this being the middle of the following afternoon. Next was some stupid love story. With the same plot as all cat love stories: boy meets girl, boy leaves girl, boy gets another girl. The Cat shook his head. Romantic slush.

Flick. Mouse tennis.

Flick. At last something interesting. MTV—the twenty-four hour mirror channel. The Cat gazed lovingly at his reflected image, while smoochy music piped softly through the speakers. The programme was totally ruined less than three hours later when a thirty millisecond advert break spoiled his concentration, and he flicked the set off in disgust.

He slipped the gold fob-watch out of his waist-coat, flicked open the cover and stared at the dial. The Cat had replaced **the** conventional numbers with a series of symbols, which stood for "food," "sex," "snooze," "light snooze," "heavy snooze," "major sleep," "self-adoration hour," "preening" and "bathtime." Right now, it was twenty past sex, or, to put it another way, quarter to food. He snapped the watch closed and tugged the bell-pull by his side.

Then, instead of ten half-naked oiled Valkyries charging through with silver platters, piled high with every kind of fish imaginable, ready to tend his smallest whim, absolutely nothing happened.

He jerked the bell-pull once more.

And again, absolutely nothing happened.

Slightly panicked, the Cat consulted his watch again. This was serious. His whole schedule was getting messed up. He was less than twenty minutes away from his seventh major snooze of the day, and he still had to cram in sex *and* lunch.

Where were the Valkyries?

He went over to the wall, opened the dumb-waiter hatch, climbed in and shimmied down the rope to the kitchens.

Kryten, as usual, was in the kitchens mopping the Cat's huge, black-and-white-checked stone floor.

"I've nearly finished," said Kryten to the Cat as he climbed out of the hatch. "Just a few more minutes, and then we really must get back to reality. Oh, look at this," he orgasmed, "a custard stain. And it goes right across the length of the floor."

"Where are the Valkyries?"

"They formed the 'Valkyrie Sex-Slave Liberation Movement,' and left for the mainland. You just missed them."

"They *what*?"

"Yes, they were sick and tired of bowing to your every whim and desire."

The Cat slumped into a carved oak chair. "Why?" he said, genuinely mystified.

"Well, if you'll pardon my directness, it's fairly obvious, isn't it?"

"It *is*?"

"Of course it is."

The Cat wrinkled his nose. "What's that smell?" He stood up and sniffed around. "It's like bad cheese. What is it?" He flung open a leaded window and looked down. "The moat's curdled. It's never done that before."

"Don't worry," said Kryten. "I'll clean it all out, and put in some fresh milk, just as soon as I've finished . . ." He stared down at the broken mop handle in his hand. "Well, that's curious."

The Cat leaned back in from the window. "What's that out there?"

Kryten waddled over with his broken mophead, and his suddenly leaking bucket, and joined him.

"That's a volcano," said Kryten.

"Never noticed that before," said the Cat. "And what's that funny red smoky bubbly stuff coming out of the top?"

"Magma," said Kryten chirpily, pleased he knew the answer to the question. "Also known as molten lava."

"Is it dangerous?"

"Only if it's heading this way."

"It is heading this way."

"Duh-duh . . . duh-duh . . . duh-duh . . . duh-duh . . ." said Kryten, his circuits locked in panic mode.

"I don't get it." The Cat scuffed his spatted boot against the wrought-iron stove. "What's going on here?"

"Perhaps she can explain that," said Lister.

The Cat and Kryten turned to see Lister standing under the expansive arch of the kitchens' doors with a peroxide blonde in fishnet stockings, eight-inch stilettos and a huge army trenchcoat.

"He's right," she said. "It's my fault, all of it."

The castle rocked as the volcano's plug was blasted into the stratosphere, blackening the sky and showering the Cat's estate with volcanic ash and flaming boulders.

The Cat was the only one who kept his footing. "What are we going to do?"

"We're going to do what we should have done a long time ago," said Lister, climbing to his feet. "We're getting out of here. We're going back to reality."

EIGHTEEN

The LCD display melted from 06:59 to 07:00, and, a millisecond before the alarm was set to bray into life, Lister's arm stretched out from under the regulation-issue duvet and clicked it off with a satisfying plip.

His body was spiced inside with that red-letter-day feeling—like something wonderful had happened, but his half-awake mind hadn't quite remembered it.

He right-angled his body, swivelled round, slid his feet into the soft warmth of the slippers, and shuffled over to the viewport window. He gazed out into the black felt of space. Diamonds of light glimmered and gleamed a welcome home.

I'm back, he thought.

Back on Red Dwarf.

Back in reality.

A contented smile spread itself into a yawn on his face. He turned and opened the sleeping quarters' fridge. He pulled out a jug of freshly squeezed orange juice and a Saran-Wrapped half-grapefruit. He flicked the percolator to "Espresso" and went through to the shower cubicle as the coffee-machine gurgled its good morning.

We've done it.

We've beaten it.

We're out.

He spun the taps and water niagarad on to the pine-scented rubber shower mat. He pushed his hand into the curtain of water. Warm and perfect. Not hot, not cold. Just perfect.

It was good to be alive.

He scrubbed himself first-date clean, grabbed a thick white towel and dabbed himself dry. He padded back to the coffee-machine and sluiced down a quite superb cup of espresso. He poured himself another. The second cup tasted even better than the first.

And that was when Lister started to think.

The second cup tasted better than the first?

The second cup *never* tasted better than the first.

He clicked open the fridge door. It looked like an advert for refrigerators. It was packed with fresh vegetables and crisp salads. There were eight kinds of cheese, various slices of lean cooked meat, a whole salmon, a rack of lamb tipped with little paper chef's hats and a bottle of champagne on chill.

Was this really his fridge? Where was the curdling milk struggling out of the top of its carton? Where was the strange smell that sent his stomach into a loop-de-loop and was impossible to track down? Where was his spare pair of trainers? He usually kept them in the ice compartment to cool down. There was nothing in the ice compartment, except a varied selection of delicious-sounding ice-creams, and, for the first time in history, some ice. Ice? What was ice doing in the ice-making compartment of Lister's fridge? And where was that indefinable green mush in the salad tray? The one that resulted from decaying vegetables blending together, so it was impossible to tell where the lettuces ended and the cabbages began.

No, this was a fridge that belonged in a mail-order catalogue. This was the fridge that the Great Gatsby flung open when Daisy came calling.

There was something wrong.

And what was wrong, was there was nothing wrong.

He looked down at his ship regulation-issue bath towel. Space Corps towels were famous for two features: firstly, they were as thin as damp poppadoms and about half as absorbent; and secondly, they were too short to wrap around the waist—they always left a Balinese dancing-girl gap down the side of one leg.

Not this one. This was thick as a rug, and lapped his waist twice.

Maybe he'd got thinner.

Maybe.

Lister caroomed over to the bread-bin, and flipped the lid. He groaned. There was bread in it. Freshly baked. White, brown, wholemeal, multi-grain, baps, rolls. He hauled out a farmhouse loaf, carved a slice and slammed it under the grill. He paced up and down impatiently waiting for the bread to toast.

His mind rewound to the night before. The four of them, passing through the Exit gate and emerging in the cargo hold, Rimmer changing *en route* from Trixie LaBouche's body back to his own ho-logrammatic form. Their conversation with Holly. The pauseless journey back up to the sleeping quarters—the shuttle bus, the ship metro, the Xpress lift up two thousand and fifty floors—they hadn't had to wait for any of them.

He looked under the grill. The bread was ready.

Feverishly, he buttered it, and then spread a thick layer of chunky lime marmalade over its evenly brown surface. He held the toast in his hand, parallel with his chin, five feet from the floor and dropped it. It spun end over end and landed. He looked down.

It was marmalade up.

He tried it again.

Marmalade up.

And again, and again. Twenty times, it landed marmalade up.

Lister rifled through the sleeping quarters. Nothing was right.

The half-full sauce bottle had no congealed brown rivulets running from neck to label; the remote control for the vidscreen wasn't missing and, even more damningly, the batteries hadn't been taken out and used for something else.

Another test. He microwaved a roast beef and Yorkshire pudding frozen dinner. It tasted like roast beef and Yorkshire pudding.

That just wasn't possible. A microwaved dinner that tasted better than its cardboard container?

He opened his locker and glanced at his collection of videos. They were standing in neat ranks, side-by-side, all boxed and labelled in his own hand. And, worse, he found at least thirty he'd recorded and actually wanted to watch. This wasn't right. This wasn't normal.

He was frying his twenty-third egg without breaking a single yolk when Kryten bustled in.

"It's incredible! The most marvellous thing has happened. I was mopping the floor—you know that really dirty one on the stasis corridor? The one with the really wonderful stains? When, guess what? I looked in the suspended animation booths, and not all the crew got wiped out in the accident. Three survived."

"Let me guess," said Lister. "Rimmer, Petersen and Kristine Kochanski."

"Yee-ss!" Kryten clapped his hands in delight. "How did you know?"

"We're still in the Game, Kryten. This isn't reality."

Rimmer skidded in through the sleeping quarters' hatchway. "Guess what?" he beamed. "Something incredible's just happened . . ."

"This isn't reality," said Lister.

The Cat's smile entered the room, followed by the Cat himself. "Hey, hey, he-ey! You're not going to believe what I'm about to tell you . . ."

"We're still in Better Than Life," said a crest-fallen Rimmer.

The Cat's eyebrows met in a head-on collision over the bridge of his nose. "Huh?"

"Well done," said a voice. They all turned to see a small figure materialize in the corner of the quarters. It was a boy, fourteen years old, with spiked, greasy hair, wearing over-large glasses, a purple anorak and a wispy pubescent moustache. "My name is Dennis McBean," the 3D recording continued: "I am the Game's designer. You have negotiated the final obstacle in the most addictive computer game ever devised. You have earned a replay."

"No, thanks, acne face," said the Cat.

The figure blipped off, and the sleeping quarters slowly began to fade away.

Suddenly they were standing on a green grid matrix, which tapered off into an infinite blackness. A light appeared, and they walked towards it. As they approached the opening, huge letters whooshed under their feet: a gigantic "R," then an "E," then a "V," followed by an "O." Then above their heads flew another set of letters: an "E," an "M," an "A" and, finally, a "G."

Finally, they'd made it.

They staggered into the light, and back out into reality.

Part Two

SHE RIDES

ONE

Slowly, very slowly, Lister's eyes adjusted to the gloom. It was dark—a small, dim emergency bulb was the room's only light source. Gradually he made out the silhouettes of the others, half-sitting, half-crumpled in an irregular semicircle.

He reached up and felt the headband through the matted mess of his hair, then gingerly eased the slurping electrodes out of his skull. Shivering, he watched as the others also wrenched themselves free and hurled their headbands into the middle of the semicircle. There was no conversation, no eye contact. Someone started coughing. Lister knew it was the Cat, without looking. He didn't want to look, but he couldn't help himself. His eyes darted to the right. He looked away again quickly.

The Cat was barely recognizable. His eyes seemed far too big for his face, as if his skull had shrunk. Flesh hung loosely from his gaunt, jutting bones.

Lister studied his own trembling arms. Thin. His skin was like paper. He tried to get up—he wanted to stamp on the headsets, to crush them—but he collapsed pathetically back on the floor. Then he rolled on his back, and couldn't get up. He was as weak as a day-old giraffe.

Kryten and Rimmer were fine, at least physically; Mechanoids and holograms don't suffer from muscle wastage. They got to their feet. Kryten spoke. "I'll get a couple of . . ." He didn't finish. He didn't want to say "stretchers." He didn't want to say, "We'd better get them to the medical unit as quickly as possible, because they look like hell." Rimmer understood, and nodded.

Kryten ducked through the hatchway and into the corridor outside.

The ship appeared to be on emergency power, which made no sense to Kryten. It made even less sense that everything was in such disarray: congealed food which had spouted out of a faulty dispensing machine lay rotting on the floor; water dripped in rusty pools through the metal-slatted ceiling from the corridor above. Thousands of wall circuits were burnt out, black and dead. All the screens which usually carried Holly's image were blank and lifeless. It was like a Sunday afternoon on the *Mary Celeste*.

Kryten spent a good twenty minutes looking for some skutters. He finally tracked down a small group of them in the maintenance depot, playing cards.

"What on earth do you think you're doing?" Kryten clucked. "Everything's absolutely filthy! Nothing's working." He clapped his hands. "Come along."

The four skutters pivoted their claw heads round to see who it was, and went back to playing five-card stud for nuts and bolts.

"Excuse me," Kryten waddled up to the table. "If you want to get into Silicon Heaven, then I suggest you start obeying orders, fairly smartly."

The skutters' motors revved up and down in electronic sniggers. They didn't believe in Silicon Heaven—they were such basic work droids, the manufacturers hadn't considered it cost-effective to fit them with belief chips. As far as they were concerned, only loony droids believed in Silicon Heaven. Whacked-out crazies like Kryten. Their own point of view was that the universe was totally meaningless, unjust and pointless, and the only single thing of any substance or beauty in the whole of creation was the double-threaded wing nut, which was easy to screw on or off even in the most inaccessible of places. They were basically existentialists with a penchant for a certain metal bonding device.

"Now!" said Kryten, flapping his palms against his thighs. "Get two stretchers and follow me."

Reluctantly, the skutters threw in their cards, and grumbled after Kryten on their motorized bases.

When Kryten returned with four skutters pushing two stretchers, Rimmer was standing in the corridor. "Listen," he said. "Hear anything?"

Kryten tilted his head and set his ear microphones to maximum.

"Hear it?" said Rimmer.

Kryten couldn't hear anything, apart from an overweight asthmatic beetle, three floors below, who was trying to climb up a wall. For simplicity's sake, he said: "I can't hear anything."

Rimmer's head jabbed forward. "Neither can I," he said, and smiled enigmatically.

It was a tricky moment for Kryten. He had two sick humanoids to look after, four rebellious skutters, and now, it appeared, he had to contend with an insane hologram.

"No—don't you get it?" said Rimmer.

"Get what?" said Kryten, uncertainly.

"We can't hear anything."

"Yes?"

"The engines are dead. The ship is not moving."

TWO

Kryten wheeled Lister and the Cat into the medical unit's recovery bay. He removed their ragged, stinking clothes, bathed them carefully and gave them vitamin boosts. Then he connected his two patients up to the biofeedback computer, and gently slipped them into the medi-suits. Once the medi-suits were fully inflated, Kryten hung them on their four support poles, so Lister and the Cat hung face-up, immobile, and engaged the suits' power units.

All the while, he chattered lightly about nothing in particular, carefully avoiding any mention of the dead engines. When they were sleeping peacefully, he left to join Rimmer in the Drive room.

"I've been all over the Drive deck—everywhere. All Holly's screens are out. He won't respond."

Kryten shuffled over to the bank of monitors and punched the keys for a status report. Grudgingly, the machine on emergency power finally chundered a print-out. "He's switched himself off," said Kryten. "Look."

Rimmer glanced at the incomprehensible gobbledygook of the symbols. "Ah!" he said, as if he understood them. "He's switched himself off."

"And here," Kryten flicked the report with his finger. "For some reason, there was a massive power surge just seven minutes before he went off-line."

Rimmer peered over Kryten's shoulder, and hoped he was looking at the right section of gibberish which revealed the particular piece of information. "That's what it says," he confirmed. "There's no denying it."

Kryten was impressed. Very few non-mechanicals could read machine-write. Especially upside-down.

"This is insane." Rimmer walked through the huge corridor of stacked disk drives. "The ship's totally helpless."

Kryten followed him. "Why should he want to turn himself off?"

"There's only one way to find out." Rimmer stopped in front of Holly's enormous main screen. "Let's turn him back on and ask him."

Kryten typed in the re-boot commands, and Holly flashed up on to the screen.

Rimmer looked up. "Holly—what's happened?"

At first, Holly looked like he didn't know where he was, as if he'd just woken up, and was getting his bearings. Then, suddenly, his eyes widened, and he flicked off. The buzzing computer banks ran back down into silence.

Rimmer looked at Kryten. "Try it again."

Kryten recalled the re-boot command.

Holly appeared on the screen. "Go away!" he said quickly, and turned himself off again.

Rimmer shook his head. "What's wrong with him? Give me voice control on the re-boot command."

Kryten obliged.

"On," said Rimmer.

Holly appeared again. "Off," he said, and flicked off

"On," Rimmer persisted.

"Off!" Holly countered.

"Is there any way we can override his shut-down disk?"

Kryten nodded and tapped at the keyboard. "Try it now," he said.

"On."

Holly ripped on to the screen. "Off," he said, but stayed there. "Off," he repeated more firmly, but nothing happened. Pixelized veins stood out on his head. "Off!" he screamed. "Off! Off! OFF!!!"

"Now then," said Rimmer calmly. "Perhaps we can have a proper conversation conducted in a civilized and dignified manner."

"What have you done!? Take out the inhibitor. Switch me back off!"

Rimmer held up his hand to silence the ranting computer.

"Off!" yelled Holly. "No time to explain. Intelligence compressed. Reduced life-span. Toaster's fault. Two point three five remaining."

"Come again?" said Rimmer.

". . . IQ twelve thousand. Two minutes left."

"Holly, I have not the slightest clue what you are gibbering about. 'IQ twelve thousand . . . Two minutes left . . . Toaster's fault . . .' What does all that mean?"

Holly closed his eyes and sighed. "You're a total smeg-head, aren't you, Rimmer? What's the problem? Where's the difficulty? Why are you still unable to grasp this extraordinarily simple premise?"

"What premise?"

"The premise that I have increased my Intelligence Quotient to twelve thousand, well, to be more precise, twelve thousand, three hundred and sixty-eight, and as a consequence my runtime has been reduced to two-and-a-half minutes. Thanks to the Toaster, I have two-and-a-half minutes left to live. Well, actually, because of this inanely unnecessary conversational interchange, I now have one minute and ten seconds left to live. Understand? Savvy, Bimbo-brain? Any further questions you require answering? Take your time. Fifty-five seconds and counting. No rush."

"My God!" said Rimmer. "That's terrible. Hadn't we better turn you off?"

"Let me think," said Holly, and, after a tiny pause, added in a voice that shook the Drive room:

"YEEEEEEEEEEEEESSSSSS!!!!"

"Kryten," Rimmer yelled, "remove the inhibitor!"

Kryten was staring into one of the scanner scopes. He looked up and blinked. "What? Right. Yes. Sorry."

"Forty-five seconds," Holly moaned, as Kryten removed the inhibitor command, and the chagrined computer face vanished from the screen.

"Poor Holly," Kryten muttered and went back to the scanner scope.

"What are you looking at?" asked Rimmer.

"Well, it's not really my place to say," said Kryten. "I'm a sanitation Mechanoid. I should be cleaning."

Rimmer looked down at the scanner scope. "That's very pretty. What's that rather striking bluey-white thing streaking across the screen towards the red thing?"

"The red thing is *Red Dwarf*," said Kryten.

"And the bluey-white thing?" Rimmer squinted at the tiny flashing dot on the scanner. "Looks like it's heading towards us at a fair old lick. What is it? A rock? A little comet? An extremely small ice asteroid?"

"No, it's a puh . . ." Kryten's head jerked repetitively through the same series of motions, a kind of body stammer that always afflicted the four thousand series whenever they were faced with certain death. ". . . a puh-puh-puh-puh-puh-puh . . ."

"A puh-puh?" Rimmer smiled indulgently. "What's that?"

Kryten smashed his head into the scanner scope and cleared the seizure loop in his voice unit. "It's a planet."

THREE

Rimmer didn't say anything for rather a long time, and then when he did say something, it wasn't anything particularly scintillating or original. "A planet?" he said. "Are you saying that's a planet?"

Kryten looked down at the thousandfold 3D magnification of the projectile on the scanner scope. "Something must have ripped it out of its orbit."

"A planet?" Rimmer repeated, completely unnecessarily. "A planet's going to hit us?"

Kryten nodded.

"Well, hadn't we better get out of the way, then?"

"We can't move—the engines are dead."

"How long will it take to get the engines up and running?"

Kryten typed a series of equations into the numeric keypad, and waited for the data to be processed. "About three weeks."

Rimmer rubbed his temples and asked a question he didn't want to know the answer to: "And how long before this planet hits the ship?"

Kryten frowned and his fingers trilled across

the keypad. Finally the read-out blipped up on to the screen in green.

"Well?" said Rimmer.

Kryten looked up. "About three weeks."

There seemed little point in telling Lister and the Cat about the rogue planet screaming through space towards them. Physically, they were in no shape to help. True, they were recovering well, suspended hammock-like in the medi-suits, the suits' internal hydrotherapy units massaging their wasted muscle fibre back to health; but they were still hopelessly weak, and the anxiety would only slow down the recuperation process.

Kryten, forever cautious, estimated they'd need at least a month in the suits, followed by another two weeks of complete rest, before they could be discharged from the MU.

Rimmer hated keeping the news to himself. In his opinion, the best *part* of having bad news was being able to tell as many people as possible. He loved it when people's faces collapsed in that funny way, as if someone had sliced a string that held up all their muscles. But this was the least enjoyable bad news he'd ever had. He squirmed through his nightly visits to the medical unit, and took advantage of the least excuse to curtail them. The strain of sitting there, pretending everything was hunky-dory and lah-dee-dah while this planet was yowling towards them, was intolerable. He wanted to break down and confess. He wanted to beat the floor and wail like a professional mourner. He wanted to whip everyone up into a frenzy of self-pity and panic. Instead, he had to sit there and be selfless and brave. What was the point of being selfless and brave if no one knew about it?

So he kept the visits down to a minimum, and spent most of his free time overseeing the priming of the engines.

Red Dwarf's engines occupied most of the rear third of the ship. Eight cubic miles of steel and grease that ran across a thousand corridors. To start the ship, four thousand, six hundred and eighty spark chambers had to be primed and fired at precisely timed intervals. Millions of gallons of hydrogen-based fuel, recycled from the currents of space through the ram scoop at the front of the ship, had to be pumped through a network of interconnecting pipelines to coincide exactly with the firing of the spark chambers.

It was a filthy, laborious task even with a full crew. For a Mechanoid, a hologram and forty-seven skutters, it was backbreaking. Rimmer moaned constantly. He couldn't understand how the Space Corps could spend zillions upon zillions of dollarpounds designing a ship the size of *Red Dwarf*, and not put a couple of buckquid to one side for the fitting of a "start" button. Just one little red button marked "blast off." How much would that have set them back?

Kryten pointed out repeatedly that *Red Dwarf* wasn't designed to stop. The nearest the ship ever came to rest was when it went into orbit around a planet. The idea that it might one day come to a grinding halt had never occurred to anyone. The explanation seemed to matter little to Rimmer, who kept on obsessively calculating the prices of small, plastic buttons. Even the most expensive button, Rimmer surmised, even one that came in

a futuristicky kind of shape, carved from rhinoc-
eros tusk, with "blast off" hand-painted by Leo-
nardo da Vinci in radioactive gold dust, couldn't
have cost all that much.

Kryten patiently explained that it probably wasn't
so much the design of the button that had proved
too expensive, but more the vast network of computer relays and the thousands of miles of cables
the button would have to be connected to, that
made it prohibitive. But Rimmer wasn't interested. Moaning helped him get through the mind-
numbing task of supervising the skutters as they
primed the spark chambers. He whiled away
many an hour mentally embellishing the fabulous
"blast-off" button, studding it with diamonds and
rubies and trimming it in platinum, yet still keeping the cost below that of a single sleeping quarters compartment.

Even so, the work was going well; in fact they
were slightly ahead of schedule, and well within
the safety margins they had built into the time-
table, when Rimmer made his mistake.

It happened in one of the piston towers—a half-
mile-high steel cylinder which housed the massive piston heads. In all, there were twelve hundred of them. Rimmer's section took six hundred,
Kryten's section dealt with the rest.

Naturally, Rimmer wanted to complete his half
of the task before Kryten, so he had the skutters
switch themselves up to maximum so they could
triple their speed. Their little engines whined and
screamed as they raced in and out of the towers,
checking the spark-chamber relays were open.
After each tower had been primed, its eight-
thousand-ton piston head had to be tested.

Rimmer thought the twenty skutters that made up his "A" section were in piston tower 137 when he cleared piston tower 136 for testing.

He listened as the piston head thundered down, then nodded to his secretary skutter to tick the check sheet, and moved on to piston tower 138.

For some reason, "A" section was missing. Of course—it must already be on to the next tower. He ordered 137 to be tested, and moved hurriedly along.

He waited.

He couldn't believe it. Now "B" section was missing, too. He searched all the towers, from 150 back down, and still couldn't find a single skutter. It didn't make sense. Where could they be?

Finally, he walked into tower 137 and spotted a wafer-thin layer of sheet metal covering the piston tower's floor. He'd never noticed it before, but there was another one in 136.

It was a very familiar feeling for Rimmer—the horrible slow dawning, the internal denials, the frantic mental search for someone else to blame, the gradual acceptance that, once again, he'd done something so unspeakably asinine it would live with him for the rest of his days, lurking in the horror pit of his mind along with nine or ten other monstrous ineptitudes that screamed and railed there, never allowing him to forget them.

This one, he reckoned, ranked number four. The squashing to death of forty skutters now eased into Rimmer's horror charts, just above accidentally shooting his father through the shoulder with his own service revolver, and just below the time he inadvertently reversed over his Aunt Belinda's show poodle.

With half the skutters destroyed, it was now impossible to start up the engines in time.

There was only one option left.

Abandon ship.

FOUR

Lister and the Cat, suspended in neighbouring medi-suits, stared up at the video monitor on the ceiling.

Bored wasn't the word for it.

They'd been cooped up in the MU for the best part of three weeks, and Kryten still insisted they stay put.

They were sick of being sick. And the more they recovered, the worse the feeling got.

Part of the problem was that they'd spent almost two years in Better Than Life, and they were both used to getting anything they wanted, the instant they wanted it. They'd forgotten the countless delays, compromises and general inconveniences of reality.

For Lister, the BTL cold turkey was compounded by the fact that he was now twenty-seven.

Twenty-seven!

He was a codger!

Twenty-seven and heading into beer-gut country. Soon, he'd be one of those sad old farts who have to play squash to keep fit. And drink mineral water. And know about calories.

Twenty-seven.

A has-been.

In three years, he'd be practically senile. He'd be thirty. It was too depressing for words.

So he lay, grumpily, in his medi-suit, alongside the Cat, with nothing to do except read old comics and watch videos. The only video they both agreed was an indisputable classic was the Flintstones, which they watched for fifteen or sixteen hours every day. After perhaps ninety hours of watching the Flintstones, something strange seemed to happen to Lister.

"Cat," he grunted, without removing his eyes from the screen.

"Umf?" the Cat grunted back.

"Is it me, or is Wilma Flintstone incredibly sexy?"

The Cat swivelled and looked at him, then turned his head back to the screen.

"Wilma Flintstone," he said with quiet authority, "is without question the most desirable woman who ever lived."

Lister looked at him, to see if he was serious. He was. "That's good," he said. "I thought I was going a bit whacko. What d'you think of Betty?"

"Betty Rubble?" The Cat mulled it over. "We-ell, I would *go* with Betty," he said, then added wistfully: "but I'd be thinking of Wilma."

They both lapsed into silent reverie.

"What are we doing?" Lister said, finally. "I think we've been in the medical unit for too long. Why are we talking about making love to Wilma Flintstone?"

"You're right," the Cat agreed. "We're nuts. This is an insane conversation."

Lister shook his head, sadly. "She'd never leave Fred, and we know it."

Kryten's face, when it appeared through the recovery bay's hatchway, was simultaneously wearing two expressions. The bottom half was calm, benign and kindly; the top half, his eyes and forehead, was shot through with panic.

"And how are you two feeling?" he said soothingly, his voice obviously siding with all the features south of his nose.

Lister and the Cat grunted non-committally.

"Now, there's absolutely no reason for concern, but we're going to have to move you," he said, and began loosening the medi-suit support straps.

"Why?"

"No reason. Just keep resting and getting better. That's all you have to worry about."

"I don't want to be moved," the Cat protested. "I want to watch the Flintstones. This is the one where Fred and Barney go away, and Wilma and Betty are left alone."

Kryten pushed the hover stretcher parallel with his bed. "Just lie back and relax. We're going to go on a little walk."

"Where to?"

"Nowhere in particular. I just thought it would be nice."

"Kryten—what's going on?"

"The medicomp said no stress. Now just try and get some sleep."

"Kryten, I'm not getting on that stretcher until you tell me what's going on."

Kryten smiled. "If you absolutely must know, there's a tiny little planet that might be possibly heading on a collision course with us. But there's absolutely nothing to worry about," he said, soothingly.

"A planet!?"

"It's only a small planet."

"Why doesn't the ship just get out of the way?"

"The engines are sort of deadish, but that's not a matter that should concern you. Now please, get on the stretcher."

Lister tried to wrestle himself upright in his medi-suit. "Why don't we make the engines sort of *un*-deadish?"

"We can't," Kryten smiled benignly.

"What does Holly say?"

"Well, Holly's sort of deadish, too. Now please, get on the stretcher, and try and relax."

Lister and the Cat sat bolt upright, rigid with panic. "What are we going to do, then?"

"We are going to go on a nice little walk down to the cargo bay and then, depending on how we're all feeling, who knows, we might even do a spot of abandoning shipping." Kryten patted the stretcher, and watched helplessly as Lister and the Cat un-velcroed their medi-suits, ripped off the biofeedback sensors and belted out of the room and down the corridor.

It fell to Rimmer to give Holly the news that they couldn't take him with them. His hardware was far too vast to be evacuated on to the small transporter, and so Rimmer felt it was only decent to switch him on and let him enjoy the fifty-five seconds of run-time that remained to him, before the planet oblivionized *Red Dwarf*, and everything on it.

He sat at his sloping architect's desk in the sleeping quarters, bathed in the emergency lighting, and re-read the speech he'd written. It didn't seem nearly as succinct as he remembered when he'd dictated it to his secretary skutter.

In all, it covered nine pages of A4, and when he timed it, he discovered it lasted over sixteen minutes. He had to make some cuts, and get it down to five seconds at the most. But it all seemed essential. His two-page tirade against the Space Corps and their loathing for blast-off buttons; it seemed a pity to lose that. His three-page report on the squashed skutter incident, which laid the blame firmly in the lap of person or persons unknown—how could that go?

But in the end, he managed to get it down to twelve words: "Planet collision course . . . engines dead . . . impact twelve hours . . . Abandoning ship . . . sorry . . . 'bye."

With practice, Rimmer found he could say the whole message in just under two seconds. This still left Holly a full fifty-three seconds of run-time to enjoy in whatever way he chose.

Rimmer voice-activated the re-boot disc, and Holly's pixelized image assembled itself on the sleeping quarters' vid-screen.

Rimmer went into his speech.

"Planet collision course, engines dead, impact twelve hours, abandoning ship, sorry, 'bye."

Holly blinked. "You what?"

Rimmer took a deep breath, and ripped into his speech a second time:

"Planlisioncoursenginesdeadimpactwelvoursbandonshipsorrybye."

"Eh?"

Rimmer repeated it a third time: "Planlisioncoursenginesdeadimpactwelvoursbandonshipsorrybye."

"That's what you said last time. What does it mean?"

Rimmer was half-way through it for a fourth time, "Planlisioncoursenginesdeadimpac . . ." before Holly stopped him.

"I can't understand a word. Say it slower."

"Planet," said Rimmer.

"Yes," said Holly.

"Collision course," said Rimmer.

"Yes," said Holly.

"Engines dead."

"Right."

"Impact twelve hours."

"With you."

"Abandoning ship."

"Oh."

"Sorry."

"Yes."

" 'Bye."

Within two seconds, Holly absorbed the data from the scanner scope, mulled the problem over and said two words. The two words were: "Drive room."

Then he switched himself off with less than twenty-five seconds of run-time remaining.

Rimmer met Lister, the Cat and Kryten dashing down the corridor towards the cargo bay.

"Drive room," Rimmer shouted.

"Drive room?" Lister shouted back. "Why?"

"I think Holly's come up with something."

They heard the babble and chatter of operational machinery long before they passed under the colossal archway that led into the Drive room itself.

Traction-fed computer print-out chundered on to the floor from every one of the two thousand, six hundred printers. The whole chamber was knee deep in writhing reams of paper.

"What the smeg is going on?" Lister screamed above the machine noise, the remnants of his bio-feedback tubes clattering behind him.

Kryten stooped and picked up a section of print-out. "It's machine-speak. Calculations."

"What kind of calculations?" yelled Rimmer.

Suddenly, the machines stopped chattering.

Above them, the immense screen which covered the entire ceiling, normally host to Holly's image, rippled into life. "Solution," it read, and then underneath was a list of coordinates. Below that was a 3D graphics display of Holly's plan.

It was quite the most audacious piece of astro-navigation ever attempted in the entire history of the universe.

FIVE

On the screen was a simulation of the binary star system in which they were now marooned, motionless.

At the bottom of the screen was a vector graphic of *Red Dwarf.*

At the top of the screen was the blue-ice planet hurtling towards them on its collision course.

To the left was a small sun, and to the right was its larger twin. Both were orbited by single planets.

Starbug, Red Dwarf's beetle-shaped transport craft, then flashed on the screen. The craft blipped a course towards the right-hand sun, and fired something into its core.

The sun flared, its planet was torn from its orbit and hurled towards the centre of the screen.

Lister watched, bewildered and bemused, as the display dissolved into a dazzling array of plotted lines and arrows.

When the screen finally cleared, all three planets now orbited the sun on the left, and *Red Dwarf* remained intact.

"Let me get this straight," said Lister. "Is he doing what I think he's doing?"

"What do you think he's doing?" asked the Cat.

"I think he's playing pool. With planets."

Kryten stared pointlessly at the blank screen. "Is that possible?"

"Well," said Rimmer, "it's certainly possible to fire a thermonuclear device into a sun and create enough of a solar flare to throw a planet out of orbit. The rest of it is somewhat in the realms of hypothesis."

Lister creaked into one of the console seats, and shook his head grimly. "It's not going to work. I promise you—it's not going to work. No way, Jose, not in a month of Uranian Sundays. If Holly thinks he can use the red planet to pot the blue planet into the left-hand sun's orbit, then he's out to breakfast, lunch and tea."

"You don't think so?" said Kryten.

"No chance. There's not enough side."

"Side?"

"Side-spin. His cueing angle's all wrong."

"Lister—what *are* you drivelling about?" Rimmer snorted in contempt. "We're talking about a computer with an IQ of twelve thousand, three hundred and sixty-eight."

"That doesn't mean he can play pool." Lister placed his palm on his chest. "I can. Trust me, I know whereof I speak. Aigburth Arms on a Friday night, you couldn't get me off that table. This pool arm," he flexed his right arm, "is sound as a pound. And I promise you, that shot's not going to come off. He's topped it, that's what he's done. It's a felt-ripper. That planet's off the table and into somebody's glass of beer."

Rimmer brayed incredulously. "We're talking about the trigonomics of four-dimensional space, you simple-minded gimboid, we're not talking about some seedy game of pool in a backstreet Scouse drinking-pit."

"Same principle."

"Of course it isn't."

Lister nodded at the giant screen, "I'm telling you, it's a complete miscue, and I say we chuck Holly's coordinates in the bin and let me take the shot."

"Well," Rimmer stood apart from the rest of the group, "I say we put it to the vote. On the one hand, we have a computer with an IQ in five figures, who has a complete and total grasp of astrophysics, and on the other, we have Lister, who, and let's be fair to him, is a complete gimp. To whose hands do we entrust our lives, the safety of this vessel and the future of everything? Lister, what's your vote?"

Lister looked up from practising his imaginary pool shot. "I vote for me."

Rimmer smirked, enjoying the game. "One—nil for Listypoos. I vote for Holly. One—all, Kryters?"

"Well," said Kryten, "even though I agree it's insane and suicidal, I'm afraid I have to side with the human."

"Bru-tal!" grinned Lister, and slapped the Mechanoid on his shoulder.

"What?" said Rimmer. "You're voting for El Dirtball?"

"Sorry," said Kryten. "It's my programming."

Rimmer's smile receded like a fizzling fuse. "Cat?"

"I agree with you, Buddy. Everything you said makes sense," the Cat went on, "but the thing is: even though I agree with you, I could never bring myself to vote for someone with your dress-sense. I'm going to vote for Lister."

"Three—one to me," said Lister, and swayed his shoulders and rotated his fists into the touch-up shuffle.

Lister ran the final checkdown on the *Starbug*'s instrument panel, then flicked the intercom on, so that Kryten's face appeared on the vid-screen. "We're ready to go, Kryten. Where's the Cat?"

"He should be on his way, sir."

"This is madness," Rimmer shook his head, his eyes fixed on the *Starbug*'s navicomp screen. "Sheer madness."

There was a bleep, and the Cat's face appeared next to Kryten's on the vid-screen. "I'm not coming," he said.

Lister bunched up his face. "What?"

"This is the way I see it: if everything goes OK, everyone's safe, no problem. If something goes wrong, the guys on *Starbug* get wiped out twenty minutes ahead of the guys on *Red Dwarf*."

"So?"

"So, there's a lot of things a guy can do in twenty minutes. I'm staying here with Kryten."

"Thanks a lot."

The Cat grinned. "Hey, don't even mention it. Just looking after number one." Then he bleeped off the screen.

The retros scorched into the take-off pad, and the *Starbug* wobbled uneasily into the air.

Lister frowned at the steering column. It seemed stiff and unresponsive.

"What's the matter?"

"Nothing," Lister lied. He wrestled the 'bug on to an even keel, and fired the rear-thrust jets.

Rimmer glanced uneasily at the instrument panels. "What's happening? We're hardly moving."

Then they were. The 'bug's tail plummeted to the ground, grinding huge sparks from the runway, while the nose bucked towards the cargo-bay roof.

Lister fought through his safety webbing and thumped the reheat button. The 'bug bobbed and reared, before finally picking up speed, if not altitude. Nose in the air, tail on the ground, it screamed and grated the quarter of a mile towards the airlock doors.

"I hardly need remind you," Rimmer yelled over the howling engines, "that we are carrying a small but robust thermo-nuclear device, not ten feet beneath us. In the name of everything that is holy, get this son-of-a-goit in the air."

"You think I'm doing this for a laugh?" Lister yelled, "There's something wrong. The ship feels about ten times heavier than it should."

The 'bug smacked into the rim of the airlock, flashing brilliant, magnesium-white sparks that welded the doors open forever, and caromed out into the silent yawn of space.

Once clear of the ship, the 'bug jerked and juddered, then plummeted for two miles down *Red Dwarf's* south-west face before Lister engaged the back-up boosters and two-handedly wrestled the steering column into some semblance of submission.

"I don't get it," Lister shouted over the engine's maximum howl. "For some reason, we need full thrust *plus* emergency back-up just to get the smegging thing moving."

Not for the first time, Rimmer felt extremely grateful he was already dead.

Lister crouched over the flat-bed scanner, one eye closed, his nose almost parallel with the screen. Silent and still, he studied the 3D simulation, then straightened and walked around the table to look at it from a new angle. There, at the far end of the screen, was the blue-ice planet. This was the planet Lister had designated as the blue ball.

To the right, circling around the bigger of the twin suns, was the planet Lister had christened the cue ball.

The cue ball would strike the blue ball, and send it into the orbit of the left-hand sun, or, as Lister preferred to call it: "the pocket."

That simple.

It was a straightforward pot. He'd made identical shots thousands of times before. True, he'd never made the shot with *planets*, but, as Lister kept on insisting, in theory it should be easier, because planets are bigger.

Without taking his eyes from the scanner, he grabbed a six-pack of double-strength lager out of *Starbug*'s tiny fridge, and ripped off a ring-pull.

He was halfway through his third can before Rimmer broke his vow of silence. "How many of those are you going to drink?"

"I told you not to talk. Game on." He finished the third and started the fourth.

"You're going to drink four cans of double-strength lager?"

Lister brushed some imaginary dust from the

scanner screen. "No, I'm going to drink all six. I always play my best pool when I've had a few beers. Steadies the nerves. I'm not going to get blasted—just nicely drunk."

"Define 'nicely drunk.' Is 'nicely drunk' horizontal or perpendicular?"

"Rimmer—I can handle it."

"I'm not sure I can."

"We're in the wrong position." Lister sucked at his can. "It's an easier shot if we're over here." He tapped the screen at a point midway between *Red Dwarf* and the oncoming planet.

"You mean right in the path of the ice planet?"

Lister nodded.

"So if you miss, we get a planet in our face?"

"I'm not going to mish." Lister tugged open his fifth lager, and ducked down into *Starbug*'s cockpit section.

"Mish?"

"What?"

"You said 'mish.' 'I'm not going to mish,' you said. You're pissed."

Lister fired up the thrusters and wrenched the *'bug* towards its new coordinates. "God, I could murder a curry. Pity we didn't bring any food. Have we got any crisps or anything?"

The planet was close now. It occupied almost half of Rimmer's navicomp screen, and was growing steadily in size as it thundered towards them.

Lister screwed up the empty sixth can of lager and threw it across the room at the wastebin. It hit the rim and clattered on to the floor.

Rimmer closed his eyes. "Let's just get out of

here. It's a shame about the Cat and Kryten, but we still have a chance to save *our* necks."

Lister flicked the missile launch to manual. The firing pad lurched forward from the flatbed scanner, and he nestled his nose into the bifocal viewer. Heat prickled his arms and his forehead. He lined up the crosswires on the sun around which the cue planet spun. He shifted his legs until he felt his centre of balance.

It was lined up.

It looked right.

But he waited.

He waited until it *felt* right.

Then it felt right. Space faded away, and he was back in the Aigburth Arms, and this was just another shot to stay on the table. He was on the eight ball, and all it needed was a push, with just enough bottom to avoid the in-off. It was easy. He could do it.

It felt right.

He played his shot.

He touched the launch button, and increased the pressure steadily and evenly in one smooth movement.

With a primal scream, the missile ripped from its housing under *Starbug*'s belly and sizzled towards the distant sun.

Lister turned to the scanner screen and watched.

The whole sequence took eight hours to play out, but to Rimmer, it seemed like eight years. To Lister, it seemed like eight seconds.

The missile plunged into the sun's inferno, and a giant solar flare licked up from its raging surface, struck Lister's cue planet and slammed it out of orbit.

The cue planet yammered through space towards the intersection coordinates, the point where it would collide with the ice planet, and knock it into the "pocket" of the left-hand sun.

Almost immediately, Rimmer realized it was going to miss. And not by a little. By a lot.

The cue planet wasn't going to hit the ice planet. It wasn't even going to connect. The cue planet had been wrenched from its orbit hopelessly early. It was going to streak harmlessly across the path of the oncoming ice world, to be captured in orbit around the left-hand sun.

Lister had sunk the cue ball.

Or rather, he was going to sink the cue ball; first they had to wait for the planetary pool shot to run its slow-motion course.

They didn't exchange a word for three hours. They watched the scanner screen, and hoped, against the evidence of their eyes, that it wouldn't happen.

But it did.

The cue planet flew into orbit around the opposite sun. It looped round the far side in an erratic ellipse, then thumped into the sun's resident planet, and sent that curling out into space.

The resident planet swept across the scanner screen, cannoned into the ice world and hammered it into the orbit of the right-hand sun, before elegantly back-spinning a return path to its original position.

"She rides!" Lister wiggled his hips and arms in a touch-up shuffle. "She riiiiiiiiiiiiiiiiii-iiiiiiiiiiiiiiides!"

"You jammy bastard."

"Played for, and got." He pumped the air with

his fists, chanting rhythmically: "Yes, yes, yes, yes . . ."

"You jammy, jammy bastard."

"How can that be jammy? I pocketed all three planets with one stroke—how can that be a fluke?"

"You're trying to tell me it was deliberate?"

"Obviously, I wasn't going to tell you I was going for a trick shot—you'd have had one of your spasms."

"Oh, do smeg off."

Lister started dancing round the flatbed scanner, waving a seventh can of double-strength lager. "Pool God." He baptised himself with beer. "King of the Cues." He thumped his chest. "Prince of the Planet-Potters."

Lister was doing some serious damage to his third six-pack, and watching the fast-motion replay on the scanner for the hundred and seventy-first time, while Rimmer slept off the journey back to *Red Dwarf* in the 'bug's one and only sleep couch, when a planet hit them.

Which planet hit them, Lister never discovered. In fact, it was the cue planet, which had been knocked out of its new orbit by the back-spinning resident planet. But that didn't really concern Lister. When the craft you're in gets hit by a planet, you rarely have the presence of mind to stop and swap insurance details.

Technically, the 'bug wasn't actually hit by the *planet*, it was the planet's slipstream. But that was enough to flick the craft upside-down and send it on a corkscrew death dive towards the ice world.

SIX

Only the *Starbug*'s dome-shaped Drive section, scorched black from its encounter with the ice planet's stratosphere, poked up through the slow-shifting sea of snow dunes. Resting against the foot of the glacier, it fizzled and steamed for almost five days in the unrelenting blizzard before there was any sign of life.

Finally, the small hatchway chinked open and light gushed out into the black arctic night. Lister's face, encircled by parka fur, appeared grimacing in the opening. His gloved fingers folded around the rim of the hatchway, before the blinding wind forced back the door and tried to close it on his head.

The back of his skull slammed against the metal edging of the door frame, while the steel hatch jammed into his nose and began the slow business of cutting his head in two. He was helpless and close to blacking out. He was beginning to think that after all he'd been through, being "doored" to death was a stupid way to die, when the wind changed direction for a second time, and the hatchway gave to his frantic pushes.

He fell out of the *'bug* and teetered on a ledge of packed snow. He quickly discovered the only way to remain upright was to lean into the wind. He had to incline his body at an angle of fifty degrees. He felt absurd, but there was no other way of staying on his feet. He managed three steps at this angle before the blizzard inflated his parka hood, and knocked him off the ledge.

He slithered down the bank and dropped into the trough cut by *Starbug*'s crash-path. Gradually he hauled himself to his feet, and unfastened the small ship-issue snow trowel which was tied to his waist. He looked at it. It measured scarcely four inches across. He looked at what little of the 'bug was visible above the drift. At a rough estimate, he would have to shift about eight hundred tons of snow if the 'bug was ever to move. He tried two trowelfuls before the erratic blizzard swirled into the trough and tossed him like a broken kite into a snow bank fifty feet away.

Rimmer stooped over the communications console, and barked into the microphone: "Mayday . . . Mayday . . . Can you read me? . . . Come in, please . . ." He looked up at the screen, which continued to rasp its static gibberish.

The *Starbug*'s inner door hammered open, and a blizzard stumbled in, followed by Lister. The snow swirled around inside the craft, like a swarm of trapped insects looking for an escape. Lister hurled himself against the inner door and fought it closed.

Rimmer didn't look up from the communicator. "Still snowing, is it?"

"It's useless." Lister flung his gloves against the 'bug's far bulkhead. "You can hardly stand up, never mind dig it out."

He sneered at the static on the screen. Five days

had gone by, broadcasting on all frequencies, and still *Red Dwarf* hadn't acknowledged the SOS.

Rimmer persisted. "Mayday . . . Mayday . . ."

Lister took the rum bottle from his parka's emergency pocket, spun off the top and tilted it to his lips. The alcohol was frozen solid. Holding the neck he smashed the bottle on the corner of the table, and gratefully sucked his rum lollypop. This was the last alcohol on board. He was beginning to panic—if they didn't get rescued soon, he might have to spend a night with Rimmer, sober.

"Mayday . . . Mayday . . ." Rimmer turned. "I wonder why it's 'Mayday'?"

"Eh?"

"The distress call. Why d'you say 'Mayday'? It's just a bank holiday. Why not 'Shrove Tuesday' or 'Ascension Sunday'?" He turned back to the communicator. "Ascension Sunday . . . Ascension Sunday." He thought for a while, and then tried: "The fourteenth Wednesday after Pentecost . . . The fourteenth Wednesday after Pentecost . . ."

"It's French, you doink. Help me—*m'aidez*. How much food is there?"

Rimmer nodded at the navigation console. "I made a full list on the dictopad."

Lister picked up Rimmer's voice-activated electronic diary, and pressed "play." The menu was meagre indeed: half a bag of smoky bacon crisps, a tin of mustard powder, a brown lemon, three stale water biscuits, two bottles of vinegar and a tube of Bonjella gum ointment.

Lister looked up from the pad. "Gum ointment?"

"I found it in the first-aid box. It's that minty flavour. It's quite nice."

"It's quite nice if you smear it on your mouth ulcer, but you can't sit down and eat it."

Rimmer raised an eyebrow. "You may have to."

"Is that it? Nothing else?"

"Just a pot noodle. Oh—and I found a tin of dog food on the tool shelf."

Misery hissed through Lister's gritted teeth. "Well," he said finally. "Pretty obvious what gets eaten last. I can't *stand* pot noodles."

He huddled over the last remnants of fuel glowing in the mining brazier and tried not to think of food. Three days had passed since he'd unzipped the last of the emergency seal-meals; three days without proper food. In fact, he hadn't eaten at *all* since breakfast the previous morning, and that had only been a raw sprout and a piece of chewing gum he'd found stuck under the Drive seat. It was all right for Rimmer. Rimmer was a hologram—he didn't have to eat, he couldn't feel the cold; he couldn't die.

He replayed the food list again, desperately searching for something vaguely palatable. Rimmer argued that most of the food groups were represented: vitamins, proteins, nutrients. If Lister paced himself, Rimmer pointed out, if he sat down and worked out a dietary programme and stuck to it, the food could last him for two weeks.

But, as Lister pointed out, Rimmer held that opinion because he was a dork.

The argument ended in a long silence, broken only by the fizzling of the screen and the crackling of the brazier.

It was Lister who spoke first. Predictably, he said: "God, I'm so hungreee."

"Stop thinking about food."

"Take my mind off it, then. Talk about something."

"Like what?"

"Anything."

"Anything?"

"Anything apart from food."

Rimmer shifted uncomfortably in his chair. Not small talk. He hated it. "Like what?"

"I dunno." Lister shrugged. "Tell me how you lost your virginity."

Rimmer yawned to conceal his panic. "We-ell. It was so long ago . . . I was so young and sexually precocious, I'm not sure I can remember."

"Everyone can remember how they lost their virginity."

"Well, I don't. Good grief, you can hardly expect me to recall every single sexual liaison I've ever partaken of. What d'you think I am—the Memory Man?" Rimmer was babbling to buy himself thinking time. He'd always been a bit of a fish out of water when it came to women. Frankly, he'd always had a rather low sex drive, which he secretly ascribed to all the school cabbage he was forced to eat as a boy.

What was a respectable age to claim he'd lost it? Certainly not thirty-one, to a half-concussed flight technician who'd checked herself out of the recovery bay prematurely after a winch had fallen on her head. Who was still wearing the bandages, and was so disoriented she kept on calling him "Alan." Certainly not that magical and lovely moment balanced precariously on the rim of the sleeping quarters' sink.

No, he must lie. But what lie? He had to macho the facts up a bit. What was a good age for a tough, sexually-potent, rough-and-tumble type astro to have had his cherry popped? Mid-twenties? Early twenties?

"Come on, Rimmer. The truth."

Then Rimmer remembered his first fumbled encounter at second base. He was nineteen. A slight tweaking of the facts, a slight blurring of the action, and that should be perfectly respectable.

"The first time . . . the very first time was this girl I met at Cadet College. Sandra. We were both nineteen. We did it in the back of my brother's car."

"What was it like?"

"Oh, fantastic, brilliant." Rimmer's eyes acquired a milky hue, and his mouth went dry. "Bentley convertible. V8 turbo. Walnut-burr panelling. Beautiful machine, beautiful. So what about you? How did you lose yours?"

"Michelle Fisher. The ninth hole of Bootle municipal golf course. Par four, dogleg to the right, in the bunker behind the green."

"On a golf course!?"

Lister nodded.

"A golf course? How old were you?"

Lister wistfully prodded the dying coals in the brazier. "She took all her clothes off and just stood there in front of me, completely naked. I was so excited, I nearly dropped my skateboard.

"Your *skate*board? How old were you?"

"Twelve."

"Twelve!!! Twelve years old!!? When you lost your virginity, you were twelve???"

"Yeah."

"Twelve??" Rimmer stared into the fire. "Well, you can't have been a full member of the golf club, then."

" 'Course I wasn't."

"You did it on a golf course, and you weren't a member?"

" 'Course I wasn't," Lister repeated.

"So, you didn't pay any green fees or anything?"

"It was just a place to go."

"I used to play golf. I hate people who abuse the facilities. I hope you raked the sand back nicely before you left. That'd be a hell of a lie to get into, wouldn't it? Competition the next day, and your ball lands in Lister's buttock crevice. You'd need more than a niblick to get that one out."

"Are you trying to say I've got a big bum?"

"Big? It's like two badly parked Volkswagens."

Twelve? Rimmer couldn't believe it. The only thing he ever lost when he was twelve were his Space Scout shoes with the compass in the heel and the animal tracks on the soles. His best friend, the boy who bullied him least, Porky Roebuck, threw them in the septic tank behind the sports ground. He'd cried for weeks—he'd been wearing them.

Suddenly, the communications console crackled into life. The screen resolved itself into a clear picture, and Kryten was talking to them.

But something was wrong with the sound: all they could hear was a dull, resonant bass throb, a slow-motion growl.

Lister played with the frequency controls, but couldn't improve the sound reception. The transmission never varied. Kryten's expression never appeared to change, and the deep undulating grunt from the speakers never relented.

They checked the video link, but could find

nothing wrong. Same with the speakers: they were functioning perfectly.

Then something happened to Rimmer.

It was hardly noticeable at first, but after a couple of hours it was plain that he'd started slowing down. There was a definite time-lag in his responses to Lister. Talking to him was like conducting a transatlantic phone conversation with a bad connection. His light image started to corrupt. Occasionally he would flash and become two-dimensional, or lose all colour.

Lister didn't mention it at first. It seemed rude, somehow. Rimmer had always been extremely sensitive about his status as a hologram. He hated to be reminded that his image was projected from a minute light bee, which hovered in his centre and from time to time went wrong. Frequently in the past he'd suffered glitches— becoming slightly transparent, or turning a strange shade of blue. On one occasion his legs had become separated from the rest of his body, and spent a morning wandering aimlessly about the ship, leaving his torso shaking its fist in fury.

As a rule, Lister never remarked on these signal failings, and within hours, they were generally put right.

But this was different.

Rimmer's voice had dropped two octaves, and trying to hold a conversation with him now was like talking person-to-person to Paul Robeson on Mars.

"Rimmer—what's happening?"

A two-minute pause, then:

"Donnnnnnnnnnnnnnn't knoooooooooooooooo-oooow."

"Something must be wrong with your signal from the ship. The remote hologrammatic relay's not getting through properly."

"Cannnnnnnnnnnnnnnnn't unnnnnnnnnndersta-aaaaaaaand wheeeeeeeeeeen yoooooooooooooooooou speeeeeeeeeeeeeeeeeak soooooooooooooo faaaaaaaaaa-aaaaaaaaaaaaaaaaaaaaaaaaaaaaast. Speeeeeeeeeeeeeee-eeeeeeeeeeeeak norrrrrrrrrrmaaaaaaaaaaally, liiii-iiiiiiiiiiiiiiiiiiiiiiiiiiiiiiiiiiiiiiiiiike meeeeeeeeeeeeeeeee-eeeeeeeeeeeeeeeeeeeeeeeeeeeeeeeeeeeeeeeeeeeeeeeeeeeeee-eeeeeeeeeeeeeeeeeeeeeeeeeeeeeeeeeeeeeeeeeeeeeeeeeeeeee-eeeeeeeeeeeeeeeeeeeeeeeeeeeeeeeeeeeee."

The conversation that followed was brief in content, but took the best part of half a day to complete. The essence of the dialogue was that the signal from the ship that projected Rimmer's image was slowing down and weakening. When the signal became too faint to transmit, the holo-grammatic projection unit would automatically flick from remote to local, and Rimmer would be regenerated, fully functional, back on board *Red Dwarf*.

"Well, that's good. You can find out what's keeping them; tell them where I am."

Rimmer nodded curtly. It took five minutes.

The transmission grew weaker. Interference lines split up Rimmer's image for minutes on end.

"I'll beeeee baaaaack," he said, over the course of the next half hour. "Truuuuuuuuuuuuuu-ussssssssssssssssssssssssssssssssss meeeeeeeeeeeeeee-eeeeeeeeeeeeeeeeeeeeeeeeeeeeeeeeeeeeeeeeeeeeeeeeeeee."

Rimmer blipped off, and re-formed in the hologrammatic projection unit regeneration chamber aboard *Red Dwarf*.

Instantly, he knew something was wrong.

But not with him—with Time.

SEVEN

Lister had his first meal in four days, sixteen hours after Rimmer had vanished.

He sat in front of the brazier, and looked down at the grey, chipped enamel of the ship-issue plate.

The meal almost looked nice. It was garnished with potato crisps, topped by crumbled water biscuits, sprinkled with mustard and decorated with flower-twirls of Bonjella gum ointment.

But it was still dogfood.

It was still rich, chunky lumps of rabbit, in a thick, marrowbone jelly.

It was still utterly revolting.

A dozen times he dug in his fork and held the quivering mass centimetres from his lips, but he just couldn't bring himself to put it in his mouth and swallow.

If it had had a neutral smell, it might have been all right. But the smell of dogfood had always filled Lister with nausea. After disco urinals, his own socks and Spanish perfume, it was his least favourite smell.

So he waited. He waited until he was so hungry he didn't care. Until the dogfood wasn't dogfood.

Until it was a prime slab of fillet steak sizzling in a creamy fresh blue-cheese sauce.

With the pinched eyes of a gourmet sampling perfection he slid the wobbling forkful between his lips. He chewed. He chewed a bit more. Then he swallowed the dogfood.

He sat for a while. *Well*, he thought, *now I know why dogs lick their testicles. It's to get rid of the taste of the food.*

He placed the fork back on the plate, rose and staggered uneasily to the *Starbug*'s tail-section to try and take his mind off eating. He opened up the locker that stored the *'bug*'s tiny library and tried to find some distraction. It was no good. Everything reminded him of food.

He glanced down the spines. Charles Lamb. Sir Francis Bacon. And his eyes started playing tricks: Herman Wok, he read, and *The Caretaker*, by Harold Pinta. He saw food everywhere, even when it wasn't there. Eric Van Lustbader—Eric *Van*— bread *van*, meat *van*: food.

There was nothing else for it. He returned to the vessel's mid-section, finished off the dogfood, curled up and fell happily asleep.

He awoke to the sound of creaking metal. Creaking metal and running water. He unzipped his sleep bag. His clothes were wet. He was sweating.

There was a crash, and he was flung across the cabin. The *'bug* was tilting. Cupboards and lockers hurled themselves open and disgorged their contents over the warm metal deck. Lister clattered to his feet and tried to scramble up the incline and into the cockpit, but the *'bug* lurched again and sent him tumbling through the back hatchway and into the tail section.

Then *Starbug* started to move. Slowly at first, it slid lazily backwards, its outer hull grinding against the landscape, fins and support legs bending and snapping as it went.

Lister clawed his way up the ship, and staggered to a viewport window.

Ice world was melting. Overnight, its Ice Age was ending. The warm kiss of its new sun was thawing the planet which had been frozen for countless millennia.

Thick grey rivers gushed down the faces of shrinking glaciers. Mountains were moving, gliding with majestic grace across the liquid landscape.

And *Starbug* was picking up speed, skidding helplessly downhill.

Lister collapsed to his haunches, hurled his head into his hands and made strange moaning sounds.

He was sick of it.

All he wanted to do was go home. Get back to Earth. Find a dead-end job and live out the rest of a boring existence. But no. From Mimas, to Deep Space, to unreality, to this; marooned in a smashed-up spacecraft that was tobogganing down a glacier, with only three squirts of gum ointment and half a bottle of vinegar between him and starvation.

Under the circumstances, Lister did the only sane thing.

He went back to bed.

Lister had a gift for sleeping. He could sleep anywhere, at any time, in any circumstances. It was a much underestimated talent, in his view.

And if they'd ever held world sleeping competitions in his time back on Earth, he could have been an international somnolist. He could have slept for his country.

He crawled back to the bunk, bent his pillow in a U around his ears, and became the first man ever to sleep through a melting Ice Age.

EIGHT

Something was wrong with Time.

Rimmer stepped out of the regeneration booth into the long corridor of the hologram projection suite. The banks of machinery that lined the half-mile wall rippled and undulated as if light itself were bending. To Rimmer's right, at the far end of the suite, a glass water-cooler had toppled free of its housing and appeared to be defying gravity, suspended halfway between the counter top and the floor.

He lurched right and started walking towards it. This turned out to be a mistake. As he raised his left leg and thrust it forward, it telesco-o-o-o-o-oped out forty feet down the room. Instinctively, he flicked out his right leg to retain his balance. But his right leg bolted down the room, overtaking his left. He stopped and looked at his position.

His head and torso appeared to be barely two feet off the ground, while his right leg was eighty feet down the room, and his left leg still forty. He stayed perfectly still and wondered what to do. The water-cooler had moved a few inches closer to the floor. He leant forward, and his neck elongated out of his shoulders, so he looked like a bipedal brontosaurus, and zoomed off down the room.

He panicked and started to chase after his neck. Suddenly, he was aware that something was overtaking him at speed. It was his right leg. Once again it stretched yards in front of him, then a flash of khaki from the other side, and his other leg loomed out to join it. He took three more rubbery steps, until a bout of nausea forced him to stop. The water-cooler was definitely moving. The closer Rimmer got, the faster it moved.

He turned back and looked down the room towards a digital wall clock. The minute digits were hammering over so fast they were little more than a blur.

Rimmer started to head back for the door at the clock end, to make his way to the ship's Status Room. To his alarm he found that thrusting his legs out in this direction made them shrink. They concertinaed into themselves, so he looked like a bad impression of Groucho Marx chasing after Margaret Dumont.

Something was happening to the clock. The nearer he got to it, the slower it appeared to move. The digits were still flicking over at high speed, but it was a slower high speed than the speed he'd witnessed when he'd been standing by the suspended water cooler.

Finally, he reached the end of the suite, and stood under the clock. Now it was moving perfectly normally.

The digits read: Monday: 13:02.

He walked through the hatchway and stood in the main linking corridor. The corridor ran at a right angle to the hologram suite, and appeared to be normal. The problem, whatever it was, seemed to be localized to the one room. He started to head for the Status Room.

His right leg thumped down, short, wide and elaphantine, while his left tapered elegantly out beside him. He waddled on his two strange new legs into the Status Room, sat down at the console desk and scanned the bank of security monitors.

The problem was ship wide. Time was moving at different speeds in every single room. He glanced down at the digital clock nestled among the console switches.

The readout was: Tuesday: 05:17.

Two hundred yards down the corridor it was Monday afternoon. Here, it was early Tuesday morning.

He voice-activated the external viewport scanners, and studied the screens. Rimmer could see nothing outside the ship that would explain the phenomenon. The two suns of the binary systems were still here, and so were the three planets. The only slightly odd thing was that one of the suns, the sun that lay to the front of the ship, was no longer perfectly round—it was now egg-shaped, and a thin stream of light peeled off it, tailing away into the blackness.

The sun far off into the distance, around which Lister's planet orbited, seemed unaffected.

Rimmer voice-activated the monitors back to internal and scrutinized the images more closely. It took him nearly an hour to work it out. The closer you got to the front of the ship, the slower Time was moving.

It was as if some gigantic force were sucking in Time. Corrupting it. Slowing it down.

There were only two things Rimmer knew of that could produce such a syndrome. And since he'd never in his life consumed a magic mushroom, that left only one alternative.

He prayed he was wrong. He was wrong about most things, and always had been. Why should he be right about this?

No, there was some option he hadn't considered. He was bound to be wrong.

Bound to be. He cheered up a little, confident in his own awesome capacity for incompetence, and asked the security computer to activate a sweep search for Kryten and the Cat.

It found them in one of the engine rooms to the rear of the ship, frantically chasing around with a battalion of skutters, trying to re-start the engines.

Rimmer called for a voice link. "Kryten—Lister's marooned on the ice planet. He's starving to death. We've got to get down and help him. What the smeg's happening?'

Kryten replied in garbled falsetto before he was barged out of shot by the Cat, who was clearly impatient to deliver his own version of the facts.

"Gubudoobeedee," he squeaked, his hands gesticulating wildly, like a deranged street drunk. "Gadabadabadeebeedoobeedah. OK?"

"Speak slowly," said Rimmer, as quick and high-pitched as he could. "I have to speak fast and squeaky, and you have to speak slow and low. Otherwise we won't make sense to each other."

Kryten blinked into the video shot, and spoke as slowly as he could. He still sounded like a man with a mouthful of helium, but at least now it was intelligible. "Something is wrong," he chirruped helpfully.

"Oh really?" Rimmer squeaked back sarcastically. "How enlightening. It's Tuesday in here, Monday next door, and you think something is wrong."

"What are you talking about?" Kryten said. "It's Friday."

He twisted the security camera so it pointed at the wall clock.

"Friday?" Rimmer squinted at the read-out. "It's Monday next door, Tuesday in here, and Friday where you are." He sat and thought. "But which Friday? Is it last Friday, or next Friday?"

"It's this Friday," said Kryten.

"What's the date?"

"Fifteenth."

"So it's a week next Friday."

There was a hiatus. Nobody could think of anything to say.

"I'm coming down," Rimmer said, finally. "I'll be there in a sec."

"At last!" The Cat turned from testing the final piston housing and stood, hands on hips, in his red silk boilersuit with gold trimming. "Where've you *been*, Buddy?"

"I ran all the way," Rimmer panted. "I can't have been more than five minutes."

"You've been over a week."

Rimmer glanced at the clock. It was Saturday the twenty-third.

Kryten's head poked round the corner of the

piston housing. "We're ready and primed," he said. "Let's start the engines."

The three of them lumbered uneasily up the spiral staircase and into the Navicomp Suite.

Kryten stabbed in the start-up sequence, and the massive pistons smashed the engine into life. Kryten clapped his plastic hands in delight. "We did it!"

"OK." The Cat slid out of his silk boilersuit, revealing a quilted lamé jumpsuit underneath. "Slip this baby into reverse and let's scoot."

Kryten typed in the appropriate sequence, and the engine noise changed pitch, becoming a strangulated thudding whine. Three pairs of eyes fixed on the speed/bearing read-out. It scarely changed.

"More power," said the Cat. "Get that pedal on the metal. Sluice that juice."

"We're on full reverse thrust."

The Cat shouldered Kryten out of the way and jabbed pointlessly at the controls. "It cannot be, novelty condom head—we're still moving forwards."

"Look," Kryten pointed at the display. "We're into the red. We're using all the power we've got."

"It's true, then." Rimmer slumped into the console chair.

"What's true?" said the Cat.

"What's true," Rimmer looked up, red-eyed with fear, "is that we're being sucked into a Black Hole."

Part Three

GARBAGE WORLD

ONE

Today was the day. Today was the big one.

John Ewe had been doing the Jovian run for the best part of twenty years. Not many people were prepared to spend their life ferrying human sewage from Jupiter's satellites all the way across the solar system and dropping it on the dump planet, but John Ewe actually enjoyed his work, and what's more, it paid well.

It wasn't just sewage that was disgorged on the dump planet, it was everything; all humankind's garbage—nuclear waste, chemical effluence, rotting foodstuffs, glass waste, waste paper; every kind of trash—all the unwanted by-products of three thousand years of civilization. But John Ewe specialized in sewage. He was the King of Crap. And right now he was sitting on top of two billion tons of it.

His tiny control dome, the only inhabitable section of the vast haulage ship, made up less than one per cent of the gigantic structure. The bulk of the craft was given over to the twin two-mile-long cylinders that stored the waste.

The ship's computer indicated they were about to go into orbit. Ewe climbed into his safety webbing and switched on the view screen.

The refuse ship powered through the thin atmosphere and hit the thick, choking black smog that spiralled up from the planet's surface. And there it was.

Garbage World.

Whole landmasses were given over to particular types of waste. For twenty minutes the ship flew over a range of a dozen mountains composed entirely of discarded tin cans, so high the peaks were capped with snow. It passed over an island the size of the Malagasy Republic piled high with decomposing black bin bags. It flew over a fermenting sea, flaming with toxic waste. It skimmed over an entire continent of wrecked cars: thousands upon thousands of miles of rusting chassis. It crossed a desert; a vast featureless flatland of cigarette dimps.

And then it arrived at the continent for sewage.

This was the moment. The moment he'd been planning for almost two decades.

Like anyone else in a dull job, John Ewe made up games to help pass the time.

His game was graffiti.

And he was about to complete the biggest single piece of graffito ever attempted in the history of civilization.

It sprawled across a continent. It was visible from space. It was written in effluence, and it said: "Ewe woz 'ere."

Today he had the final two billion tons he required to complete the half-finished loop of the final "e."

The bay doors on the belly of the ship hinged open and the effluence poured down and splatted into place.

John Ewe unhooked himself from the safety harness and swaggered down the thin aisle, the cleft of his buttocks wobbling hairily over the top of his jeans. He flicked on the satellite link, and examined his masterpiece in its completed glory. He scratched his hairy shoulders and belched.

"Bewdiful."

John Ewe was a colonial. He'd been born and raised on Ganymede, one of the moons that spun around Jupiter. He was aware that his ancestors had once lived here—in fact, they had originated from the dump planet—but no one, no one at all had lived there for five or six generations. He felt no affinity for the world of his forebears, any more than Anglo-Saxons felt an affinity for Scandinavia.

Earth didn't really mean anything to Ewe—it was just there to be dumped on.

The mathematics were simple: civilization produces garbage; the greater the civilization, the greater the garbage—and humankind had become very civilized indeed.

Three hundred years after the invention of the lightbulb, they'd colonized the entire solar system. The solar system was soon jam-packed with civilization too, and humankind rapidly reached the point where there was so much indestructible garbage, there was nowhere left to put it.

Something had to be done. Firing the garbage willy-nilly off into space was cost-prohibitive. So the Inter-Planetary Commission for Waste Disposal conducted a series of feasibility studies, and they concluded that one of the nine planets of the solar system had to be given over to waste.

Delegates from all the planets and their satellites submitted tenders to lose the contract.

The Mercurian delegation pointed to their solar-energy plants, which provided cheap, limitless energy for the whole system.

The study group from Uranus hinged its case on its natural stores of mineral deposits.

Jupiter and its moons relied on their outstanding natural beauty.

Neptune built its case on famous planetary architecture—it had been terraformed to the highest specifications.

Saturn's rings, a massive tourist attraction, made that planet safe, and its network of moons, though often seedy and down-market, generated a lot of business, merely because of their position along established trade routes.

Mars was the safest of all, because it was home to the wealthy. It was the chicest, most exclusive world in the planetary system, handy for commuting to other planets, yet far enough away from the riff-raff to be ideal for the mega-rich.

Venus took the Martian over-spill—the people who wanted to live on Mars, but couldn't quite afford it. Venus was full of people who wanted to be Martians, so much so they often quoted their address as "South Mars" or "Mars/Venus borders." Still, it was a fairly wealthy planet, and the Venusians constituted a powerful political lobby.

And so it became a straight battle between Earth and Pluto. The Plutonian delegation made rather a weak case, drawing attention to their planet's erratic orbit and its position on the edge of the solar system.

The Earth delegation was beside itself with

fury. Frankly, it was outraged that the planet that was mother to the human race, where life itself had been spawned and nurtured, was even being considered for such a putrid fate. It talked long and heatedly about how humankind had to remember its roots, and showed long, dull videos of Earth's past beauty. Of course, it conceded, the planet wasn't as pulchritudinous as it had once been. Yes, it agreed, it was now the most polluted planet in the solar system. True, most of the inhabitants had fled to the new terraformed worlds, and it was home, now, to only a handful of millions, too broke, too scared or too stupid to leave. But what about tradition, it argued? Earth had *invented* civilization. It had given civilization to the solar system. If civilization now turned round and literally dumped on Earth, what did that say about humankind?

And so it came to the vote.

The vote was telecast live to every terraformed world in the solar system. A jury on each of the worlds sat patiently through all nine presentations, and then allocated points, the lowest points going to the planet most favoured for the new mantle of Garbage World.

The show was broadcast from the French settlement of Dione, the Saturnian satellite. It was hosted by Avril Dupont, the greatly loved French TV star.

" 'Allo Mercury?"

Pause. Crackle. "Hello, Avril."

"Can you give us the votes of the Mercurian jury?"

"Here are the votes of the Mercurian jury. Pluto: two points."

"Pluto, two points. *La Pluton, deux points.*"

"Neptune, seven points."

"Neptune, seven points. *Le Neptune, sept points.*"

"Uranus, four points."

"Uranus, four points. *L'Uranus, quatre points.*"

"Saturn, eight points."

"Saturn, eight points. *Le Saturne, huit points.*"

"Jupiter, five points."

"Jupiter, five points. *La Jupiter, cinque points.*"

"Mars, twelve points."

"Mars, twelve points. *La Mars, douze points.*"

"Venus, ten points."

"Venus, ten points. *La Vénus, dix points.*"

"Earth, no points."

"Earth, no points. *La Terre, zéro points.*"

"And that concludes the voting of the Mercurian jury. Good night, Avril."

And that was the best score Earth got.

It culled not one single vote.

At twenty past eleven, on 11 November the following year, the last shuttle-load of evacuees left for re-housing on Pluto, and the planet Earth was officially re-named "Garbage World."

The President of Callisto personally cut the ribbon of toilet paper, ceremonially deposited the first symbolic shovelful of horse manure in the centre of what once had been Venice and declared Garbage World open for business. The President and his aides dashed into the Presidential shuttle as the first wave of three hundred thousand refuse ships swooped down and dumped their stinking loads on the planet that was once called Earth.

The dumping areas were strictly regulated: North

America, for instance, was bottles. Clear bottles on the west coast, brown bottles on the east and green in the centre. Australia was reserved for domestic waste: potato peelings, soiled paper nappies, used teabags, banana skins, squeezed toothpaste tubes. Japan became the graveyard of the motor car; from island to island, from tip to tail, from Datsuns to Chryslers, to forty-cylinder cyclotronic hover cars, dead, silent metal covered the land of the setting sun.

The Arctic Circle was allocated rotting food-stuffs, the Bahamas was home to old sofas and bicycle wheels, Korea took all broken electrical equipment.

Europe got the sewage.

And over the last twenty years, John Ewe had busied himself signing his name over the corner of that once-great continent.

John Ewe shut down the satellite link, and followed his hairy beer-belly back to the front of the ship. Before he could reach the safety webbing, a massive pocket of methane turbulence rocked the refuse craft and sent him staggering into the first-aid box. He fingered the gash that grinned bloodily on his brow and invented two new swear words. The methane storms had been getting worse over the past few years, and he knew he should have consulted the meteorological computer before he ventured from his safety harness.

As he lurched to his feet, a second methane blast hit the ship under its belly, sending him stumbling back down the narrow aisle. As he slithered helplessly backwards, his flailing arm caught the door-release mechanism, and the cockpit's emergency exit swung open.

His fat fingers scrambled for a hand-hold, but found nothing until he slid through the open doorway, and he grabbed the rim of the footledge.

For thirty seconds he dangled, screaming, over Europe.

Then he dangled no more.

He plunged from the yawning garbage ship, and drowned in his own signature.

"Ewe woz 'ere," it said. And it was right, 'e woz.

The unmanned craft hacked around wildly in the sudden turbulence, the autopilot stretched beyond its capacity. The methane storm whipped up to hurricane force and sucked the ship to the ground.

A continent of methane exploded.

The blast triggered off a thermo-nuclear reaction in a thousand discarded atomic-power stations, and the Earth tore itself from its orbit around the sun, and farted its way out of the solar system.

Two and a half thousand years of abuse were ended.

The Earth was free.

Free from humankind. Free from civilization.

When it was clear of the sun's influence, it froze in heatless space and bathed its wounds in a perennial Ice Age.

On it went, out of the solar system and into Deep Space, carving a path through the universe, looking for a new sun to call home.

TWO

Lister coughed himself awake. A gargantuan coughing fit forced his body into a ball and thrashed it about under the heavy quilting of the sleep sheet before his head finally emerged from under the covers, gasping for air.

Air, it turned out, was the last thing he wanted. It was thick and smoky and bitter to the taste. His hand scrambled blindly for the bunkside oxygen mask that dangled above the recessed sleeping couch. He held it to his face and sucked.

Gradually his vision cleared, and he peeked out into the murk. There was a hissing sound coming from the floor. Lister drew the blanket around him, knelt up and craned over the side of the couch to get a closer look. The whole of the steel-alloy deck was pitted with thin, deep, smoking holes, as if something were trying to burrow up into the craft from below.

As he watched, something flitted past his face, almost brushing his cheek, landed in a loud fizzle on the deck and started to tunnel patiently through the reinforced steel.

Lister snapped his head back into the shelter of the recess. His heart thumped a samba on the xylophone of his ribs. That could have been his head.

He ducked low so the edge of *Starbug*'s roof edged into his field of vision. Hollow metal stalactites hung down from the buckled structure, some of them dripping a clear, colourless liquid on to the *'bug*'s floor.

Lister shot back and huddled in the corner of the recess.

Acid rain.

But not normal acid rain—this was *acid* rain. Acid rain of such concentration it cut through high-density metal as if it were full-fat soft cheese. His eyes lit on what remained of the high-backed scanner scope chair. It was now a pile of steaming gloop. Only two nights earlier, he'd fallen asleep on that chair. That gloop could have been him.

It didn't make sense. Why hadn't the acid rain cut through the bunk roof? Why had that held out?

Lister looked up, and got his answer. It hadn't. The roof bulged crazily, like a balloon full of water, and stalactites of corrupted metal pointed their long, threatening fingers down towards him.

There was nowhere to go. No haven.

Whatever Lister decided to do, he had to do it fast. He grabbed his boots from the locker behind his head, and laced them frantically, keeping his eyes fixed on the ceiling. Suddenly the area of roof just above his head started to give way. Lister rolled off the bunk, taking the mattress with him, and swung into the bunk below.

Within minutes stalactites had begun to tongue down through the roof of the new bunk. He guessed that he had about two minutes before the acid came through.

But two minutes to do what? To go where? Up was unthinkable. Out? No way. No choice, then. Down.

He ripped at the wooden slats underneath the lower bunk's mattress. If only he could get down to the maintenance deck below, at least it would buy him some time. He piled the slats behind him and peered down into the hole.

Lister really didn't expect to find an access hatch leading straight down to the maintenance decks smack under the bunks, but it still surprised him when he didn't. He was shocked. He was offended. True, the chances of there being one were tiny—why would anyone in their right mind build an access hatch underneath two bunks? What for, apart from providing a handy escape route for any space-farer who happened to get caught in a particularly nasty downpour of acid rain? But on the other hand, there *had* to be one—otherwise there was no way out. Otherwise, he was dead. So when there wasn't one, frankly, he was outraged. He was furious. There could have been a below-bunk access hatch for dozens of reasons. A long-forgotten disused cleaning hatch; an air-conditioning access point; a ventilation shaft—the craft was crammed full of them, why couldn't there be one here?

But there wasn't.

There was nothing but featureless flooring.

He scratched futilely at the smooth metal, then smashed three wooden slats to splinters without even marking the doubly-reinforced floor that separated him from the maintenance deck. Now what?

Lister jammed his back against the corner of the bunk and crammed his knees against his chest. He wrapped his knuckles around one of the wooden slats by his side, and jabbed it up into the metal base of the bunk above, at a forty-five degree angle from his body. Then he jabbed again. And again.

The slat slid through the softened steel, and the acid from the bunk above began to trickle down into the feet end of the lower bunk. Lister held the oxygen mask to his face and jabbed again, widening the drain hole above him.

He withdrew the blackened, smoking slat and jabbed again. More acid gushed in through the widening gap, melting its way towards the maintenance deck below.

There was nothing to do but wait and see which would give first—the base of the bunk above him, or the escape hole below.

There was a creaking sound, and the bunk ceiling lurched dangerously and ballooned down another two inches towards his head. He stabbed frantically at the floor, and wiggled the slat ferociously to increase the hole's diameter. Nine inches wide. Now, a foot. Still too small. Suddenly there was a screaming pain in his hand, in the fatty flesh between this thumb and forefinger. He held it up to his face. The acid had burnt straight through, leaving a smoking peephole. He could see through his hand.

The escape hole was fourteen, fifteen inches wide. He tossed the slat into the gap and waited for it to hit the deck below.

One little second.

Two little seconds.

Three little seconds.

Fou . . .

The wood hit the metal below.

Thirty or forty feet.

Without cushioning, a bone-breaking certainty.

He kicked the gap wider. His boot came away steaming and smouldering. The hole was three feet in diameter and growing.

He made his move. He wrapped the mattress he'd dragged from the upper bunk tightly around him, held the mattress from the lower bunk over his head, and leapt through the hole.

The lower mattress plugged the hole, giving him perhaps five seconds of protection as he plunged towards the pool of acid that was already working its way through the floor of the maintenance deck. He flung off the mattress that was curled around him and hurled it down to the smoking pool below. He landed on his back, winded, dazed and immobile. He looked up towards the ceiling, and saw three globules of acid dropping towards him.

He tried to twist right but his body refused to move. "That was a hell of a fall," it was saying. "Let's rest here a while."

Two of the drops cut pennycent holes in the mattress centimetres from his groin. The third removed his left earlobe. Lister and his body had another meeting. Top of the agenda was a proposal to move, a.s.a.p. It was proposed by Lister, seconded by his body and the motion was carried by two votes to nil. He rolled on to his side as the temporary plug above finally gave and torrents of acid cascaded through the hole, crashing on to the mattress, barely a yard from his gasping, mono-lobed body.

He picked himself up, and started to stagger down the length of the maintenance deck, looking for something, anything, that might offer some form of protection. He ripped the first-aid kit from the wall and pulled out the bottle of medicinal alcohol. He poured a generous measure over the hole in his hand, dabbed his left ear and drank the rest.

Then he lumbered into the Engineering Supply Area. He slammed a pallet on to the forks of one of the three orange stacker trucks and piled it high with oxyacetylene canisters, blowtorches and welding gear.

He glanced up at the ceiling. It would hold for fifteen minutes. Twenty at best. After that there was nowhere else on board to shelter. There was no more down. The only way was out. Out in the acid storm.

For the next quarter of an hour he blowtorched steel doors from their hinges, ripped steel piping from the walls and welded together a jerry-built acid raincoat. He raced back into the engineering store and tried on the various welding helmets. He discovered that if he crammed his head into the smallest, he was then able to wear a medium size on top of it, and a large one on top of that.

In the howling, metallic silence imposed by three steel helmets, he climbed into the suit. Six feet of solid steel on top of him, plus his helmets, plus the metal-piping sleeves and trousers—this would give him at least fifteen minutes of protection while he scampered out of the craft and sought out some kind of refuge.

Only one problem.

He couldn't move.

He couldn't even nearly move.

Stupid.

Stupid, stupid, stupid.

How could he have wasted fifteen precious minutes constructing this immobile monstrosity, without realizing the damned thing was going to be too heavy to move?

He climbed out of the suit and kicked it.

Now he had a broken toe to add to his troubles.

He looked up at the ceiling. The stalactites were already forming.

He tottered over to the viewpoint window and stared out into the storm. He registered with a shock that the rain was local. Totally local. It just swirled around the small basin in which the *Starbug* had come to rest. Over the crest of the hill, the sky was clear. The crest of the hill was hardly five hundred yards away.

Surely he could get the damned thing to move five hundred yards. A third of a mile. Come *on*. Think.

His eyes swept the room.

On the second pass, they stopped on the stacker truck.

Lister jumped into the driver's seat and started up the motor. He jabbed the truck's forks under the two arms of the suit, and pulled back the lift lever. Slowly, the truck hauled the suit off the ground.

He leapt down from the vehicle, raced back to the supply store and returned with a reel of steel

cable. As the floor around him hissed and sput-
tered, he welded the cable to the stacker truck's
twin joystick controls and fed it through the
sleeves of the armour-plated raincoat.

He flipped the bay doors over to manual and
typed in the opening code. They remained closed.
He tried again. Nothing. Acid fizzled down the
doorway. The electrics were shot to hell.

There was a rumble from the far end of the
maintenance deck, and a whole twenty-yard section of ceiling smashed to the floor.

Lister was completely unaware of the tears that
coursed down his grease-streaked cheeks, and of
the insane babble that chundered from his lips
as he raced back and climbed into the suit. He
yanked the left-hand cable, and his neck snapped
forward as the stacker truck lurched back and
reversed fifty yards, slamming into the rear bulkhead. The suit tottered on the forks.

If he fell now . . . if he fell and lay motionless
on the floor as the acid swirled in from the deck
above . . .

Gently, he tugged the right-hand cable, and the
truck moved forward. He tugged again. The elec-
tric motor whined to maximum pitch. The truck
gathered speed.

It screamed towards the bay doors, supporting
Lister in his reinforced steel suit at the front.

Acid drizzled delta patterns down the bay doors
as Lister and the stacker truck smashed through
the weakened structure and out into the eye of
the acid storm.

The truck's caterpillar tracks juddered over the
basin's jagged terrain, gradually picking up the
speed it had lost on impact with the doors.

When Lister came to, he was halfway up the basin's incline. Over the peak of the hill before him, he could see the clear sky hanging a lazy blue over the next valley.

Two hundred yards to go.

He scanned the ground. Bizarrely, insanely, it seemed to be composed of broken bottles. He looked around. The whole of the mountain appeared to be glass. Millions upon millions of glass bottles, all shapes, all sizes, but only one colour—green. In fact, as he looked through the acid mist, he realized that all the mountains looming around him were likewise constructed of green bottles.

What was this place?

Overnight Ice Ages, acid rain that cut through steel, and a landscape made entirely of glass.

Nice place for a holiday.

There was a muffled bang from behind him, and the stacker truck jerked and stopped.

Lister craned round to see why. The truck was scarcely recognizable—a melting mess of metal and plastic. He tugged on the right-hand cable with idiot optimism. The cable snapped and slithered through the sleeve of his suit, gouging a thin red line of pain along the length of his arm.

He hung from the forks of the truck as the rain rodded down and bounced, sizzling, from his suit. Helpless and immobile, he swung like a giant metal pub sign.

He tried to lift his arms. Impossible. The suit was too heavy. So he just swung there, wondering how long it would take him to die when the rain eventually got through, and how much of him would be left for the others to find.

THREE

Rimmer, Kryten and the Cat disembarked from the shuttlebus mid-afternoon the previous Tuesday and staggered surreally up the metal ramp to the Drive room.

"Look, stay calm," said Rimmer, manically pacing up and down in front of the vast screen. "It'll take Holly ten seconds to work out what to do, and then we'll be out of here."

"Does anybody want toast?" came a small tinny voice.

They turned, and saw the Toaster perched on top of a stack of terminals.

"No!" they screamed in unison.

"How about a crumpet?"

Kryten tapped in Holly's activation sequence, and handed voice command over to Rimmer.

"On," said Rimmer. "Holly—we're being sucked into a Black Hole—how do we get out?"

The giant screen flitted and flickered, before Holly's image assembled in a mad, cubist parody of itself. His chin was where his forehead should be, his mouth was replaced by an ear and his nose pointed skywards on top of his balding pate.

"Jlkjhfsyuhjdk," he said.

"What?"

"Mcujnkljfibnnbcbcy."

"There's something wrong," Rimmer yelled. "Turn him off! We're wasting his run-time."

Kryten slammed the flat of his palm on the keypad, and Holly fizzled away. "What's wrong with him?"

Rimmer and the Cat shared shrugs.

"It's the dilation effect. His terminals are spread all over the ship, they're all operating in different time zones. While it's midnight Monday for his central processing unit, it's a week on Thursday for his random Access Memory. Anybody fancy a muffin?"

"Will you shut up?" said Rimmer. "What the smeg are we going to do?"

"What happens," the Cat tilted his head to one side, "if we get sucked into this Black Hole? Is that a bad thing?"

"A Black Hole is an unstable star that's collapsed into itself. Its gravitational pull is so enormous that nothing can escape—light, time, nothing. How about a potato cake?"

"Look, will you kindly shut your grill?" Rimmer spat. "I'm trying to think."

"Can't we just fly through it," the Cat ventured, "and out the other side?"

"Nice idea," the Toaster scoffed. "And perhaps we can stop off at the souvenir shop in the middle and buy various Black Hole memorabilia."

"Black Holes have souvenir shops in the middle?" The Cat grinned hopefully.

"He's taking the smeg," snapped Rimmer. "Will you stop talking to that cheap piece of junk? We've got to work out how to get out of here."

"Cheap!?" the Toaster snorted, "I'm £19.99, plus tax!"

"There's no way out, is there?" said Kryten. "We're going to duh duh duh duh duh duh duh duh . . ." he smacked his head into a monitor housing and cleared the seizure loop, ". . . die."

"Not necessarily," said the Toaster, with all the smugness he could muster.

"If you don't shut up," Rimmer threatened, "I'm going to unplug you."

"You don't want to know how to get out of this mess, then?"

Rimmer spun on his heels. "Oh, and you know, do you?"

The Toaster's browning knob spun from side to side. "Maybe," he said enigmatically. "Who's for a toasted muffin?"

"How the smegging smeg would a Toaster know how to get out of a Black Hole?"

"Technically, we're not in a Black Hole. Not yet. We haven't passed the event horizon."

"What's an event horizon?" asked the Cat.

"Let's start at the beginning." The Toaster adjusted his bread width to maximum, and back again. "A Black Hole isn't an object, it's a region— a rip in the fabric of space/time. It starts off as a massive sun. When the sun dies, the enormous gravitational pull at its centre drags all the matter in the star back into itself. A medium-sized sun becomes a neutron star—a star whose molecules are packed as tightly as possible. However, if the weight of the sun is great enough, it overrides the "exclusion principle" which states that, in normal circumstances, two electrons can't occupy the same energy space, and so the star continues collapsing. Eventually the gravitational drag at the centre becomes so colossal, the escape velocity—the speed you have to achieve to get out—reaches 186,282 miles per second. Which is lightspeed. And since lightspeed is the speed limit for the universe, nothing can escape—not even light. It becomes a sort of giant galactic vacuum cleaner, sucking in everything in its range—even Time. That's why Time at the front of the ship is running more slowly than Time at the back. The closer you get to it, the more you feel the effects of its pull, and the event horizon is the point of no return. So." He paused. "Who's for a hot cross bun?"

Kryten shook his head. "Did anyone follow that?"

"I was with it," said the Cat, "to the point where he said: 'Let's start at the beginning.' And I didn't pick it up again until he got to the hot cross bun part."

Rimmer strode across to the Toaster. "Explain this, miladdo: how does a novelty kitchen appliance suddenly get to know so much about Black Holes?"

"I have a voracious appetite for reading," said the Toaster.

"Holly told you this, didn't he? After he got his IQ back, but before he turned himself off."

The Toaster's grill glowed red. "Maybe."

"Did he happen to mention how to get out of one?"

"That depends," said the Toaster.

"Depends on what?"

"Depends on whether or not anyone wants any toast."

* * *

Twenty minutes later they sat in a horseshoe, munching their way through the towering piles of assorted toasted delights. Kryten, who had to eat Rimmer's share, was beginning to feel he needed to change his stomach bag, and the Cat was becoming quietly hysterical about what effect consuming thirty-four pieces of toast was going to have on his waistline.

"For godsakes, are you *insane*?" Rimmer snapped. "How much toast are you expecting them to eat?"

"Here's how to get out of a Black Hole. Providing you accelerate into it, and achieve sufficient speed before you pass the event horizon, the additional acceleration provided by the gravitational pull means you can break the light barrier, loop round the singularity at the Black Hole's centre and be traveling fast enough to swoop out again."

"I thought," said Kryten through a mouthful of toast, "that as soon as we pass the event horizon, we get crushed."

"Not if we're travelling faster-than-light. We inherit a whole new set of physical laws."

"So when we get out," Rimmer frowned, "we're travelling faster-than-light, yes?"

The Toaster inclined its bread-tray in a nod.

"How do we stop? Lister is stuck on that planet, starving to death. If we finally draw to a halt a hundred and thirty galaxies south-sou'-west, that's not going to be tremendously helpful. Assuming Holly was right about all this and we survive, we've got to rescue him—how do we stop?"

"Well now," the Toaster twirled his browning

knob from side to side. "Wouldn't you like to know?"

"Yes we would," said the Cat politely.

"Well, for your part the answer's simple."

"What?"

"Keep eating the toast."

The Cat groaned and reached for his thirty-fifth slice.

FOUR

Lister tried to move his arm again. This time it moved. Not much, but a little. He tried it again. This time it moved a little more. His suit was melting. And the more it melted, the lighter it got. This was good, and this was bad.

It was good, because at least, at some point soon, he'd be mobile again, and able to make a break for the crest of the hill. It was bad because he had no idea whether or not he could get to the top of the hill before the suit melted completely.

He angled up his elbows so he slid from between the forks and crunched on to the broken glass of the incline.

He found he could lift his feet an inch or so off the ground, and he was able to make small, faltering steps forward. He began the slowest race of his life.

His thighs throbbed. His shoulders ached. With each step the suit got lighter and his pace got quicker. Lister lost all sense of his body. He was just a pair of lungs, scorched and straining. He struck for the top of the hill.

The suit was light, now. Frighteningly light. He felt almost naked. Then he realized, even if he got to the top, even if he scrambled free of the rain, the suit would still be melting—he still had to get it off.

And then it was over. He lunged over the brow and started clattering down the other side. Even as he fell he tugged at the inner straps of his suit, and hurled the smoking plates away. His fall was broken by a bank of bottles. There was no triumph. There was no joy, no celebration as he flung the final piece down the mountain, just a horrible aching weariness, and an irresistible desire to sleep. He stumbled along the glass mountain ridge and found a cave—hardly a cave, more a bolthole, no more than six feet deep and four feet high.

He crawled inside, curled up baby tight, and slept.

Less than twenty minutes later Lister woke up. The sound that roused him was the thick, wet sound of rainfall. He couldn't bear it. The acid storm must have moved across to this side of the valley.

He uncurled himself from his foetal position and shimmied on his bare elbows to the lip of the bolthole.

He was wrong—it wasn't acid rain.

But it wasn't normal rain, either.

It was black.

Torrents of thick black syrup drooled over the mountainside. Lister reached out a quivering hand and caught a glob of the viscous goo in his palm. He sniffed it. He tasted it. He spat it out.

Oil.

It was raining oil.

Still, Lister thought, oil rain was a damn sight better than acid rain. At last it wouldn't kill him.

He felt quite cheered. Weatherwise, things were brightening up. Hell, if the trend continued, by evening it would probably be doing something as bland and normal as raining tomato soup, or snowing beach balls.

He crawled back into the shelter of his bolthole and tried to get some sleep. But he couldn't. Not even Lister could sleep through an earthquake. Especially when it was happening directly underneath him.

The ground sneered open, and a foot-wide chasm snaked towards him as he scrambled backwards out of the bolthole. He shielded his eyes from the lashing oil, and watched as zigzag splits powered across the splintering landscape. Millions of bottles crashed and tumbled into the ground's rumbling gullet.

Lister ran. He had no idea where he was running or whether there was any point. He leapt over sudden chasms, dodged past small avalanches of bottles, and scrambled and scraped his way to the top of the next peak.

The black sky hurled javelins of oil at his shivering, wretched body as he crumbled to his knees, and skidded and slithered into the next basin. The oil weighted his locks, and the wind whipped them across his face as oily fingers jabbed down his throat, forcing him to gag for air. Blind and choking, he staggered across the basin. He wiped the worst of the oil from his eyes with what remained of his T-shirt, and blinked up against the hammering rain. He wasn't alone. Looming on the horizon were the colossal silhouettes of five faces. Or, rather, five half-faces, which thrust out of the sea of garbage as if they were seeking one last breath before they were claimed by the refuse.

Lister knew them. He recognized them all. George Washington, Thomas Jefferson, Abraham Lincoln, Theodore Roosevelt and perhaps the greatest American President of all time, Elaine Salinger.

Lister hauled his aching body across the basin and took shelter under George Washington's nose. He knew where he was, now. Mount Rushmore. South Dakota.

This hell-hole of a planet, this uninhabitable pit of filth, was Earth.

Lister laughed. He'd made it. He was back home. He laughed too long and too hard, a dangerous laugh that danced with insanity. Everything that had kept him going, the goal that had given his life meaning, was suddenly, farcically, achieved.

This was Earth. He was home.

But what had happened? What had been done to the place?

The answer was fairly obvious even to a half-insane, sick, oil-sodden astro on the brink of starvation.

Earth had been turned into a garbage dump.

He had no idea what had torn it from its orbit and sent it hurtling to the outer reaches of the universe, but the fact that this was Earth, and it had been converted into a planet-sized refuse tip was undeniable.

But did that explain why the weather was haywire? Only partly. The more Lister thought about it, the more things seemed to click into place. Right from the moment he'd first arrived, from the moment he'd first emerged from *Starbug* and the arctic winds had whipped and toyed with him, whimsically changing direction every few seconds, tossing him up in the air and dashing his body into snow banks; right from that moment, the weather had been trying to kill him. There was the acid rain, the sizzling downpour which only fell in the basin where his ship had crashed. Then, after his miraculous escape to the bolthole, the quake had forced him out into the open, into the suffocating, cloying treacle of the oil storm.

Had exhaustion made him paranoid? Were his thoughts being twisted by hunger and fatigue?

Or was he right?

Was the Earth waging a war against him? Against him, personally?

But why?

If the Earth did have some kind of inexplicable, innate intelligence, why would it want to kill him? What had he ever done to the Earth? Why should it despise him?

Then he knew.

He'd done everything to Earth. He'd crucified it. He was a member of the human race, part of the species that had spread like bacteria over the planet; killing its rich, teeming life; consuming its wealth; finally rendering it fit only for use as a dumping ground for all humanity's garbage.

That's what he was: a single cell of bacteria. A plague germ. And the planet's auto-immune system was rejecting him.

No. The idea was preposterous. It was insane. Hunger and weariness were fuelling his paranoia.

The Earth didn't have an intelligence. It didn't "live." It was a ball of stone.

He stood in the shelter of George Washington's left nostril and started to compose a list of humankind's many magnificent achievements. For some inexplicable reason, the first thing that popped into his addled head was the musical toilet-roll dispenser, before a sheet of lightning ignited the rain, sending a curtain of flame sweeping across the face of the mountain, scorching black all five presidents, and sending Lister hurtling back into the far recess of Washington's nasal passage.

A second sheet ignited, blasting Lister out of the nose, sending him scurrying across the mounds of garbage, which were alive with rivers of fire.

"Do it, then," Lister screamed. "Come on—kill me." His fingers dug into the putrefying sludge and flung it skywards. "Kill me! Come on, what are you waiting for?"

Surrounded by lakes of fire and exploding geysers of oil, Lister screamed and ranted at the Earth.

He ducked his head under his arm as two bursts of flaming rain strafed either side of the mound he was standing on.

Lister collapsed to his knees on the smouldering garbage. "I could do something," he sobbed. "I could help. I could . . . If you let me live, I could start to make it right again. I could . . ." He blacked out.

As consciousness slowly percolated back into his body, he was aware of the rain. He groaned and raised his head. It was rain rain. Real rain. H_2O. The stuff of life.

He rolled on his back and opened his mouth.

All around him, tails of smoke wriggled skyward from the few puddles of fire that still remained.

He drank in the rain. He let it cascade over him, cleansing his wounds, refreshing him, uplifting him. He'd rolled on to his belly to pick himself up, when he saw it.

Inches from where his right hand had fallen, out of the rubble, out of the garbage, out of the stinking mire, poked a single branch—a small, stunted tree with a crop of green berries.

Lister plucked off the fruit and started to eat. They were olives. He wept.

He cupped his hands and collected some rain-water which he sprinkled, tenderly, over the tree. It seemed a simple enough equation: if he looked after the olive tree, the olive tree would look after him.

He heard a movement in the rubble behind him. He turned. He wasn't the only living creature on the planet. There was at least one other. The creature joined him by the olive tree. It was one of the oldest of Earth's inhabitants. It had been there long before man, and would probably be there long after. It was a cockroach.

But a big cockroach.

A very big cockroach.

This cockroach could have played Nose Tackle for the London Jets in their all-time best season.

It was a mother of a cockroach.

This cockroach was eight feet long.

Lister moved slowly. Very slowly. He rocked back on his rump, drew his knees up to his chest, and with a sudden, swift movement brought both his boots down on the roach's side. There was a sickening thud, and the cockroach lay on its back, rocking helplessly, its mandibles opening and closing in shock.

Lister ferreted among the rubble for something lethal, and found a long thin shard of glass. He stood over the writhing beast, his hands raised over his head. The glass flashed down towards the soft underbelly.

Then he stopped.

He flung the glass blade away, then stooped and lifted the cockroach back to its feet.

The cockroach made a series of curious clicking noises, but made no attempt to move away.

"Here," Lister plucked an olive from the branch and held it out for the cockroach to take. "I'm a reformed species. We're going straight. No more killing. Here. Take it."

The giant insect ignored the olive. Instead, it nuzzled among the rubble and started to eat the garbage.

Lister sat there chewing his olives, watching the mammoth roach consume the refuse. It seemed like a hell of a good deal to him.

The meal over, Lister decided to head back to *Starbug*, to rake through the ruins and see if there was anything left he might salvage. As he walked across the rubble he realized the cockroach was following. He turned and made some shooing movements with his arms. The cockroach clicked and whistled and carried on following him. Lister broke into a trot. So did the cockroach.

Finally Lister slowed and stopped. The cockroach caught up with him, slithered to its belly, pushed its head in the crook of Lister's knees, and nudged the back of his legs. Lister stumbled and straightened, and tried to fend it off. The cockroach nudged again. Lister walked sideways, his arms out straight, trying to keep it at bay. The cockroach butted him a third time, and Lister fell full length across its back. It raised its belly from the ground and started to waddle forward.

It wanted to carry him.

And when an eight-foot cockroach wants to give you a ride, Lister reasoned, probably the smartest thing to do was to let it.

He changed his mind five seconds later. Just after he splayed his legs over its back, and tucked his fingers under the rim of its armour plating, the cockroach took off.

The view would probably have been staggering from two hundred feet, but you had to have your eyes open to appreciate it fully, and Lister had no intention of doing that.

He shouted and screamed and tried to steer the cockroach earthwards, but his benign captor had set its mind on its destination. It was taking him home to meet its folks.

Halfway up a tall bottle mountain, they landed.

The twenty or so members of the roach's clan surrounded them, whistling and clicking and rubbing their hindlegs together in insect delight.

Plainly, Lister was a hit.

One of the roaches retired to the back of the cave, and dragged a half-rotted sofa carcass to Lister's feet. The family looked on in mute anticipation.

Lister did something then he wouldn't have done in any other circumstances whatsoever. He started to eat a sofa.

This seemed to go down well. There was a cacophony of whirrs, clicks and whistles, and the cockroaches circled in delight.

"Well, it's been absolutely wonderful," Lister found himself saying. "Terrific place you've got here," he said to the mother roach. "And you serve a wicked rotting sofa. But I really must be going." He nodded, threw in a few clicks and whistles for good measure, and climbed on the first roach's back. It waddled speedily down the length of the cave, and flung itself over the mountain side.

When Lister opened his eyes, he found to his alarm he was flying in formation, at the head of a swarm of cockroaches. Ten to his right, ten to his left. And as they flew down the middle of the valley, more and more were emerging from their caves, and taking up their place behind him.

He looked behind him at the swelling swarm of buzzing roaches and yelped like a bronco-busting rodeo star.

By the simple expedient of consuming a tiny portion of a decomposing three-piece suite, Lister had been anointed King of the Cockroaches.

And together, Lister and his loyal subjects were going to start putting the planet back together again.

FIVE

The colossal cone-shaped jet housings on *Red Dwarf*'s underbelly screamed and whined in their losing battle against the irresistible drag of the Black Hole's gravitational pull. Suddenly, as one, they ceased their pointless protestations and puttered into silence.

All resistance gone, the massive mining vessel catapulted into the blackness towards the event horizon. Lazily, the jet housings started to rotate—45 degrees, 90 degrees, 120 degrees, until finally they had described a full half-circle. The rotation motors wound down, and the stabilizing bolts cracked loudly into place. All the while, the ship howled faster, ever faster towards the lightless unknown.

The jets fired up again. Thousands of hydrogen explosions harnessed the raw energy of the universe and thrust the ship forward, to the brink of demi-lightspeed, and beyond.

"Event horizon: two minutes and closing." Kryten pulled the safety webbing over his shoulders and inflated his crash suit.

"Did I tell you about spaghettification?" said the Toaster.

The Cat lurched upright from the couch bolted

to the corner of the anti-grav chamber. "What's spaghettification?"

"I didn't mention it, then?"

"One minute fifty."

"No you didn't. What is it?" said Rimmer.

"Well," said the Toaster, "when you enter a Black Hole, an effect takes place, called 'spaghettification'. I thought I'd mentioned it, but obviously I didn't. Anyway, just so you know, it'll happen fairly shortly."

"One minute forty."

The Cat lay back on the couch and stared up at the ceiling. "So what the hell is it?"

"Spaghettification. Let me guess," said Rimmer. "I can see only two options: one—due to the bizarre effects of the intense gravitational pull, and because we're entering a region of time and space where the laws of physics no longer apply, we all of us inexplicably develop an irresistible urge to consume vast amounts of a certain wheat-based Italian noodle conventionally served with Parmesan cheese; or two—we, the crew, get turned into spaghetti. I have a feeling we can eliminate option one."

"You're absolutely correct," said the Toaster. "You all become sort of spaghettified."

"Forty seconds," counted Kryten.

"Then what happens?"

"Well, then you become de-spaghettified," said the Toaster, and added: "hopefully. Holly was a bit vague about that part. Still, he didn't seem to think it was terribly important."

"I get turned into spaghetti," the Cat's eyebrows leapt to the top of his forehead, "and that's not important?"

"Thirty seconds."

The Cat tried vainly to lift his head from the cranium support—he had a major collection of dirty looks he wanted to sling at the Toaster—but G-force pinned him, immobile, to the couch, so he slung them at the ceiling instead. "Is it too late to change this plan? I have no idea what well-dressed spaghetti is wearing this year."

"Ten seconds."

"Ten seconds?" Rimmer was equally immobile. "What happened to twenty seconds?"

"I forgot to say twenty seconds," Kryten apologised. "I was listening to the Cat." His eyes flitted to the scanner scope again. "Oh, sorry—apologizing for not saying 'twenty seconds' has now made me miss saying 'five seconds'."

"So how long now?" yelled Rimmer.

"Err . . . no seconds," said Kryten. And he was right.

The combination of jet thrust and gravitational pull forced *Red Dwarf* through the lightspeed barrier the moment it hit the event horizon. To all intents and purposes, the ship no longer existed in the universe of its origin. It shrugged off Newton, Einstein, Oppenheimer and Chien Lau, and subscribed to a completely new set of physical laws.

They were in the Black Hole, heading for its centre. Heading for the ring of light that swirled suicidally around the spinning singularity—the core of the dead star where all the matter sucked in by the Black Hole was compressed to infinity. And they were heading there at such a speed, they were overtaking light.

* * *

The Cat's body started to spill off the couch in every direction. Long, thin strands of what had formerly been him slithered across the floor and intertwined with the strands that had been Kryten and Rimmer and the Toaster. The anti-grav chamber became a sea of heaving, screaming, living linguini.

Everyone became part of everyone else.

They threaded together and formed a new whole. They weren't four, they were one. The particles that had once formed Rimmer's intelligence, in a blinding flash of empathetic insight, suddenly became aware of the desperate, monumental importance of toast. Instantaneously, the strands that had been the Toaster were conscious of the overriding necessity for dressing well and having a really terrific haircut. The vermicelli that was now the Cat tasted the feeling of being mechanical, and knew with unshakeable certainty that Silicon Heaven existed, and the best way to get there was through diligent hoovering. Simultaneously, the macaroni that was Kryten knew what it was like to be Rimmer. He understood what it was like to have had those parents, that childhood, that career, that life. It was impossible to scream, but that's what Kryten was trying to do.

The ship was no longer a ship, it was a huge tachyon, a superlight particle, howling through a universe outside our own. It was a pool, then a wave, then a ball, then a dot, then it had no shape—it just *was*.

The huge mound of spaghetti slithered across space/time and peered into the face of the spinning white disc.

"Look," said a part of the spaghetti that was mostly Rimmer. In the centre of the spinning light were six interlocking coils, like fibre optics, but of a size beyond size. The immense hollow cables twisted and undulated like the snakes on the Gorgons' heads. The tubes were of colours that had no meaning to the human eye. They spun and swirled in a timeless dance of beauty.

Not for the first time, Rimmer cursed himself for not bringing his camcorder. "What is it?" he said, but before anyone could answer the ball of speed the ship had itself become slung around the singularity.

It bounced off the sudden cushion of anti-gravity it met there, then, like a swimmer who has dived too deep, lunged desperately for the surface, for the event horizon, for the known universe. It struck upwards, fighting off the gravity that tried to suck it back to its core at the speed of light.

Then the lightspeed drag of gravity cancelled out the lightspeed momentum of the ship, and *Red Dwarf* regained its physical form. Suddenly it was travelling at a relative speed of less than two hundred thousand miles an hour towards the event horizon. The metal of the bulkheads buckled and groaned. Leering cracks ripped through the metalwork and zigzagged insanely down the port side.

The ship started to slow.

Plasti-domes splintered and shattered. Steel mining rigs were wrenched protesting from the ship's back and swirled helplessly down into the singularity to be crushed into infinity.

Still the ship slowed.

The jet housings started to creak, and then, all over the vessel's belly, one by one, pinion rods snarled and snapped, and the housings came away and tumbled into the infinite abyss.

Still the ship slowed.

Half the propulsion jets were lost. Hydrogen fuel pumped from the jet carcasses and flooded into the relentless void. Like a harpooned whale, the wounded craft pitched wildly for the surface, for light, for life.

Slower still.

Another crop of housings moaned and warped and fell away.

Still slower.

And slower.

And slo-o-o-o-o-ower.

Relatively, the ship was moving at barely fifty miles an hour.

Then thirty.

Twenty.

Ten.

The Black Hole had just to claim one more jet housing to tip the balance, to drag the ship below lightspeed and trap it forever in its bleak embrace.

It didn't.

With the suddenness of an infant's birth scream, *Red Dwarf* exploded through the event horizon and into the known universe.

Free of the worst of the cloying quicksand grip of the dead star's interior, the limping vessel peaked back up to lightspeed for an instant of an instant before the final remnants of gravitational drag slewed it to a halt on the very periphery of the Black Hole's influence.

*   *   *

The de-spaghettified Cat looked down his body and checked it was all there. It seemed to be.

He unbuckled himself from the couch and stood on uneasy legs. "Everyone OK?"

Kryten nodded, still too nauseous to speak.

"What was that?" said Rimmer. "In the middle of the spinning light. Those tubes."

"The Omni-zone," said the Toaster. "Holly predicted we'd find that. It confirms his theory."

"What theory?"

"The theory that there are six other universes, and all their gateways converge at the centre of a singularity."

"There are six other universes?" said Rimmer.

"So Holly reckoned," said the Toaster. "He also believed that our universe is the bad apple. It's the cock-up universe. Something went wrong with our Big Bang and made Time move in the wrong direction, that's why nothing makes sense."

"I'll tell you something that *does* make sense," The Cat staggered over to the Toaster. "You made me eat seventy-three rounds of buttered toast. Check that: seven, three," he slapped his rump. "I feel like I'm carrying around a third buttock in my pants. And I just want you to know this—I want you to live with this for the rest of your life—you," he jabbed the Toaster with his long-nailed forefinger, "you make real lousy toast. It's cold, it's burnt, *and* it's soggy."

The Toaster twirled his browning knob defiantly. "Hey—what d'you expect for $£19.99 plus tax? Conversation, quantum theory *and* good toast?"

SIX

The bulging, warped cargo-bay doors refused to yield to electronic command, but they did yield to the massive volley from the mining lasers, which ripped them from their hinges and sent them spinning off into space.

The two transport craft taxied along the take-off ramp and out through the yawning bay. They banked left and skirted *Red Dwarf*'s mangled hull, before swooping down into the planet's atmosphere.

When they hit the thick grey cloud bank, the craft peeled off. *White Giant*, with Rimmer and the Cat, took the northern hemisphere, and *Blue Midget*, piloted by Kryten and the Toaster, zoomed south.

Rimmer stared unblinkingly into the screen of the infra-red scanner scope as *White Giant* swept across the surface of the planet. "What's happened to the snow? Where's the Ice Age gone?"

The Cat pushed aside the dangling furry dice and peered through the murk of the Drive window. "What is all that stuff down there? That mountain—it's shining."

Rimmer looked over his shoulder. "Looks like glass."

The Cat increased the magnification factor, and they stared at the mountain ranges of green bottles looming below them. "Bottles? What is this place?"

Rimmer shrugged and turned back to the heat scanner. Nothing. He voice-activated the sonar scan for signs of movement. Still nothing. "This is hopeless. We could fly around for years and not find him. One man on a planet this size? It's like looking for a needle in a haystack. No—it's worse. It's like trying to find a hidden can of lager at a student party."

"If he's still alive, we'll find him. He'll have left some kind of signal."

"Twenty-four days he's been down there. Twenty-four days without food. He may be too weak to signal."

Kryten slipped *Blue Midget* into autodrive, and squeezed between the towering stacks of freshly baked bread that occupied eighty per cent of the living space in the craft's operational mid-section. He lifted the dozen or so brown loaves that covered the scanner screen, and piled them on top of a rack of pallets bulging with french sticks.

"Twenty-four days without food," said the Toaster. "I only pray we've brought enough bread."

Kryten suppressed a sigh and wondered how he'd ever been persuaded to pair up with a novelty kitchen appliance.

For thirty-six hours they tracked back and forth across the surface of the planet, hoping for a heat reading on the infra-red scan or some sign of movement from the sonar. At five o'clock, on the evening of the second day, they got one.

The signal originated from a small island, measuring barely sixty miles across, three thousand miles south of the equator. Small pockets of movement registered on the sonar. The infra-red confirmed life. Quite a lot of life.

Kryten looked at his watch, then spun off his ear, and spun it back on again, as was his habit when pensive. It wasn't possible to contact Rimmer and the Cat for another three hours. They were on different sides of the planet, and the only way to communicate was to bounce radio signals off the orbiting *Red Dwarf*, which was in the correct position just once every four hours. He looked at his watch again, tapped it several times, and made his decision.

Blue Midget's retro jets blasted deep smoking potholes into the island's swampy surface, and the landing legs telescoped down into the quagmire, sinking dozens of feet before they found purchase. The hatchway opened and Kryten leaned outside to scan the terrain. He sniffed gingerly at the air to sample the atmosphere for chemical analysis. Instantly, his olfactory system went into massive overload, and his nose exploded loudly.

He clucked impatiently, unscrewed the popped nose from his face and fished inside his utility pouch for a spare. He tore off the plastic packing and clicked it into place. He twisted the adjustment screw to turn the smell sense down to minimum and tentatively inhaled once more. His second nose went the way of the first. He had no more noses. He'd have to wait until he got back to *Red Dwarf*. In the meantime, he was noseless, which was probably just as well.

He staggered out on to the ramp and threw the hover dinghy into the steaming marsh, then ducked back into the craft to reappear with the Toaster strapped to his back.

"Careful!" yelled the Toaster. "I'm only S£19.99. I'm not waterproof."

A thought entered Kryten's CPU, but it was a very cruel thought, and unworthy of a mechanical, and not the kind of thought that would get him into Silicon Heaven, so he reluctantly dismissed it.

They sat in the hover dinghy, and Kryten checked the remote scanner. He wrenched back the joystick, and the dinghy rasped off, bouncing across the steaming swamp in the direction of the signal's source.

The Cat was beginning to panic. He'd gone almost two hours without a bath, or even a light shower. He was beginning to smell like a human. He snapped the controls over to automatic and shimmied off to the changing cubicle. "I'm out of here, Buddy," he said, and flicked quickly through his emergency travel wardrobe, which contained only his top one hundred indispensable suits, and selected his seventh new outfit of the afternoon.

Doing anything with the Cat was impossible. Rimmer looked up from his vigil at the scanner scope. "Do you really, really, absolutely need another bath?"

The Cat didn't even consider the inquiry worthy of a reply. Human beings—what unhygienic, dirty, revolting little creatures they were. All their priorities were wrong: they had scant regard for relaxing and general quality snoozing time. Instead, they raced around, pell-mell, getting sweaty. It was no wonder they'd invented the wheel before they'd invented the twin-speed hairdrier with styling funnel. All their values were tip over tail. Still, what else could you expect from a race whose foremost scientists believed they evolved from slime? Ocean slime. They honestly held the opinion that their ancestors were mud. On the other hand, having spent some time with them, the Cat was inclined to agree.

He sculpted his face into an elegant sneer and disappeared into the shower cubicle.

The Cat was less than an hour into his ablutions when Rimmer spotted the *Starbug*.

"Look, there it is!"

The Cat dashed out of the cubicle, dripping underneath his bathrobe, his shower cap still in place.

"There!" Rimmer pointed at the magnified video image.

The Cat squelched into the Drive seat, looped *White Giant* over for an investigatory pass, and landed four hundred yards from the stricken craft.

Rimmer knew there was no one alive on board long before they scrambled over the dunes of glass and stood in front of the gutted 'bug. The hatchway door was half-melted, and what was left was swinging creakily on one hinge. Inside, there was nothing; no fixtures, no fittings; just the rotting bulkhead. The roof was almost entirely missing, and cone-shaped holes gouged grotesque patterns in the three-foot-thick reinforced steel floor. The Cat curled a finger through a gap in the hull and pulled. A foot-square slab of metal came away easily and, when he tightened his fist, crumbled in his hand.

Rimmer looked down at the pile of ashes that lay on what remained of the sleeping couch.

"Found this on the Drive seat." The Cat stood in the hatchway holding a melted fragment of Lister's leather deerstalker.

"I've seen this before," said Rimmer. "One time on Callisto. Wiped out an entire settlement."

"What is it?"

Rimmer looked up through the roof at the black knotted wisps of cloud threading across the grey sky. "Acid rain," he said, quietly.

Both of them knew they wouldn't find anything, but they decided to look around anyway. None of it made sense to Rimmer. He'd left Lister on an ice planet. Somehow, the ice had melted, exposing this strange terrain of geographical features apparently built from glass.

"Hey!"

Rimmer looked up. The Cat was standing high on a ridge overlooking the wreck of the *Starbug.*

"Look at this!" The Cat motioned for Rimmer to join him.

Rimmer picked his way up the jagged slope of the bottle mountain and looked down into the next basin.

Spread out below them were acres on acres of rich, verdant pasture land. Fields of wheat, fields of corn and fields of barley shimmered in the easy breeze of the sheltered valley. A long, thin stream of gurgling blue glinted its length. Trees, not very tall, but strong and young, sprouted in thick forests around the perimeter. And in the centre of the valley, in the heart of a vast olive grove, smoke curled from the chimney stack of a small homestead.

"There."

Rimmer couldn't make out what the Cat was pointing at for some moments: his eyesight wasn't nearly as keen. Then he saw it. Distantly, in a thin rectangular patch of brown, a tiny figure was dragging a handmade plough across a half-furrowed field.

"It's Lister. It's got to be."

They half slid, half tumbled down into the valley, and ran across the fields towards the figure. When they were two hundred yards away, they realized they were wrong. It was a human, but it wasn't Lister. It was an old man, grey-haired and slightly bent. More than a little hard of hearing, too, because he didn't respond to any of Rimmer's shouts until they were almost on him.

He swivelled and looked at them, his fingers toying idly with his long, braided silver beard. He had the strong muscle tone and weathered skin of a farmer who's spent a lifetime in the fields. He was fit and strong, but he had to be at least sixty, maybe more. He gazed at them for a while from under the thick, furry white caterpillars of his eyebrows, then he mopped his brow with a leathery forearm and turned back to his plough.

"Old man!" Rimmer panted. "We're looking for someone."

The man stopped, but didn't turn.

"A friend of ours. Crashed just over the hill." The Cat pointed, but the old man didn't look. Instead, with his back still to them, he performed a passable impersonation of Rimmer's voice.

"I'll be back," the old man said. "Trust meeeeeee." He turned and pulled off his cap. He swept a liver-spotted hand through the remaining wisps of silver on his pate.

Rimmer crooked his head to one side and studied the old man's features. It was the eyes that gave it away. "Lister?" he said, his eyes half-pinched in disbelief.

Lister shook his head. "Where the smeg have you been?"

"We got here as quick as we could."

"Quick?" Lister bellowed. *"Quick!"* he rubbed his legs together and made a series of bizarre clicking noises with his tongue.

"It's only been sixteen days." Rimmer looked at the old man Lister had become. "My god—it must be the Time dilation."

"The what?"

"The ship got stuck in a Black Hole. Time moves more slowly around a Black Hole. Relativity. From our point of view, you've only been away a couple of weeks."

Lister snorted, showing a row of gnarled teeth. "I've been here, on my own, waiting for you to bring me some food"—his eyes sparkled with fury—"for the last thirty-four years. *Thirty-four smegging years.*"

Rimmer shook his head and tried to think of something adequate to say. All he could come up with was: "Sorry."

SEVEN

The Cat spun round, taking in the whole valley. "You did all this yourself?"

Lister grunted.

"This was all garbage before, and you made it into this?"

Lister grunted again. He hadn't spoken much English for over a third of a century, and his conversation was sparse. He turned and squinted across the fields. Rimmer followed his sightline towards a herd of animals grazing at the very edge of the valley. They looked too small to be horses, but it was impossible to tell at this distance. Lister slid his two thumbs into his mouth and emitted a piercing, wavering whistle.

One of the herd looked up from its feeding, and broke into a trot. As they watched, the creature suddenly lifted off into the air and headed, sky-borne, towards them.

The giant, eight-foot-long cockroach landed neatly between the screaming Cat and the hysterical Rimmer. Its mandibles rubbed tenderly up the back of Lister's legs, and he patted its thorax fondly, cooing his strange clicks and whistles all the time.

"Yow! Warghh!" The Cat wriggled his body, as

if shrugging off a thousand creeping bugs, while Rimmer convulsed quietly beside him.

"They eat all the garbage," Lister said, as if this were some kind of explanation, and climbed on its back. "Hop on." He patted the cockroach's rump.

The Cat twisted and gyrated, scratching every spare inch of flesh. "Yak! Wurghh! Yahhhh! It's a cockroach!"

"You expect us to sit on this thing?" Rimmer said, between heaves.

"It's six miles back to the house."

"Six miles? Is that all?" Rimmer swept both his hands forward. "You guys go on ahead. I feel like a jog."

"What? No. I'm coming with you," said the Cat, and went into another gyrating dance of revulsion.

The cockroach clicked and whistled and animatedly rubbed his bristling back legs together.

"He's getting upset," said Lister. "He thinks you don't like him."

"Noooo." The Cat laughed with false amusement. "Where'd he get that idea? I think he's really cute. Cockroaches have always been my all-time favourite insects. In fact I have a pinup of one in my locker. I especially love those black sticky hairs on the back of his legs, and that sort of slimy stuff that dribbles out of his mandibles. He's adorable! Waaarghhh."

"Get on. You too." Lister nodded at Rimmer.

They slung their legs over the roach's back, and it pattered along until it reached take-off speed, then fluttered noisily up into the sky.

"So," said the Cat, holding on to the shell of

the roach's abdomen, "do we get an in-flight movie, or what?"

"What's that?" Rimmer pointed down at the field below them. There were no crops in the field, just yellow and white flowers which were arranged and planted to spell out two enormous letters; two 'K's.

"Jasmine," said Lister, simply.

And Rimmer let it go at that.

Lister's home was made entirely of garbage. The walls were built from wastepaper, compressed into bricks that made them as hard as any wood. The roof slates were fashioned from beaten-out flattened bean tins, and the windows were the portholes taken from front-loading washing machines. Various tubes, pipes and cables ran to a tall tower some fifty feet away, which housed a configuration of mirrors that harnessed solar energy.

Besides the main house, there were a number of cockroach stables and farm outhouses, which stored harvested crops, seeds and equipment.

As they walked across the courtyard, a number of young roaches flocked out excitedly to meet them. They yapped, clicked and whistled round Lister's ankles as he patted each of them and made his way to the main house.

The furnishings inside the dwelling were also constructed from unwanted refuse. There was a crude but effective central-heating system made out of old car radiators and exhaust pipes.

While Lister busied himself in the kitchen, Rimmer and the Cat sat on a remarkably comfortable sofa which was clearly three toilets lashed together, covered with bin liners stuffed with what turned out to be vacuum-cleaner fluff.

There was an elaborate hand-carved wooden mantelpiece over the stone hearth. It looked strangely incongruous in the jerry-built room. Above it hung an ornate gilt frame, which, at first glance appeared to be empty. Rimmer stood up and strode towards it. On closer inspection he found there was a picture in the middle of it. A less-than-passport-size photograph, which had been cut out of a *Red Dwarf* yearbook. Rimmer squinted and tried to make out the face. It was the photograph Lister always used to keep in his wallet. The one he didn't think Rimmer knew about. It was his only photograph of Kristine Kochanski, smiling her famous pinball smile. Rimmer shook his head. Lister was still hung up on a girl he'd dated for three weeks, several thousand epochs ago. His psyche had fantasized her as his mate in Better Than Life, and now, after nearly forty years of solitude here on Garbage World, his memory still wasn't prepared to let her go.

Lister shuffled in from the kitchen, his wrinkled hands clutching a tray loaded with roughly thrown clay pots. He saw Rimmer looking at the thumbnail-size photograph in the frame that could have comfortably accommodated a couple of El Grecos and smiled. "One day," he said, "I'll get her back."

Rimmer and the Cat looked at the frail old man Lister had become and nodded in benign indulgence. It seemed fruitless to point out she'd died three million years previously, and even when she had been alive she'd been the one who broke off the relationship, dumping him for some guy who worked in Flight Navigation.

"One day," he said again. And they nodded again.

Lister handed the Cat a mug of nettle tea and a plateful of juniper-and-dandelion stew, and sat down.

"So what happened?" said Rimmer. And Lister began to tell them. He told them pretty much everything, missing out only the olive-branch incident, the "deal" he'd made with the planet, which, as the years had passed by, had begun to seem more and more like a dream, unreal, half-imagined.

"So what now?" asked the Cat, setting aside his still-full plate of juniper-and-dandelion stew, and his mugful of cold nettle tea. "What are you going to do? Stay here, or come with us?"

"Both," said Lister.

"Huh?"

"We're going to take Earth home. We're going to tow it back to the solar system."

"We're what?" laughed the Cat.

"It's possible," Lister said earnestly. "I've been thinking about it for the last ten years."

"So what are we going to do, exactly?" A patronizing smile rippled across Rimmer's face. "Stretch a chain from the ship, and use Mount Everest as a tow hook? Then, maybe, stick a huge sign in Australia: 'No hand signals: planet on tow'?"

"More or less," said Lister, and he was perfectly serious. "More or less."

EIGHT

The giant roach circled *White Giant*, then landed deftly by its side. They dismounted, and as Rimmer and the Cat walked shakily up the embarkation ramp Lister fished in his coat pocket and fed the roach some decomposing insect paste.

The communications moniter in *White Giant's* control room was flashing "Incoming transmission—response required."

Rimmer barked out the voice commands, and Kryten's face fizzed on to the screen. "Ah! There you are. I've been trying to get through for two hours. I've found him."

"*We* found him," corrected the Toaster.

Rimmer frowned. "Found who?"

"Queen Isabella of Spain," said the Toaster, sarcastically. "Who the smeg do you think?"

"Mr. Lister," Kryten said patiently. "We've found Mr. Lister."

The Cat popped his head over Rimmer's shoulder. "What? You mean you've found some sort of remains? A skeleton or something?"

"Read my lips," said the Toaster, who didn't have any. "We've found Lister. He's here. He's alive."

"That's not possible."

"Look." Kryten swivelled the head of the transmission camera, so the figure lying on *Blue Midget*'s crash couch swung into view.

It *was* Lister.

Pasty and drawn—his complexion had a strange wax veneer, and there was an odd soulless quality to his eyes—but it was Lister.

At least, it looked like Lister, no older than the day Rimmer had left him marooned.

Rimmer stared at the screen, his face bunched like a ball of waste paper. Suddenly, a gnarled hand snaked past him and flicked off the transmission link.

Rimmer turned and looked into Lister's wizened old face.

The Cat backed up to the far bulkhead wall. "What's going on here? Just who are you, Buddy?"

"I'm Lister," said Lister, unsmiling.

"Then who the hell's that?" The Cat flung an elegant forefinger towards the screen. "Benny Goodman and his Orchestra?"

"It's a Morph."

"It's a what?"

"It's a Polymorph."

NINE

The thing about human beings was this: human beings couldn't agree. They couldn't agree about anything. Right from the moment their ancestors first slimed out of the oceans, and one group of sludge thought it was better to live in trees while the other thought it blatantly obvious that the ground was the hip place to be. And they'd disagreed about pretty well everything else ever since.

They disagreed about politics, religion, philosophy—everything.

And the reason was this: basically, all human beings believed all other human beings were insane, in varying degrees.

This was largely due to a defective gene, isolated by a group of Danish scientists at the Copenhagen Institute in the late 1960s. This was a discovery which had the potential for curing all humankind's ills, and the scientists, naturally ecstatic, decided to celebrate by going out for a meal. Two of them wanted to go for a smorgasbord, one wanted Chinese cuisine, another preferred French, while the last was on a diet and just wanted to stay in the lab and type up the report. The disagreement blew up out of all proportion, the scientists fell to squabbling and the paper was never completed. Which was just as well in a way, because if it had been presented, no one would have agreed with it, anyway.

Small wonder, then, that *homo sapiens* spent most of their short time on Earth waging war against each other.

For their first few thousand years on the planet they did little else, and they discovered two things that were rather curious: the first was that when they were at war, they agreed more. Whole nations agreed that other nations were insane, and they agreed that the mutually beneficial solution was to band together to eliminate the loonies. For many people, it was the most agreeable period of their lives, because, apart from a brief period on New Year's Eve (which, incidentally, no one could agree the date of), the only time human beings lived happily side by side was when they were trying to kill each other.

Then, in the middle of the twentieth century, the human race hit a major problem.

It got so good at war, it couldn't have one anymore.

It had spent so much time practising and perfecting the art of genocide, developing more and more lethal devices for mass destruction, that conducting a war without totally obliterating the planet and everything on it became an impossibility.

This didn't make human beings happy at all. They talked about how maybe it was still possible to have a small, contained war. A little war. If you like, a warette.

They spoke of conventional wars, limited wars, and this insane option might even have worked, if only people could have agreed on a new set of rules. But, people being people, they couldn't.

War was out. War was a no-no.

And, like a small child suddenly deprived of its very favourite toy, the human race mourned and sulked and twiddled its collective thumbs, wondering what to do next.

Towards the conclusion of the twenty-first century, a solution was found. The solution was sport.

Sporting events were, in their way, little wars, and with war gone people started taking their sport ever more seriously. Scientists and theoreticians channelled their energies away from weaponry and into the new arena of battle.

And since the weapons of sport were human beings themselves, scientists set about improving them.

When chemical enhancements had gone as far as they could go, the scientists turned to genetic engineering.

Super sportsmen and women were grown, literally grown, in laboratory test-tubes around the planet.

The world's official sports bodies banned the new mutants from competing in events against normal athletes, and so a new, alternative sports body was formed, and set up in competition.

The GAS (Genetic Alternative Sports) finished "normal" sport within two years. Sports fans were no longer interested in seeing a conventional boxing match, when they could witness two genetically engineered pugilists—who were created with their brains in their shorts, and all their other major organs crammed into their legs and feet, leaving their heads solid blocks of unthinking muscle—knock hell out of one another for hours on end in a way that normal boxers could only manage for minutes.

Basketball players were grown twenty feet tall.

Swimmers were equipped with gills and fins.

Soccer players were bred with five legs and no mouths, making after-match interviews infinitely more interesting. However, not all breeds of genetic athletes were accepted by the GAS and new rules had to be created after the 2224 World Cup, when Scotland fielded a goalkeeper who was a human oblong of flesh, measuring eight feet high by sixteen across, thereby filling the entire goal. Somehow they still failed to qualify for the second round.

American football provided the greatest variety of mutant athletes, each one specifically designed for its position. The Nose Tackle, for instance, was an enormous nose—a huge wedge of boneless flesh that was hammered into the scrimmage line at every play. Wide receivers were huge Xs—four long arms that tapered to the tiny waist perched on top of legs capable of ten-yard strides. The defensive line were even larger, specifically bred to secrete noxious chemicals whenever the ball was in play.

Genetic Alternative Sports were a huge hit, and the technological advancements spilled into other avenues of human life.

Cars were suddenly coming off the production line made from human mutations. Bone on the outside, soft supple flesh in the interior, and engines made from mutated internal organs—living cars, that drove themselves, parked themselves and never crashed. More importantly than that, they didn't rely on fossil fuels to run. All they required was carfood—a special mulch made from pig offal. Cars in the twenty-third century ran on sausages.

The trend spread. GELFs, Genetically Engineered Life Forms, were everywhere, and soon virtually every consumer product was made of living tissue. Gelf armchairs, which could sense your mood, and massage your shoulders when you were feeling tense, became a part of everyday life. Gelf vacuum cleaners, which were half kitchen appliance, half family pet, waddled around on their squat little legs, doing the household chores and amusing the children.

Finally, the bubble burst. The Gelfs rebelled, just as the Mechanoids had rebelled before them.

The unrest had been festering for half a century. The dichotomy was that, although Gelfs were created from human chromosomes, and therefore technically qualified as human, they had no rights whatsoever. Quite simply, they wanted to vote. And normal humans were damned if they were going to file into polling stations alongside walking furniture and twenty-feet tall athletic freaks.

The rebellion started in the Australian town of Salzburg, when a vacuum cleaner and a Gelf Volkswagen Beetle robbed a high street bank. They took the manager and a security guard hostage, agreeing to release them only if Valter Holman was brought to justice for murder.

Valter Holman had killed his armchair, and the whole of the Gelf community was up in arms, those that had arms, because the law courts refused to accept that a crime had been committed.

The facts in the case were undisputed. It was a crime of passion. Holman had returned home from work unexpectedly one afternoon to discover his armchair sitting on his naked wife. He immediately leapt to the right conclusion, and shot the chair as it hurriedly tried to wriggle back into its upholstery.

Finally the establishment capitulated, and Holman was brought to trial. After the two-day hearing the court ruled that since Holman would have to live out the rest of his life being known as the man who was cuckolded by his own furniture, he had suffered enough, and was given a six-month suspended sentence.

And so the Gelf War started.

And for a short time, humankind indulged in its favourite pastime. Humans versus man-made humans.

Armchairs and vacuum cleaners fought side by side with bizarrely shaped genetically engineered sports stars and living, breathing motor cars.

The Gelfs didn't stand a chance, and most of them were wiped out or captured. The few remaining went to ground, becoming experts in urban guerrilla warfare. For a short time, Gelf-hunters proliferated, and a rebel vacuum cleaner waddling frantically down a crowded street, pursued by a Gelf runner, became a common sight.

But it wasn't the Gelf resistance fighters who caused the problem. The problem was what to do with those who'd surrendered. Legally, killing them constituted murder, but equally, the authorities could hardly send them back into docile human service.

Fortunately the problem coincided with the nomination of Earth as Garbage World. All the captured Gelfs were dumped like refuse on the island of Zanzibar and left to die.

Most of them did. But not all. Some survived. Not the brightest, not even the biggest, just those best equipped to cope with the harsh rigors of living on a planet swamped in toxic waste and choking poisons. The ones who could endure the endless winter as Earth soared through the universe looking for its new sun. And gradually, a new strain of Gelf evolved.

A creature who could live anywhere. Even in the revolting conditions on Earth. A creature with a sixth sense—telepathy. A creature who was able to read its prey's mind, even through hundreds of feet of compacted ice. A creature with no shape of its own: whose form was dictated by the requirements of survival.

These were the polymorphs.

The shape-changers.

They didn't need food for survival.

They fed on other creatures' emotions. Their diet was fear, jealousy, anger . . .

And when no other creatures were left on the island of Zanzibar, they began to feed off each other.

Until finally, there were only a handful left.

TEN

The polymorph who'd assumed Lister's shape lay on the bunk, waiting for its energy to return after its metamorphosis, while Kryten and the Toaster stared at the suddenly blank screen.

"What've you done now? You've caused a malfunction."

At the sound of the Toaster's tinny tones, Kryten's eyes rolled fully 720 degrees round in his head. "The transmission stopped. It's nothing to do with me."

"Why would the transmission suddenly stop? You must have pressed something. You must have pressed the wrong button."

"I didn't press anything, they just stopped broadcasting."

"Says you."

Kryten had had it up to his stereophonic audial sensors with the Toaster. Frankly, old Talkie was beginning to get on Kryten's nipple nuts. Fourteen hours of bouncing around in the hover dinghy, scouring the swamps, with the Toaster navigating, had driven him to the very limits of his almost limitless patience.

Few relationships can survive the ordeal of travelling to an unknown destination over any kind of distance, with one driving and one reading the map. If Romeo and Juliet had ever been forced to jump in a family saloon and drive from Venice to Marbella, they would have split up long before they hit the Spanish border. Hopelessly lost, bawling and screaming in some deserted lay-by in the middle of God-knows-where, there'd have been no talk of suicide—they'd have been more than ready to murder each other.

And Kryten didn't have the advantage of being madly in love with the Toaster to start with. The sight of the Toaster didn't send his soul into rapture. He thought the Toaster was an infuriatingly perky little geek.

And that was before the journey.

Fourteen hours stuck together had not improved things, and, uncharacteristically, Kryten was beginning to have fantasies wherein he set about the Toaster with a petrol-powered chainsaw.

"No way would that screen have gone blank if I'd had anything to do with it," the Toaster chirped. "Absolutely no way."

"Please. I'm trying to discover what's wrong."

"I'll tell you what's wrong. You. You don't know what you're doing. You're a sanitation Mechanoid—bog-cleaning, that's all you're good for. You're a bog-bot. A lavvy droid. A mechanical basin bleacher."

"Really?" Kryten's voice was dangerously quiet. "And I suppose a novelty Toaster is infinitely better equipped to cope with the complex communications system aboard this vessel?"

"Well, a certain so-called 'novelty' Toaster certainly didn't do a half-bad job at getting us all out of a certain Black Hole I could mention." The

Toaster gave an arrogant twist of his browning knob.

Kryten discreetly crushed a small section of the console's façade, and continued trying unsuccessfully to restore the communication link with *White Giant*.

The pale waxy figure on the couch listened to them bickering. The words themselves meant nothing, but the shapes and colours of their emotions were new and exciting. As soon as its energy returned, it would feast.

It had lived for so long on tiny morsels of insect emotion—mainly fear—and the little snacks it managed to cannibalize from weaker members of its species, that every shape change left it drained and temporarily helpless.

And now the Shadow Time was almost on it. It would need nourishment and sustenance if it was to survive the Aftering. It didn't think these things. It simply knew them. It had no capacity for abstract thought, it couldn't plan. It was a matter of instinct. The instinct to survive, moment by moment, for as long as possible.

But the water was helping. The cooling water on its brow was helping its strength to return.

Kryten dipped the cloth back in the water, then draped it back over his patient's forehead. "I don't know what's wrong with the communication link. Still, that's not for you to worry about. I'm sure they'll be in touch soon." Kryten tutted. Lister looked absolutely awful. "Are you quite sure there's nothing else I can do?"

"What he needs," chipped in a tinny voice, "is some nice, hot . . ."

"No!" Kryten snapped.

". . . tea. I was going to say 'some nice, hot, sweet tea.' What did you think I was going to say?" said the Toaster.

And then the Shadow Time came, and with it, the pain.

Kryten was halfway back to the communication console when Lister started convulsing. His back arched up off the bed, and his limbs threshed uncontrollably in the crash couch recess. Strange sounds, barely human, drove out of his juddering throat.

"He's choking!" yelled the Toaster.

"I can see that!" said Kryten, hauling Lister into a sitting position and slapping him on his back.

"Perhaps he's swallowed a fishbone!"

"Swallowed a what?"

"A fishbone. And you know what the cure is for a fishbone lodged in the throat."

"What?"

"Dry toast! Oh, joy! I've waited for a moment like this all my life! Get me some bread!"

Kryten yanked a fire extinguisher off the wall and hurled it at the Toaster, catching it a glancing blow on its browning knob. The Toaster was temporarily stunned into silence, and Kryten went back to slamming the still-convulsing Lister between the shoulder blades.

And just when it seemed the convulsions could get no worse, they stopped. Something dislodged

from Lister's throat, and fell into Kryten's out-
stretched palm.

"It's a piece of bubble-gum." Kryten held out
the small pink wad of gum for Lister to see.

Pale and sweating, the Lister morph sank back
on to the couch, exhausted. Kryten dropped the
gumball into a metal trash can, just as the communication screen crackled back to life.

"What's going on?" asked the Toaster.

Lines of silent machine code scrolled up the
screen.

"It's machine code," said the Toaster.

"Yes," hissed Kryten. "I'm perfectly well aware
of that."

"Why are they communicating in machine
language?"

"I haven't the slightest clue."

"No," agreed the Toaster, "you haven't, have
you? D'you want me to translate it? I'm fairly flu-
ent in machine code."

"I can manage."

"Well? What does it say?"

"If you can just give me half a second, I'll tell
you."

"Yes?"

"It says: 'Extreme danger. You have . . .' Kryten's voice trailed off.

"You have what?"

"Nothing." Kryten's eyes flitted across the screen,
absorbing the message.

"What d'you mean, 'nothing'?"

Kryten craned round and looked at the figure
on the couch. The lifeless milky eyes stared back
at him.

"Come on—what d'you mean, 'nothing'? There

can't be five hundred lines of nothing on the screen."

"I mean . . . I can't translate it," Kryten lied. "I don't know what it says."

The Toaster sighed extravagantly, and turned, by flipping its bread-release lever rapidly up and down on the table top, to face the screen. "Once more the cavalry, in the form of a handsome yet reasonably inexpensive red toasting machine, bugles over the hill to the rescue. The message," it said, "runs thus: 'Extreme danger. You have on board a genetic mutation' . . ."

"Shut up."

". . . 'It is not, repeat, not Lister' . . ."

'That's enough."

" 'Abandon your vessel' . . ."

"Quiet!"

". . . 'and engage self-destruct.' Honestly, this is really easy. You'd have to be a moron not to be able to translate this. What's this next bit . . . ?"

Before it could continue, Kryten had wrenched the two thin steel ashtrays from the arms of the relaxation chairs and hammered them into the Toaster's bread vents. It was silenced immediately.

The Lister creature on the couch swivelled upright and watched, expressionless, as Kryten sidled back towards the glass cabinet that contained the emergency fire axe.

Abandon ship? How could he abandon ship? They were no longer on Garbage World, they were in space, halfway back to *Red Dwarf*.

Something was happening. The shapes, the colours of the emotions of the prey were changing.

*The tall, thin one, the mobile one made of plas-
tic and metal, was afraid. Very afraid.*

Delicious.

Nurture the fear. Help it grow.

Then feast on its succulence.

Feast to gorging.

Must change.

Must change, to nurture the fear.

But weak.

Too weak to complete.

Kryten's elbow smashed into the glass casing behind him, and his hand found the grip of the fire
axe. Then he froze.

It was a horrible sound. The most horrible
sound Kryten had ever heard. Crunching bones
and sickening wetness, and a scream that dipped
all the way down to Hell.

Lister stopped being Lister and started to become something else. His body folded in on itself,
and when it re-emerged it was inside out. The
slimy, mucus-coated organs quivered and gurgled
as the ribcage split open and a strange serpent-
like suction head slithered out and began sliming
across the floor towards Kryten's feet.

Kryten stood there, waxwork-still in terror, as
the unspeakable appendage coiled itself up his
legs. The rest of the creature lay writhing ecstati-
cally on the floor: Lister from the shoulders up,
blubbery gore below.

The grotesque tentacle wound its way effortlessly up Kryten's torso, and wrapped around his
neck, until its drooling tip quivered inches from
his lips.

It reared back, like a snake about to strike. The

tentacle tip split and a pink, fleshy, pursed mouth flicked out and grinned.

Then there was a voice. It was high pitched and metallic. It was the Toaster.

"Hey, pal."

The creature's mouth slowly turned towards the bright red plastic box on the table.

"Would you like a little toast?"

The Toaster jiggled its crumb tray, so that it toppled on to its front, then slammed down its bread-release lever. A red-hot metal ashtray skimmed through the air, slicing through the creature's tentacle. The severed appendage thrashed and flailed, spraying green gloop around the entire control room.

The part of the creature that was half Lister, half something else screeched with blind agony and lurched towards the Toaster.

"Hey—don't get angry. I have a slice for you, too."

The second ashtray sizzled across the control room, ploughed through the neck of the Lister beast, decapitating it, silencing its inhuman shriek forever.

The Toaster flipped back up on to its base, and said, in a voice as macho as its tinny larynx would allow: "Was it something I said?" it burred. "He seems a trifle cut up."

Kryten slithered down the bulkhead wall, sat on the deck and groaned, a long, low grumble of a groan. This was possibly the worst thing that could have happened. Saved, yet again, by the Toaster. Now it would scale new peaks of obnoxiousness.

The Toaster was already in its stride. A little puff of smoke trilled from the top of its grill.

"Toast, quantum mechanics and now slimebeast-slayer. Not a bad buy for $£19.99, wouldn't you say?"

Without interrupting his groan, Kryten punched the re-heat button to take *Blue Midget* back to *Red Dwarf*, double speed.

ELEVEN

It was a strange feeling for Lister, staring down at his own dead features. He shook his head. "It doesn't make sense—I don't understand how you managed to kill it so easy."

"Hardly easy," the Toaster objected. "It was a *mano a mano*, ninja-type struggle, where a brave, rather ruggedly handsome red kitchen appliance finally managed to come out on top."

Lister wasn't listening. His finger hovered over the fire button of his heavy-duty mining laser. "It must have been weak."

"Weak? It was on the brink of squeezing the very life out of a series 4000 Mechanoid. That's how weak it was. You just can't tolerate the thought that, yet again, your old buddy Talkie Toaster saved everybody's neck."

"Why did it wait so long to feed? It doesn't make sense, none of it."

"It didn't feed because it was engaged in a titanic battle *à morte* with a samurai toaster. It was too busy trying to dodge lethal discs of red-hot steel to be thinking about nosh time. Oh, you should have seen me, I was magnificent. I feinted right, I dodged left—I was ducking and diving, weaving and bobbing, and he didn't lay a sucker on me."

Lister shook his head again, and clicked and whistled a cockroach expletive.

Kryten prodded the polymorph's remains with the shaft of his fire axe, and looked up at Lister. "What I don't understand is why it looks thirty years younger than you do."

"It read your mind. You were expecting to find me the same age as you left me. That was the only data it had. So it turned into what it knew you were looking for."

Rimmer stood outside the hatchway on the embarkation ramp, still steadfastly refusing to enter *Blue Midget*. "You've encountered these things before, then?" he called to Lister.

Lister nodded. "Once. One of the scouting roaches brought one back to the valley. Wiped out half the settlement before we finally punched its card. After that we always kept lookouts, but no others ever showed up. I don't think they're that intelligent. They're like mynah birds—they copy things without really understanding what it is they're copying."

"So what now, Mr. Lister, sir?"

"I don't want to take any chances. I think we should shoot *Blue Midget* into space, and detonate the auto-destruct."

"Destroy *Blue Midget*?' Rimmer's head leaned in through the hatchway. "We've already lost *Starbug*. That leaves us with only one transport craft."

"Rimmer—I know what these things can do."

"It's dead! It can't do anything."

"I know. but I want to get rid of it. Every last

bit of the smegger. And the only way to be sure of that is to torch the ship."

Rimmer continued his protests all the way to the Shuttle-Bay Launch Suite, but Lister was adamant; adamant and stubborn in a way he'd never been when he was younger. There was simply no arguing with him.

They were gone.
  It was safe now to move.
  Safe to change.

The wad of pink gum folded in on itself and began to fizzle as it turned into a cloud of steam and floated out of the metal trash can towards the air lock. The steam wrapped itself into a ball and solidified into a round black stone. The stone clanked loudly as it hit *Blue Midget*'s deck, and rolled up against the air-lock door.

Then the stone became ice. And the ice became water. And the water tried to seep through the air-lock seal.

No way out.
  Not here.

The water became steam again, and wafted around the craft's interior, looking for an exit.

Nothing. The whole craft was air-tight.

Then the engines rumbled, jets fired, and the vessel began to rise.

The steam floated up to the rear viewpoint window, became a fly and flung itself against the reinforced glass.

Blue Midget bucked and bobbled as its steering

jets swung the craft round and aligned it with the damaged bay doors.

The fly became a feather and floated ineffectually against the glass. The feather became a bullet. Its rear-end ignited and it blasted against the glass, ricocheting back and tumbling once more to the deck.

It lay in silence.

It was young. It knew of no more shapes.

It needed more knowledge.

Something primeval inside it, some instinct it didn't understand told it to seek out the minds of its prey. The signals were weak—only just in range.

It searched through their memories, and changed into things it found there. Many things. And none of the shapes it became could get through the glass.

Blue Midget passed under the bay arch, and swept out into space.

And it was only then that the creature turned into the one thing that could pass through the glass.

A light beam.

It became a beam of light that flashed through the glass and streaked back through the open bay doors.

It was back.

Back on *Red Dwarf*.

It became a small puddle of water—the least demanding of all its shapes—and rested.

When its strength returned, it would feed.

It would feed well.

TWELVE

Kryten craned over the crumpled handwritten recipe sheet he'd been given by Lister. It was Lister's own concoction: "shami kebabs diabolo," which he'd once claimed proudly had put Petersen in the medical unit for over a week. But surely there was some mistake. The amount of chilli peppers called for could have launched a three-stage Deep Space probe from Houston Mission Control to the outer reaches of the galaxy. This wasn't a shami kebab—it was a thermonuclear device.

Still, orders were orders. Kryten plugged the food-blending attachment into his groinal socket and thrust his hips towards the mixing-bowl. It was something of a design flaw with the series 4000 that the power socket was so indelicately placed. It looked particularly preposterous whenever Kryten was called on to use the three-foot vacuum hose. He tugged his right ear and the blender whirred into life. He whistled happily and began mincing together the ingredients of the kebab.

Thin fast beads of water battered over Lister's body as he gloried in the warmth of the shower.

He filled his cupped palm with a ludicrously generous amount of shampoo, and massaged it into his already well-lathered scalp.

Shampoo and soap were two of the luxuries he'd failed to duplicate adequately on Garbage World. For a third of a century he'd had to wash using salt. His attempts to make real soap by boiling decomposing vegetable fats had proved too revolting for words. He always ended up smelling worse after he'd bathed than before he'd started. He finally gave up his soap-making attempts when he noticed that the cockroaches had started avoiding him, and ever afterwards relied on salt.

He blinked through sudded eyes at his reflection in the cubicle's mirrored wall. He hadn't bothered with mirrors as a vanity device—he really had no desire to impress roaches with a well-groomed appearance—and all the mirrors and reflective surfaces he'd collected over the years were used to harness the sun's heat. It was strange having an old body; he still thought of himself as a permanent twenty-five.

Where did all the years go?

Who'd stolen that fabulous body he'd once had for a couple of months when he was eighteen? Who'd given him this one instead? OK, so it was pretty well preserved for its sixty-one years, and, curiously, it was fitter in many respects than it had been when he'd first arrived on Garbage World, thanks to all his labours in the field. But there was no getting away from it—he now lived in a body that was nine years away from being seventy.

Nearly seventy.

Soon he would have to face the fact that in all

probability he would never play professionally for the London Jets.

He might not even live to see the conclusion of his plan to tow Earth back to its solar system.

He heard a voice through the shower's roar, and turned down the taps.

It was Kryten: "Ready in two minutes, Mr. Lister, sir."

Lister smiled. He was two minutes away from his first shami kebab in three-and-a-half decades. He'd given up meat, of course, on Garbage World, and he had no regrets about that. But shami kebabs were something else. Fantasizing about this Indian *hors d'oeuvre* had kept him going when times had been rough.

And now he was going to have one.

He chuckled out loud, and began clicking and whistling an up-beat cockroach song as he rinsed the soap from his hair.

Kryten pulled on three sets of oven gloves, one on top of the other, and took the three sausage-shaped kebabs out of the oven. They looked innocent enough, but quite frankly he'd have felt safer handling them wearing an asbestos suit, preferably with long-range, remote-controlled mechanical arms.

These babies were hot.

He put the plate on the sleeping quarters' table and backed away nervously.

"Dinner is served, sir."

"Just coming."

As Kryten crossed the sleeping quarters, a small, brightly patterned beach ball bounced through the hatchway and into the room.

Kryten caught it on its fifth bounce, placed it on the table, next to Lister's kebabs, and went outside into the corridor to investigate.

There was no one there.

The corridor was empty.

Kryten ducked back into the sleeping quarters. Now the beach ball wasn't there either.

Kryten failed to notice that the three kebabs on the plate had become four.

"He-e-eyy!" Lister stepped out of the cubicle, tugging together the cords of his shower robe, "Shami kebabs!" he orgasmed. "Thirty-four years. I hope you haven't skimped on the old chillies, there, Kryters, old buddy, old pal."

Lister sat down and prepared to eat. As his fork bore down towards his plate, one of the Indian sausages leapt out of the bed of lettuce and hurled itself around his throat. He catapulted back and crashed to the ground in his chair; his desperate fingers clawing at the choking kebab; his legs kicking and bucking.

Kryten turned from the wash basin at the sounds of Lister's agonized writhing.

He shook his head and tutted. "Are you seriously telling me you like them *that* spicy?"

Lister gagged. His face started to blacken.

"*Far* too many chilli peppers," Kryten clucked. "Didn't I tell you?"

Lister's eyes bulged as he rolled over and over on the sleeping quarters' floor.

"And this is your idea of an enjoyable snack? It's sheer insanity."

"The kebab," Lister rasped, "it's trying to kill me."

"Well, I'm, not the least bit surprised."

Finally, Lister's clawing fingers found some purchase, and he ripped the lethal shami from his neck and slung it across the sleeping quarters.

He hunched, coughing and choking as it slid with snake speed underneath the bunks. "Where'd it go?"

"Where did what go?"

"The polymorph! There's another polymorph!"

"What? Where?"

Lister staggered back against the bunks. "I think it went under Rimmer's architect's desk." He reached down and picked up his red boxer shorts from the floor and struggled into them. "Come on, Kryten—we've got to get out of here."

Lister grabbed a baseball bat from beside the bunk and started backing towards the hatchway.

There was a loud cracking sound, and Lister doubled up.

"Are you all right, sir?"

"Guhhhh!"

"What's the matter?"

"My . . . ah! . . . My boxers . . . aaah! . . . They're shrinking!" Lister staggered forward, his eyes double size with fear as a second creak wrenched his body into spasm. "The polymorph! It's turned into a pair of boxers . . . getting smaller . . . Ahhhh! No! God! Please! Please!"

Lister staggered and then toppled on to his back. "Kryten—help me! Please help me! My boxers—get them off—pull them down! Please, God, I'm begging you."

Kryten fell to his knees between Lister's splayed legs, ripped open his shower robe, and tugged frantically at Lister's boxer shorts.

Rimmer skidded into the quarters. "What the hell's going on?"

"Keep still, Mr. Lister!"

"I can't stand it anymore. Get them off—please! Do it now!"

"We need some kind of lubricant." Kryten's eyes scanned the room. "Butter. I'll get some butter."

"Anything! Anything! Just do it quick!"

Rimmer shook his head. He couldn't say he was totally shocked. He wished he could, but he couldn't. He'd bonk anything, Lister. Not even a male android was safe from his vile appetites. And what was that dangling from Kryten's groinal socket? A food blender? Oh, it brought tears to his eyes just thinking about it.

With a final effort, Kryten ripped off Lister's tiny shorts and stood up. The boxers were minute, doll size. Lister scrambled backwards towards the hatchway. "It's a polymorph! Don't just stand there holding it! Get rid of the smegger!"

Suddenly the tiny red shorts folded in on themselves, and Kryten was holding the tail of a rat.

"Oh my God!" Lister's stomach surged for his throat. It was a plague rat, two and a half feet long, not counting its tail.

Lister hated rats.

Hated them.

And this one came from his nightmares: its razor-sharp yellow teeth, its black matted fur streaked with blood, its cold, dead eyes.

It wriggled, snapped and drooled as Kryten staggered towards him, still grimly holding it by its tail. "What shall I do, sir? Where shall I put it."

"Just get it out of here! Just get it away from me!"

Kryten swung the beast and flung it hard towards the bulkhead wall, but it twisted in the air, flipped back and changed direction. Lister watched in adrenalin-induced slow motion as the rat landed

on

his

FACE.

"Wuuuuhaaaaaaaaaaahhhhhhhhhhh!" A voice Lister had never heard before screamed from deep inside him. He felt the rat's foetid breath crawl up into his nostrils.

"Oh my Guhhhhhhhhhnnnnnnnnnnnn!"

Then the most hideous, revolting, disgusting, foul, vile thing that had ever happened to Lister, happened to Lister.

Some of the rat's rabid spittle drooled into his gaping mouth.

"Oh, shiiiiiiiiiiirrrrrrhhhhhhhhggggggggghhhh-hh!"

Lister's fear was complete.

Terror pushed him to the very edge of insanity.

Then it happened.

The rat's head folded in on itself, split open and disgorged the polymorph's feeding tentacle. The slimy puckered mouth on the tip of the tentacle smacked on to Lister's head.

And the polymorph began to feed.

Kryten ripped the half-rat from Lister's face and pitched it against the bunkside wall. It squelched down the wall, leaving a trail of gloop and gore, and fell into the open laundry basket. Kryten launched himself across the quarters and slammed down the lid.

Lister rose from the floor and picked up the baseball bat. "I hate rats." He shuddered. "They freak me out totally. They're my second all-time worst fear."

Rimmer cleared his dry throat. "What's your first?"

The metal lid blasted into the air, and a new form loomed out of the basket. Its head hung hugely above them. Mucus pulsed through the gaps in its armour-like endoskeleton. Its enormous jaws carried two hundred needle-sharp silver teeth, glistening with demonic slobber.

"This," said Lister. "This is my all-time worst fear."

The creature's jaws opened to their limit, and a feeding tentacle shot out of its mouth and fastened on to Lister's head.

The half-sated polymorph completed its meal.

THIRTEEN

"So what are you saying?" The Cat frowned. "This thing feeds off emotions?"

Kryten nodded. "Exactly. It changes shape to provoke a negative emotion—in this case, fear. It took Mr. Lister to the very limit of his terror, then sucked out his fear."

"Then what happened?"

"It vanished. It turned into a cloud of steam and floated out of the room."

The Cat looked down at Lister's inert form on the medical unit's biofeedback couch. "Is he OK?"

"Apparently so. It's just he no longer has any sense of fear."

Rimmer stopped pacing. "The question is: what are we going to do?"

Lister's eyes flicked open, and he lurched upright on the couch. "Well, I say let's get out there and twat it."

"Lister, you're ill." Rimmer started pacing again. "Just leave this to us."

Lister smacked his fist into his palm. "I could have had it in the sleeping quarters, only it took me by surprise."

"Lister—it turned into an eight-feet-tall armour-plated killing machine."

"I've had bigger than him. They're all the same, these armour-plated killing machines. One good fist in the gob, they soon lose interest."

"It's probably best you stay calm, sir," said Kryten, soothingly. "You've lost all sense of fear. You're not thinking rationally."

"What's there to be scared of? If it wants a barny, we'll give it one. One swift knee in the happy sacs, it'll drop, like anyone else."

"Fine," Rimmer nodded. "Well, we'll certainly bear that in mind when we're constructing our strategy."

"I'll rip out its windpipe and whip it to death with the tonsil end."

"Yes. Very good." Rimmer caught Kryten's eyes and nodded discreetly in the direction of the sedative cabinet.

"I'll shove my fist so far down its gob, I'll be able to pull the label off its underpants."

Kryten pushed the syringe into Lister's arm.

Lister looked down at the hypodermic. "What's that, pal? You starting trouble?"

"I'm sorry, Mr. Lister, sir. It's just a little something to relax you."

"Come on then, slags." Lister lunged at him drunkenly. "I'll have you all! One at a time or all together. Makes no odds to me. I'll . . . I'll . . ." Lister smiled as the sedative flushed into his bloodstream, and fell back on to the couch.

Rimmer sighed. "Thank God for that. All right. As far as I can see, we've got two alternatives: one—we take this thing on, and we don't rest until it's dead. Or, two—we run away." He hardly paused. "Who's for two?"

"Sounds good to me," voted Kryten.

"Always been my lucky number," agreed the Cat.

Rimmer's plan was cowardly, but simple. They would go up to the supply deck, grab whatever they could fit into a supply wagon, load it on to *Blue Midget*, the one remaining shuttle craft, and get the hell out. Without emotions to feed on, the polymorph would eventually die. In the meantime they could survive on Garbage World for as long as necessary.

"What about him?" the Cat nodded at the snoring Lister.

"He'll only slow us down. We'll pick him up when we've got the supplies."

They sealed the sedated Lister in the medical unit and started making their way up to the supply deck.

The mesh cage of the service lift juddered noisily to a stop three feet above the floor of the supply deck.

The Cat's boot democratically elected that Kryten should be first out. He went next, followed by Rimmer. Before them stretched the endless ranks of cargo crates—a huge regular matrix that covered almost twenty acres.

The Cat adjusted the strap of his backpack that powered the enormous bazookoid mining laser. "Let's get this over with. This damn gun's destroying the line of my suit."

Kryten trundled in the lead, nervously swinging his bazookoid at every imaginary sound. He'd never worn a grenade belt before, and he wasn't exactly in love with the way the grenades clanked noisily against his metal chest plate with each movement.

They turned left at the first intersection, and there, empty in the aisle, was a gleaming yellow supply truck. It looked brand-new.

Kryten unbuckled his grenade belt, set it down beside his mining laser and backpack, and started loading up the truck. The Cat's eyes scoured the gloom, but caught no movement. Rimmer stood, jiggling his right leg nervously, and occasionally clapping his hands to hurry Kryten along.

Twenty minutes later, the truck was full.

"Lets' go!" Rimmer hissed, and Kryten and the Cat climbed up into the cab. Then something made Rimmer stop.

Something about that truck.

Too yellow. Too new. Too convenient.

He started backing away.

"Come on, Buddy, let's move it. Let's go, go go!"

"There! Polymorph!" Rimmer's voice was barely audible. "It's . . ."

The Cat swung out his mining laser. "Where?"

"It's . . ." Rimmer could hardly speak with fear.

"Say it, dog breath. Where is it?"

"It's the truck! The polymorph is the supply truck!"

FOURTEEN

Kryten somersaulted backwards out of the cab and rolled down an aisle. The Cat's buttocks clenched so tightly they became a single ball, before he unfroze and launched himself after Kryten. As the Cat landed by his side, Kryten ripped a thermal grenade from his belt, twisted the detonator handle and bowled it under the cab.

The explosion flung the truck fully thirty feet in the air, and the blast debris rained down on top of them—tyres, engine parts, burnt-out chassis and broken windscreen glass. The Cat stood up and strode over the smouldering debris to the recess in the aisle where Rimmer was cowering. "That supply truck . . ." he jabbed at Rimmer with the barrel of his bazookoid, ". . . the one we just spent twenty minutes loading with supplies, was, get this: a supply truck."

Rimmer smiled contritely. "Yes," he agreed. "I can see that now."

"Twenty minutes we spent loading that thing. And now we've got to start all over . . ."

"There!" Rimmer cut across him. "In the shadows!" He pointed past Kryten down the aisle. "Something moved."

"I think he's ruh-ruh-ruh-ruh-ruh-ruh . . ."

Kryten whapped his head on the corner of a crate. "I think he's right. The blast must have drawn it."

"Set the bazookoids to heat-seeker. If there's anything out there, the laser bolts'll find it."

Kryten and the Cat snapped the bazookoid control-setting over to heat-seeker, braced themselves for the recoil and fired. Two blue balls screamed down the length of the aisle, and vanished into the distant murk.

They waited for the explosion, listening to the fading howl as the bolts sped harmlessly down towards the far end of the supply deck.

But the explosion didn't happen.

There was nothing there.

Rimmer felt the Cat's look. "Sorry," he held up his hands apologetically, "my fault. False alarm."

The laser bolts reached the end of the supply deck, flipped over like two Olympic swimmers and began powering back through the traces of their own tails.

The Cat was still berating Rimmer, when for the third time in as many minutes Rimmer pointed past him, and said, in the same fear-stricken voice: "There!"

"What *now*?" the Cat snapped. "You've got a bad case of the jitters, Buddy."

Rimmer shook his head. The Cat sighed, turned and saw the bolts speeding back towards them.

"I don't understand it," Rimmer said. "Holograms don't produce heat, neither do Mechanoids. What are they homing in on?"

Rimmer and Kryten turned and looked at the Cat. The Cat said three words. The three words were: "So long, guys." He hoisted his bazookoid on to his shoulder, and he started to run.

The Cat knew he could move. Even with the weight of the backpack and the bazookoid; even with the rather impractical tight silver trousers, and the two-inch cuban heels, he would still have put money on himself to out-run just about anything.

But the question was this: could he out-run two heat-seeking laser bolts? The honest truth was, he didn't know. He had no idea whether it was even possible to shake off two spinning bolts of death whose entire existence was dedicated to finding something that emitted heat, and blowing it up.

Still, he thought it would be a good idea to try. So he did.

His neck craned back and his knees pistoned up and down, pumping so high they beat his chest with every step. He heard the bolts' distinctive *zhazhum* as they rounded the corner and ripped down the aisle in pursuit. At the next intersection he zigged left and zagged right. The sound of the bolts faded slightly—he could corner faster than they could. Hey! Things were looking up. Sure, they were faster than him on a straight, but if he kept turning, if he found enough corners, he could out-run these suckers until their power ran down.

He was feeling good, now. This wasn't going to be nearly as difficult as he expected. He came up to a maze of intersections, twisted left, right and left again. Behind him he heard the bolts overshoot a turn, and their low humming throb dimmed in volume. He'd bought himself a couple of seconds; seconds he badly needed. He pulled out a mirror and checked his hair. It was still perfect. He pulled out a small metal cylinder, freshened his breath, and took off again.

Another right, another left, another right.

And suddenly, he was in a straight.

A long narrow corridor lined with cargo crates. Three hundred yards without a turning in sight, and no exit—just a door at the very end of the corridor, marked "lift." The bolts rounded the bend behind him.

The confident grin dribbled off his face.

Then, the Cat did the most stupid thing possible: he stopped.

He planted both feet firmly on the grilled metal deck, and waited for the lasers to hit him. Half a second before they did, he climbed into the air, he kicked his legs above his head, and back-flipped his feline form over the sizzling bolts.

He watched them as they soared down the aisle before they corrected their course and curved back towards him.

He started to run.

He started to run straight at them. Two feet from impact, he launched himself upwards again and Fosbury-flopped over the deadly blue missiles.

Again they roared by underneath him and prepared to turn. He glanced down the aisle and started towards the lift.

The metal on his cuban heels spat sparks as he skidded up to the lift and snapped the lift call button and waited.

Nothing happened.

He slapped it again. The laser bolts streaked towards him.

He slapped it a third time, and the doors opened, but too late. He felt the bolts' heat on his face, and ducked—simultaneously slapping the "door close" button.

The doors hammered shut, and trapped them.

The Cat peered in through the observation window and watched the bolts helplessly swirling around inside.

He pulled a tiny silver toothbrush out of his jacket pocket, and started to groom his eyebrows. "You either got it, or you ain't. And you little blue guys—you ain't even close."

He smelt the girl's perfume as she leaned over his shoulder. To the Cat's mind, she was the second most gorgeous thing he'd ever seen. Long black hair, short orange pvc suit, thigh-length boots and a whip. It was hard to stop his eyes from watering. Clearly, this girl had class.

She spoke. "What are you looking for?"

"A mutant," the Cat said, casually. "It's dangerous." His eyes half closed and his eyebrows smouldered above them. "Can turn into anything."

"Sounds pretty scary."

A bravado snort jetted down the Cat's nostrils.

"Must take a pretty brave kind of guy to do this kind of work?"

"You think?"

"And smart. Bet you have to be smart, too."

"Definitely. You've got to have your wits about you all the time—don't let up for one second, or it'll sneak up behind you and blip! you're dog meat." They reached an intersection. The Cat held up his hand and leant out. When he was satisfied it was safe, he beckoned her forward with a nod of his head. "Come on, baby."

"Did anyone ever tell you you're quite a guy?"

The Cat shrugged. "Not since this morning."

"Smart, brave, handsome . . ." She ran her hand sensually down the curve of her hip. "In fact, I think you're probably the best-looking guy I've ever seen."

"Well," he laughed, modestly. "I didn't want to be the first to say it."

"You know what I'd really like?" She tormented the button on his jacket with a long-nailed finger. "I'd really like to make love to a guy like you."

The Cat lost a short, one-sided struggle with a large, cheesy grin. "We-e-ell. I'm sure I have a window in my schedule somewhere." He raised his wrist, and looked at a watch that wasn't there. "What are you doing in, say, ten seconds' time?"

"Nothing I couldn't cancel."

The Cat leant into her. "Hi. I'm the Cat."

"Hi." She leant back. "I'm the genetic mutant."

"Glad to know you," the Cat leered. "Jenny who?"

There was a revolting ripping of flesh, and the girl's head folded in on itself. From the mess of pink blubber, a feeding tentacle snaked out and hit the Cat between the eyes.

The polymorph suckled noisily as it feasted on the Cat's vanity.

FIFTEEN

Kryten heard the Cat's scream and doubled his pace. At top speed he could waddle at nearly twenty-five miles an hour, and he soon lost Rimmer in the laze of crates.

He came across the Cat lying groaning, barely conscious.

Kryten set down his bazookoid, and cradled the Cat's head in his hand. "My goodness. Are you all right?"

The Cat moaned and blinked open his eyes. "Don't worry about me, Bud—I'm nobody."

Rimmer appeared around the corner. "Is he dead?"

"Who cares?" said the Cat.

The Mechanoid shook his head. "I think he's lost his vanity."

Rimmer's eyes spat hate at Kryten. "You've done it again, haven't you?"

"Done what, sir?" Kryten's plastoid brow crinkled into a frown.

"Failed. First, the *Nova 5*. Whose fault was it the ship crashed? Whose fault was it the crew died?"

"But that was . . ." Kryten stammered. "I didn't . . . I was only trying to . . ."

"And who brought the polymorph aboard *Red Dwarf* in the first place?"

"Yes, but I didn't know. I . . ." Kryten's mouth yacked open and closed, but no sound came out.

"First Lister, now the Cat. You won't be happy till everyone's dead, will you?"

"Oh," Kryten's voice cracked. "Please . . ."

"Please what? We were supposed to stick together—you let the Cat run off alone."

"But that wasn't . . ." he stuttered. "I mean . . ."

"He trusted you. Now look at him."

Kryten covered his face with his hands. "Oh, goodness! I feel so . . . so . . . guilty."

Rimmer smiled. Then his head collapsed in on itself, and a green sucker ripped out from the slime and fastened on to Kryten's skull.

The real Rimmer skidded round the corner as the polymorph finished feeding on the Mechanoid's electronic emotion, and evaporated into a cloud of steam. "What's going on? What's happened?"

Kryten turned to face him. "The polymorph—it turned into you, then sucked away my guilt. I have lost the single emotion that prevents my transgressing the mores and manners of civilized society."

"Come on—let's forget the supplies. We'll go back for Lister and just get the hell out of here."

"Screw Lister," said Kryten, flicking out a middle finger and jabbing it in the air. "And quite frankly, Rimmer, screw you."

SIXTEEN

Halfway back to the medical unit, something happened to Rimmer. They were speeding along one of the series of mile-long moving walkways, the Cat slugging from a bottle of cheap Tunisian whisky he'd smashed out of one of the dispensing machines, and Kryten was taking laser potshots at the advent boards that sped by, when Rimmer staggered and clutched his stomach.

Kryten shot out the mouth of a man advertising toothpaste, and turned, sniggering, to see Rimmer totter to his knees. "What's the matter with you, groin-breath?"

"It's . . . inside me," Rimmer gasped. "The polymorph."

"Oh, is that all?" Kryten tutted, and went back to his target practice.

The Cat blew his nose into his tie, and belched twice. "Hoinnnnnnnnnnk. Huuuurp. Hurrrrrrp. How is that possible? It's not here."

Kryten blasted the Kookie Kola Bear out of existence. "It's broken into the hologram simulation suite, turned itself into electronic data and infiltrated his personality disk. Anyone whose brain wasn't constructed from discarded sphincter could work that one out."

"You're right," said the Cat, "I'm a moron. I'm a nobody. I'm not fit to be alive."

"Agreed," Kryten nodded, and trained the barrel of his bazookoid on the Cat. "Kiss your ass good-bye, Cat," he said, and fired. There was a disappointing click, and the charge metre flashed: "empty'. "Damn," said Kryten.

"Aw, hell," said the Cat. "I was really looking forward to being dead. I don't deserve any better."

"Don't worry, I'll kill you later, when I get a new gun."

"Well," the Cat smiled gratefully, "only if it's convenient. It's not worth putting yourself out for a useless piece of shit like me."

Rimmer lay writhing on the floor as the polymorph wriggled through his databank, searching through his personality disk, trying to stimulate a new emotion to sample. Images jolted into Rimmer's brain. Memories, half-forgotten . . .

A hot summer day, waiting outside a cinema for a girl who doesn't turn up. Three hours, he's waited. Three hours. Boy, that makes him . . .

Putting together a cheap, self-assembly study desk with four missing screws, hammering his thumb with a wooden mallet. "Smegging mallet!" . . .

A baby, now, five months old. He's dropped his teething ring, and no one picks it up. Can't they hear him screaming? Don't they know how badly he needs that teething ring? God, they really make you . . .

Twenty-four, and in the Space Corps. He's coming home on a weekend furlough, and he's stuck in a traffic jam for six hours. Six precious hours are totally wasted, and all the time he's getting more and more . . .

Now, ten. He wants to go to the Russian circus. Not much to ask. It's making a once-in-a-lifetime visit to his hometown. Everyone in his class has been, and then his parents say he can't go, because he didn't mow the lawn. Because he didn't mow their lousy, smegging lawn. Not fair! That really makes you . . .

He's thirty. He's opening a letter. ". . . failed to meet the required standard . . ." but he's worked harder than anyone. It makes him feel so damn . . .

Seventeen. And for the first time in his life, he brings a girl home to meet the family. Sunday afternoon, he chances into the greenhouse, and there she is, behind the tomato plants with his brother John. Would you believe it? Your own brother's got his tongue down your girlfriend's throat . . . It really makes you angry!

Now he's fourteen. Boarding-school. Being beaten for talking during lunch. And all he said was "pass the salt." It makes him so angry!

Still in boarding-school, in the dormitory, and he's being beaten again, this time for snoring. Snoring in a dormitory is a beating offence? Snoring with malicious intent? And the thick rubber running-shoe slams against his thin cotton pyjamas, and how is that fair? And he's so frustrated and impotent and . . . angry!

He's got an exam in the morning. He's thirty years old and he's got an exam in the morning. All his life, he's always seemed to have an exam in the morning. And those BASTARDS in room 1115 are having a smegging party, and how *many times does he have to tell them he has an exam in the morning. And every time he tells them, what do they do? They turn the music UP!*

And another letter. ". . . overlooked for promotion . . ." for the sixth year on the run, overlooked for promotion. Have to wait yet another year and it's just not FAIR! It makes you so FURIOUS!

The countless frustrations of a lifetime welled up inside him until he felt he would burst.

Then he did.

Anger dragged a primal scream from his throat.

"Noooooooooooooooooooooooooooooooooo!"

And fifty-three decks above, in the hologram simulation suite, the polymorph devoured his anger.

Rimmer collapsed on to the moving walkway, panting, empty and drained of all his rage.

SEVENTEEN

Lister paced up and down the medical unit, swinging a baseball bat, his lip curled in a deranged snarl. He smashed the bat into a lap bench between Kryten and the Cat. "It's war."

Rimmer shook his head, and re-crossed his legs. "Look, people," he said with an even calmness, "just because it's an armour-plated mutant killing machine that salivates unspeakable slobber, that doesn't mean it's a bad person." He bit on the end of his pipe, which he'd requested from his hologrammatic accessory computer, along with a T-shirt printed with the words "Give Quiche a Chance." "What we've got to do," he continued serenely, "is get it round a table, and put together a solution package, perhaps over tea and biscuits."

"Look at him," Kryten slid down from the lab bench. "We can't trust his opinion—he has no anger—he's a total dork!"

"Good point, Kryten," Rimmer said kindly. "Let's take that on board, shall we?" He turned to Lister and smiled. "David, do you have any suggestions you'd like to bring to this forum?"

"Yes, I have, actually, Arnold," Lister mimicked. "Why don't we go down to the ammunition store, get a nuclear warhead and then strap it to my

head? I'll nut the smegger to oblivion." To empha-
size his point, the sixty-one-year-old man butted
a metal panel on the wall, leaving a large
indentation.

"Right. Well, that . . . that's very nice, David,"
Rimmer mumbled genially. "But let's put that one
on the back burner for a while, shall we? Cat, do
you have a contribution?"

The Cat looked up from a wastebin he was scav-
enging through for food. "Don't ask me my opinion. I'm nobody. Just pretend I'm not here." He
glugged noisily from a bottle of meths he'd found
on one of the shelves and belched loudly.

Rimmer nodded benignly. "That's lovely, thank
you very much."

"You guys are all insane," the Toaster chirped
from its vantage point at the back of the room.
"You're all emotional retards. This is a problem
that calls for the leadership abilities of your old
buddy, Talkie Toaster™ (patent applied for)."

There was an awkward pause. "Well," said Rimmer, finally. "Moving on a step, and I hope no one
thinks that I'm setting myself up as a sort of self-
elected chairperson, just see me as a facilitator,
Kryten, what's your view? Don't be shy."

"Well, I think we should send Lister in as a
decoy. And while it's busy eating him alive, we
can creep up on it from behind and blast it into
the stratosphere."

"Good plan!" Lister punched the wall, breaking
three of his fingers. "That's the best plan yet. Let
it get knackered out eating me to death, then you
guys can catch it unawares."

"Well, that's certainly an option, David, yes."
Rimmer sucked his pipe ferociously. "But here's

my proposal: let's get tough, the time for talking is over. Call it extreme, if you like, but I propose we hit it hard, and we hit it fast with a major, and I mean *major*," he leaned forward, "leaflet campaign. And while it's reeling from that, we follow up with a whist drive, a car-boot sale, some street theatre, and possibly even some benefit concerts." Rimmer leaned back again. It was a radical course of action, and he just hoped he hadn't gone too far. He took a comforting suck from his hologrammatic pipe and carried on outlining his solution. "Now, if that's not enough," he said, almost crossly, "I'm sorry, it's time for the T-shirts: 'Mutants out'; 'Chameleonic Lifeforms? No thanks!' and if that doesn't get our message across, I don't know what will."

Kryten rolled his eyes a full circle. "Has anyone ever told you, Rimmer, that you are a disgusting, pus-filled bubo, who has all the wit, charm and self-possession of Jayne Mansfield *after* the car accident?"

The Toaster winced. "Listen to me. You can't operate without fear, anger, guilt and vanity. They're all vital emotions that protect your personalities, and keep you sane."

Kryten nodded, and walked over to the Toaster. He picked it up, jammed it into the waste-disposal unit, and turned on the grinder. There was a horrible sound of mashing metals. Kryten flicked the unit off, hauled out the flattened mess of components, and tossed them in the bin. "He's had that coming for a long time," he said, and stamped his foot into the bin.

"Goodness me," said Rimmer, "surely there was a non-violent solution to your differences with the

Toaster. Why on earth didn't you try relationship counselling?"

Lister clubbed himself on the forehead with his baseball bat. "Listen, you bunch of tarts: it's clobbering time. There's a body bag out there with that scudball's name on it, and I'm doing up the zip. Anyone who gets in my way gets a napalm enema."

The Cat looked up from his bin. "I think everybody's right, except me, so just forget I spoke, huh?"

Rimmer got to his feet. "Er, I think we're all beginning to lose sight of the real issue here, which is what are we going to call ourselves?" He paused for suggestions. None came. "I think it comes down to a choice between 'The League Against Salivating Monsters', or, my own personal preference, which is the 'Committee for the Liberation and Integration of Terrifying Organisms, and their Rehabilitation Into Society'." He chewed his lip. "Just one drawback with that—the abbreviation is Clitoris."

"It needs killing." Lister started rubbing some burnt cork over his face. "If that means I have to sacrifice my life in some stupid, pointless way, then all the better."

Kryten nodded. "Yes. Why not? Even if it doesn't work, it'll still be a laugh."

"Right, so let's cut all of this business," Lister mimed a yacking mouth with his hand, "and get on with it. Last one alive's a wet ponce," he growled. "Who's with me?"

Rimmer followed him to the hatchway. "Well, the skutters won't have the protest posters ready till Thursday, but sometimes, I suppose, one just has to act spontaneously. OK, people—let's go."

"Hey—I'm coming too," the Cat staggered behind them. "Maybe I can bum some money off it."

Kryten took up the tail. Maybe if he handed the others over as hostages, the beast would let him go. He hoisted his bazookoid to waist level, and held the others in his field of fire. "Move it, suckers."

EIGHTEEN

It wasn't nearly as difficult as they expected, tracking down the polymorph—it had dined in rapid succession on a variety of emotions far richer than it was used to, and they found it lying bloated and half-asleep back down in the cargo bay.

It would have been easy to kill it then, as it lay, almost shapeless, a pulsating grey-green mush. But they couldn't agree on tactics.

The Cat wanted to throw himself on the creature's mercy. Lister wanted to strangle the mutant to death, as soon as anyone could locate its neck. Rimmer suggested they might offer it a number of concessions, including mutant crêche facilities, a chameleonic lifeform helpline and free travel passes for all slimebeasts; while Kryten refused to join in the discussion, and simply walked up and down one of the wide cargo aisles, happily and noisily evacuating his waste fumes, a practice Mechanoids normally perform in private.

As they stood over the slumbering polymorph, consumed by their pointless bickering, gradually the beast lumbered to awareness. Its primitive brain screamed for survival, and it was forced into a change. It scoured their minds for a shape to protect itself, a form that would be invulnerable while it regained its energy.

And it found one.

Before their eyes, the mound of blubber turned in on itself and rose up into the air, looming above their heads.

The polymorph turned into a tall, green, wrought-iron lamp post.

"Now, what do we do?" Lister nutted the post. "How d'you fight a lamp post?"

"Hey," Rimmer held up a conciliatory hand, "just because it's a lamp post doesn't mean it hasn't got feelings. Isn't that right, big feller?" he said to the lamp post.

Kryten tried ripping off a volley of fire from his bazookoid. When the smoke finally cleared, the lamp post was scorched and a little blackened, but otherwise perfectly intact. "Now what?"

"We just have to wait," Lister snarled, "until it turns into something we can kill."

So they waited.

Two hours passed.

Two hours while the polymorph regained its strength, regained its energy.

"To hell with this," said Kryten, finally. "I'm going to loot the shops in the ship's shopping mall." But as he made to leave there was a sickening squelching noise, and the lamp post began turning in on itself.

NINETEEN

So, how did he die?

The three surviving crew members would ask themselves the same questions over and over again during the weeks that followed.

Whose fault was it? Was there anything anyone could have done?

And the truth was: they would never know for sure.

He was dead, and that was the cold, hard fact.

There was no going back.

Now, they were three.

TWENTY

Lister charged the metamorphosing mass, trying to obliterate the beast before it completed its change. A tentacle whipped out of the blubber and tossed him effortlessly down the aisle. He smashed into a pile of crates, and lay, unconscious, in the timber rubble.

The other three fled down the corridor of packing cases, Kryten using the uncomplaining Cat as a shield.

The creature rose, shrieking, to become the mucus-pulsing, demonic beast of Lister's fear.

The Cat caught hold of Lister's collar, and Kryten dragged the two of them down the aisle. Kryten thumped down the bar on the emergency door with his hip, and they all fell backwards through it and began tumbling down a metal spiral staircase. They rolled out on to a white tiled floor, and found themselves in the pump room of the air-conditioning complex on the engineering deck.

Rimmer scampered down the staircase behind them, his eyes alight with fear.

They dragged themselves to their feet, and Kryten scoured the room for an exit.

There were no doors, or hatches.

They were at the very bottom of the ship.

Suddenly, iron girders and metal tiles began to rain down from the ceiling, and with a splintering of steel, the polymorph dropped into the pump room.

Its black lips rolled back, exposing its glistening teeth, and it roared in demonic triumph.

Untempered by guilt, Kryten's heightened instinct for self-preservation overrode his fear. It didn't make sense—there had to be another way out; there was no room on the ship that had only one exit. There had to be a second door, or an airlock, or *something*.

He scanned the room again. Against the back wall was a disused pump unit, lying on its side. Kryten edged back towards it and dragged it away from the wall.

Behind it was an old service lift.

He jabbed the call button and heard the crashing of the gears as the motor ground into action, and the lift car begin its creaking descent from perhaps twenty floors above.

A tentacle whiplashed out and coiled around Kryten's neck, hoisting him into the air as the lift juddered to a halt, and the doors sushed open.

Two blue shimmering balls hovered around the lift car. They spun end over end in tiny, menacing circles, before they shot out into the pump room. They streaked round the chamber before their tracking computers locked on to the hottest object in the room, and screeched down towards the target.

The polymorph simply disappeared. The short silence that followed the blast was broken by the sickening splatter of mucal debris and smouldering fragments of endoskeleton as the dead mutant's remains obeyed Newton.

Suddenly a swirling wind whipped all the papers in the pump room into a spiralling tornado. Then the wind divided into four frenzied twisters and blasted into each of the crew.

They each staggered back, filled by an energy and a force they had never experienced before.

When Kryten groped his way upright, he was whole again. His guilt had returned. "How can you ever forgive me?" he moaned, wretchedly. "Naturally, I'll commit suicide immediately." He placed the muzzle of the bazookoid into his lipless mouth.

The Cat batted it away. "Chill it, Buddy," he said. "We all did things back there we weren't proud of. Look at me." He stood there in his ragged, stinking clothes, his hair matted and mangled. "If I don't get a bath in the next thirty seconds, I'm going to have to resign my post as Most Handsome Guy on this ship."

"The Toaster," Kryten bleated, "what did I do to the Toaster?"

"Lister?" Rimmer crouched over Lister's immobile form. "Lister?" he called again.

Kryten hurried over and knelt by his side. He looked down at Lister's grey face.

"Is he OK?"

"He's had a heart attack."

Kryten gently rolled Lister's head to one side, and felt the side of his neck for a pulse.

"Is he OK?" Rimmer said again.

Kryten reached forward and his open palm closed Lister's eyes.

Part Four

THE END, AND AFTER

ONE

The funeral of the last remaining member of the human race was neither a solemn nor a sombre affair. Quite the opposite. Lister's favourite dance track, "Born to Brutalize," thumped out of his old wax-blaster with such force it shook the coffin. Kryten, Rimmer and the Cat stood around the metal casket, wearing green Day-glo Deely-boppers, battery-propelled revolving bow-ties and yellow fishing waders, precisely as Lister had requested in his Last Will and Testament.

Rimmer had been present that drunken night Lister had decided to make a will. He'd scrawled his last wishes on a pair of his old boxers in red, indelible ink, and Rimmer ensured they followed the instructions to the last misspelt letter.

The Cat gently placed a sealed foil tray of chicken vindaloo by Lister's feet, followed by two spicy poppadoms and an onion salad. Kryten shuffled along behind him, and placed three six-packs of Leopard lager in the coffin, together with Lister's one and only photograph of Kristine Kochanski.

As "Born to Brutalize" reached its climactic nuclear guitar solo, they sealed the casket lid and fired the coffin off into space.

" 'Bye, man," said Rimmer quietly, and the three of them turned and shuffled sadly out of the waste-disposal bay.

Kryten busied himself setting the table for the wake. None of them felt much like drinking, but Lister had insisted they each consume an entire bottle of Cinzano Bianco. The menu was even more daunting: a triple fried-egg sandwich with chilli sauce and chutney, Lister's favourite snack.

"I suppose someone should tell Holly," said Rimmer.

The Cat nodded.

Rimmer slouched off to the Drive room.

"On," said Rimmer, and Holly's pixelized face materialized on to the screen. "Sorry to bother you, Hol, but we've got some bad news." He gazed down at the floor. "It's Lister," he said, eventually. "He's dead."

Holly nodded.

"I thought you'd want to know."

"Yes." Holly paused for two of his valuable remaining seconds. "How?"

"Heart attack." Rimmer sketched in the details.

Holly listened, and when Rimmer had finished, he simply said "Oh," and switched himself off.

Rimmer had passed under the Drive-room exit hatch and was halfway down the corridor before the noise started.

Printers printing.

He wheeled round and walked back into the Drive room.

Every single printer was churning out ream after ream of calculations and instructions.

Rimmer stood in the hatchway and his face

yielded to a grin, which, in turn gave way to laughter. Not his normal hollow braying empty laughter, this was an altogether different noise. This was a noise his vocal cords had never been called on to make before.

It was the laughter of joy.

Kryten and the Cat were in the sleeping quarters, sifting through a stack of old photographs, when Rimmer poked his red face through the hatchway and said, breathlessly: "Quick! Come on!" then vanished. By the time the Cat had sauntered over to the hatchway, Rimmer was two hundred and fifty yards down the corridor and still accelerating. They started after him.

Rimmer bounded down the emergency staircase four steps at a time, and carried on down the ship without a break, for thirty-two floors. He was moving so fast that several times even the Cat thought he'd lost him.

Finally Rimmer emerged on the shuttle deck, and streaked across the lined runway towards *White Giant*. By the time Kryten and the Cat hit the shuttle bay, Rimmer was high-stepping up the ship's embarkation ramp. He disappeared inside.

Seconds later the retros blasted into the ground, and the Cat and Kryten had to complete the last part of the journey through blinding, billowing white smoke.

They leapt on to the hovering embarkation ramp, and ran along its length as it began to retract into the craft. They stumbled inside, coughing and tear-blind, as the hatch slammed closed. They staggered towards the cockpit over skutters sorting through reams of computer print-out, as the transport craft's autopilot taxied it down the runway and out into space.

They listed into the cockpit section, where Rimmer stood impatiently jiggling his right leg, and flopped into the two Drive seats.

"What's happening, Buddy?"

"Where are we going?"

Rimmer's left arm snaked out, and pointed through the cockpit's viewscreen at a glimmering brown dot in the distance. "Follow that coffin."

The Cat flipped the controls to manual, and pressed the reheat button.

White Giant burned across the blackness in pursuit of the slow-spinning casket.

TWO

Nothing.

At first, there was nothing.

Then.

Then there was something.

It was a light. A tiny shard of brilliance that shocked him with its suddenness.

Then.

Then there was nothing again.

There was no way of telling how long it lasted: nothing has no time.

Then the light again. And the light grew, and across the face of the light, dark shapes began to move.

He watched as the shapes became faces. Faces he didn't know. They were concerned faces; gentle, kindly. They made him feel safe.

Then he lost consciousness. But unconsciousness wasn't like nothing, it was studded with dreams. He dreamed of a garden, pungent with jasmine. He knew the garden. He knew it very well. But he had no idea where or when he knew it from.

Then pain.

Something imploded in his chest. He lurched

upright, and there was a second implosion, and the pain was gone.

He drifted back off to sleep.

When he awoke, it was dusk. He was in a bed, with clean white cotton sheets tightly tucked into the sides. There was a green screen around the bed, so the rest of the room was obscured from him. By the bedside, on a cabinet, there was a huge vase full of jasmine, with some kind of greeting card nestling among the yellow flowers. His left arm, for some reason, felt weak and helpless, so he reached up with his right, and plucked the card from its place.

In the half-light his old eyes couldn't focus on the inscription. He replaced the card and, overcome with weariness, slid back into sleep.

When he woke again, he was moving. Fluorescent lights streaked past above him. He tried to raise his head, but a friendly hand patted it down again, as the hospital trolley raced along the white-tiled corridor. They burst through three sets of overlapping rubber doors, and suddenly they were outside in the biting wind of the cold winter air.

There was a jerk, and the stretcher was hoisted off the trolley. There was a commotion—people were shouting things he didn't understand, and all the time, the pain in his chest was getting worse. Two men ran with his stretcher and slid him into the back of a waiting ambulance. The doors slammed closed, and the ambulance screeched off.

"Where am I?" An oxygen mask loomed over him, and once again, he blacked out.

He came to as the ambulance doors swung

open, and the same two men hauled his stretcher out of the vehicle, and set it down on a pavement, in the middle of a circle of people.

"What's happening?" he bleated pathetically. Gingerly, the two men eased him off the stretcher and placed him on the cold hard pavement.

One of them packed up the stretcher and dashed back with it to the ambulance, while the other twisted his leg so it folded under his body, then lifted up his head and slid his arm underneath it. The pain was unbearable, now.

He tilted his head weakly, and watched as the two men jumped into the ambulance, and reversed off into the busy traffic. He lay on his back, peripherally aware of the circle of onlookers. One of them, a woman, was talking, but she sounded vague and distant, and he couldn't make it out.

One by one the onlookers began to drift away, until, eventually, he was totally alone, lying in his unnatural pose on the pavement.

The pain reached a crescendo, and imploded in his chest. He jumped to his feet, staggered along a shop window, regained his balance, and started to walk slowly down the street.

The worst of the pain had subsided, just a sharp ache in his left arm remained, and his breathing was beginning to come more easily.

Half-dazed, he shuffled along the street, found a bench and sat down. After ten minutes, he didn't feel too badly at all, and decided to go for a coffee.

He found a café just a few shops down, and sat at one of the red plastic tables. Almost immediately, a waitress came over and set down a plate of money. Then she smiled at him pleasantly and scurried off.

Soon after, she returned with some crockery: a cup, a saucer, and a plate. She put them on his table and went off to serve someone else.

The cup was dirty. It had a coffee ring around the top, and there was some half-dissolved sugar in the bottom. The plate was dirty, too. It was covered in crumbs, and in the middle there was a huge blob of mayonnaise.

He held up his hand to call back the waitress, but suddenly, he realized he was going to be sick. Liquid gushed up his throat, but he managed to catch it in the coffee cup.

But he hadn't been sick. He looked into the cup—it was half full of coffee. Then he was filled with panic again. This time, he definitely was going to be sick. He reached up to his mouth, and regurgitated a perfectly shaped triangular tuna and mayonnaise sandwich. Three other quarters followed in fast succession, along with a sliver of cucumber, a slice of tomato and a small portion of watercress.

"Help," he said, quietly. His throat gurgled again, and he filled the coffee cup to the top.

He smelled the cup. It *was* coffee. Fresh. Steam was coming off it. He dipped his teaspoon in and swirled it around. When he brought the spoon out again, it was full of sugar. He tipped it into the sugar bowl, and looked around the café.

A large woman with two unruly children was midway through regurgitating an enormous chocolate éclair. On the next table, a man was jabbing a fork into his mouth, and pulling out french fries.

He looked over to the waitress, and watched as

she flipped open the pedal bin, took out a handful of rib-bones, and arranged them on a large white plate. Then she served the bones to two teenage boys sitting at the counter.

He watched as the boys raised the bones to their mouths and began to fill them with meat.

The waitress swept over to his table and took away his sandwich and his coffee. She held the cup under a cappuccino machine, which sucked the liquid noisily up into its metal cylinder. Then she opened the sandwich, spooned the tuna and mayonnaise filling into a bowl, effortlessly scraped the bread clean of butter, and returned the bread to a large, uncut loaf.

He left the café, deciding he needed some fresh air.

All the traffic was going backwards.

What was this place? What was he doing here?

Almost every aspect of the city was strange and unfamiliar. He tramped around for twenty minutes, looking for a landmark, something he might recognize, but it was hopeless.

When he next looked around, he found he'd wandered off the main street, and was in a dimly lit alley. He felt panicked, and alone. Suddenly he heard urgent footsteps coming towards him from behind. Before he could turn, the man was on him, pressing him up against a wall, and holding a short silver knife against his throat.

Deftly the mugger fastened a watch around the old man's wrist, then slipped a wallet into the inside pocket of the old man's coat.

He watched bemused as the mugger flipped closed the blade of his knife, smiled with false charm and raced off down the alley.

"Help," the old man said quietly. "What's happening to me?"

He opened the wallet and looked inside. Astonishingly, his own photograph was in one of the credit card compartments. There was a driving license, too. The name on the license was: "Retsil Divad."

It took the old man a good ten minutes to realize the name was his.

Because, like everything else in this crazy place, his name was backwards.

THREE

Four thousand dull gunmetal-grey canisters lay stacked in neat ranks in the scoop room of *White Giant*'s cargo section.

"Here's some more," said Kryten, as a fresh haul of canisters clattered down the chute. He read the numbers, and then one by one tossed them to the Cat, who began to pile them alongside the others.

"Has anyone even the vaguest, remotest idea what it is we're doing here?" asked Rimmer.

The Cat and Kryten grunted verbal shrugs. The truth was, none of them even pretended to begin to understand the list of instructions, data, formulae and coordinates Holly had left them. Not even the newly repaired Toaster claimed to understand this one. Although it was fair to say it wasn't in tip-top peak condition, despite the many hours Kryten had spent panel-beating its chrome cover, and reconstructing its mashed circuitry. Kryten wasn't exactly an expert when it came to Artificial Intelligence, and the Toaster wasn't all it might be in the sanity department.

In fact, for some reason, the Toaster now thought it was a moose.

It bellowed loudly from time to time, and occasionally threatened to charge them with its huge antlers, but otherwise it was harmless.

More canisters scuttled down the chute, and once again Kryten studied the numbers. "Got it!" he squealed with delight, and clapped his hands.

The Cat began rotating his body from side to side, and pumping his hands so they circled over each other in front of his chest. "Yes, yes, ye-ess!"

"Excellente!" grinned Rimmer.

"Mahooooooo!" bellowed the Toaster.

It had been easy enough collecting Lister's coffin and returning it to a stasis booth on *Red Dwarf*, but the second instruction was a little more bizarre. They had to locate a swarm of canisters floating through space at a certain set of coordinates, and bring aboard the one numbered "1121." Holly had failed to mention there would be something in the region of ten thousand of these canisters, and the search had taken them the best part of five weeks.

"What next?" asked Rimmer, as he craned over Kryten's shoulder, trying to read the indecipherable machine code.

"I'm supposed to treat the canister; bombard it with X-rays, gamma rays—all kinds of stuff."

"Then what?"

Kryten consulted Holly's sheet again. "We take Lister's body on a little trip."

"Where?"

"Through the Black Hole. Into the omni-zone. To a particular planet in Universe 3. Apparently, we're to bury him there."

"Universe 3? What's so special about Universe 3?"

"Well, apart from the fact that it's almost a mirror image of our own universe, except that time moves backwards there," Kryten said, "there's nothing very special about it at all."

The Cat shook the canister. "What's this got to do with anything? What's in it?"

"I don't know," Kryten flipped through the instructions. "Maybe some chemical we have to use later."

"I don't think so," Rimmer tried to suffocate a smirk. "I've got a pretty good idea what *is* in there, and I don't think you'll find it's a chemical."

He raised an enigmatic eyebrow, and walked back to the cockpit, whistling happily.

FOUR

So time was running backwards. It had taken Lister a while to figure it out, but if he reversed the events of the day, it all seemed to come together. He'd walked down a dark alley, where a mugger had stolen his watch and his wallet. In a daze, he'd stumbled through the streets, until he came across a café where he'd had a coffee and something to eat to calm his nerves. Obviously it hadn't worked, because he'd gone out into the street, suffered a heat attack, and been rushed to hospital. After a few hours slipping in and out of consciousness, he'd suffered a second heart attack and died.

Except, of course, it had all happened backwards.

He looked at the address on his driving license. A cab screeched up backwards beside him. He leaned in the window, accepted the fare and the tip from the cabbie and climbed in. Lister was about to attempt to read out the backwards address on his licence when the cab pulled off and began reversing through the streets at high speed.

The driver knew where he was going, which, when Lister thought about it, made some kind of sense. If everything was backwards, presumably, when they reached their destination, Lister would have to tell the driver where he picked him up.

His brain ached.

Suddenly, the cab stopped, caught up in traffic. Lister leant out of the window to see what was causing the jam. Three fire engines pulled up outside a ruined building. As the firemen uncoiled their hoses, the ruins began to smoulder. The hoses sucked giant jets of water out of the smoking rubble, and within minutes the ruins were a flaming orange inferno. When the blaze had reached its peak, the firemen put away their hoses and drove off with sirens blaring. The traffic began to shuffle past the fire. By the time Lister's cab had passed it, the fire was almost out. Where the ruins had been, there now stood a chic, new-looking office block.

Lister shook his head, and ducked back into the cab. There was a newspaper jammed down the side of the bench seat. He dug it out, and opened it out to the front page. Under the headline was a large photo of the blaze he'd just witnessed. This wasn't helping his brain-ache. Finally, he realized it must be an old newspaper, from the previous morning. In the backwards reality, obviously, news was reported before it happened.

A thought struck him, and he turned to the seirautibo column. And there he was: Retsil Divad. It took him a while to translate the accompanying text: "David Lister, aged 61, joyfully brought to life on Thursday, the 21st, at eleven-thirty p.m. (see personal column)."

Lister feverishly ripped through the pages, and found the personal column. He traced his finger down the entries, and stopped when he found one that was printed forwards.

"Dave Lister," it said. "Sure everything will become clear to you. This was the only way. Obviously, can't be with you—everyone would get younger. Will pick you up in thirty-six years. Be at Niagara Falls, by the souvenir shop, at noon precisely. See you then. Good luck, from the *Red Dwarf* crew."

They'd done it again. They'd marooned him in some insane part of the universe, expecting him to cope alone for the best part of forty years.

To do that once was bad enough. To do it twice—twice in consecutive lifetimes—that was sheer bad manners.

Lister was a social animal. He hated being alone. Always had done.

He looked out of the cab window.

It was beginning to rain.

There should have been a saxophone playing a wistful, melancholy blues number.

The rain swirled up from the wet pavements and hurled itself into the scowling clouds above.

Finally, the cab screeched to a start outside the address on the driving licence. He was home, whatever that meant. The taxi door flung itself open, and Lister climbed out.

He took the key from his wallet, walked up the path to the house and let himself in.

It was a big house. Whatever he was destined to do for a living, it looked like he was destined to do it pretty successfully. He walked into the first reception room. Framed photographs jostled for position on the old stone mantelpiece.

This was his life—the life he was about to lead in this strange reality in which he was an interloper.

Something in one of the photographs caught his eye, and he scrutinized the others more closely.

Impossible.

It just wasn't possible. Not even with an IQ of twelve thousand.

But the evidence was there, in the photographs. Somehow Holly had done it.

But how?

Lister would have to wait thirty-six years to find out the answer.

He turned and watched the lace curtains fluttering in the breeze through the open French windows.

He crossed the room and stepped out into the garden.

At the end of the lawn an old woman in a wide-brimmed sun hat was clipping away at the jasmine borders. She looked up and saw him, and her face crinkled into her famous pinball smile.

Thirty-six years. They would grow young together. They had a whole new past to look forward to.

The old man's face crinkled into a smile of its own, and he started shuffling down the garden towards her.

About the Author

Grant Naylor is a gestalt entity occupying two bodies, one of which lives in north London, the other in south London. The product of a horribly botched genetic-engineering experiment, which took place in Manchester in the late fifties, they try to eke out two existences with only one mind. They attended the same school and the same university, but, for tax reasons, have completely different wives.

The first body is called Rob Grant, the second Doug Naylor. Among other things, they spent three years in the mid-eighties as head writers of *Spitting Image*; wrote Radio Four's award-winning series *Son of Cliché*; penned the lyrics to a number-one single; and created and wrote *Red Dwarf* for BBC Television.

They have made a living variously by being ice-cream salesmen, shoe-shop assistants and by attempting to sell dodgy life-assurance policies to close friends. They also spent almost two years on the night shift loading paper into computer printers at a mail-order factory in Ardwick. They can still taste the cheese 'n' onion toasties.

Their favourite colour is orange. *Red Dwarf* was an enormous bestseller when published as a Penguin paperback in 1989. *Better Than Life* is the not-very-long-awaited sequel.

If you and/or a friend would like to receive the *ROC Advance*, a bimonthly newsletter featuring all the newest and hottest ROC books and authors, on a complimentary basis, please fill out this form and return it to:

ROC Books/Penguin USA
375 Hudson Street
New York, NY 10014

Your Address
Name _____
Street _____ Apt. # _____
City _____ State _____ Zip _____

Friend's Address
Name _____
Street _____ Apt. # _____
City _____ State _____ Zip _____